LOGAN'S L

Playing Others' Games by his Rules

Max Holden

May you enjoy the read, as I enjoyed the write

Max Holden

DEDICATION

Logan's Rules is for my life's anchor:

Eileen

CONTENTS

ACKNOWLEDGMENTS

My wife, Eileen, whose patience and support helped me through this process.

Dawn, Kevin, Bev, Jeff, and my many other friends who've reviewed and commented on Logan's Rules, helping me build the finished article.

To all the technology companies, whose free tools I've used to research and polish the manuscript.

FOREWARD

The theme of this book has been with me for several years. While gainfully employed, there was no time to put ePen to Virtual paper. Now fully focussed on writing, I've been able to bring this all together.

I trust you'll enjoy (or in some cases, hate) the novel's characters, live the action scenes, its ebbs and flows of emotions; and I hope its unexpected twist.

*** This novel contains some bad language, which I've used judiciously for those characters' personas that require it. ***

PROLOGUE

The politician sat on the bed in his hotel room going through some papers. It was early afternoon and he'd just finished some meetings and was writing up his report.

He was one of a number of like-minded senior members of the Afghanistan government who had the country's best interests at heart. His current mission was to lobby the local influencers and explain to farmers why they should change their illegal poppy and hemp crops to more profitable and stable forms of agriculture. The financial and logistical support of the government and its western allies made for a powerful argument.

If the re-planting strategy was successful, the businesses of many influential players that benefited from the manufacture of drugs would be destroyed.

This was not only a local or in-country issue. Powerful external drug organisations would suffer from any reduction in quantities and price fluctuations. And all these had no qualms about torture, murder, and extortion.

He occupied the best room in the town's top hotel. Saying that, there were only two of what could be described as hotels in this place.

Today had been a hot day. Even with the air conditioning on maximum, it was hot inside his room.

From outside the room, the two security men could still hear the grunting and groaning of the ancient cooling appliance as it tried to lower the air temperature inside.

The politician's security team was staffed by Albatross Tactical Security personnel, a private quasi-military and security organisation with offices and interests around the globe.

Headquartered in Texas, USA, Albatross Tactical Security was one of the many private security companies used by allied forces in Afghanistan. It guarded officials, military installations, and key personnel. The organisation also helped train the local army and police forces.

For security and military work, ATS used ex-forces mercs recruited from around the globe. Their pay was double that of western military, often massively more than their own country's military. Even better, the risks were lower working for this organisation.

The two security men on protection duty, were new to working for ATS. They were experienced ex-soldiers from the Bundeswehr, the Federal Defence Forces of Germany. The men were soon to be relieved by the next pair from their team.

There wasn't much to look forward to after their shift in this town. There were no highlights for them here unless they went to a local café. And those were definitely not safe places to be. So, they'd shortly be back in their rooms having a beer or two that they brought from their base.

There were six of them on this security detail. Each team of two worked shifts of four hours on and eight hours off, except when travelling between towns. The other four, were experienced mercs from the French contingent; all ex-Armée de Terre.

Normally, new members of a security team would work with an experienced partner. This detail was considered low risk by their management; a simple babysitting exercise. So the Germans stayed together. Everyone was happier that way. In their base of operations, the different nationalities of Albatross' personnel mostly kept to themselves. It was no different for the French and the Germans on this Op.

In the gloomy light of the long corridor, the guards noticed the silhouettes of two men walking toward them. With a glance at each other, they stood up and readied their automatic weapons.

The corridor was dimly lit. Many of the strip lights were broken and some of those which worked, annoyingly flickered. The lack of illumination wasn't helped by the dark walls and carpet sucking out any light. Even the shards of sunlight peeping into the corridor from under doors and through dark curtains were of little help.

It was basically dingy.

The two men continued their approach. As they got closer, the Germans could see they were armed. They now cocked their guns in readiness.

The armed men continued towards them. They walked slowly, nonchalantly, as they approached the two guards on the door.

The German guards could see the newcomers' weapons were still shouldered and out of harm's way. So their initial concern was reduced to merely careful watchfulness.

Once the arrivals were within several metres, the two men guarding the door relaxed. They, at last, recognised the men as their relief. There were smiles all around.

One of the approaching men partly raised his hand as a wave of recognition and uttered, "bonjour mes amis."

With a glance at each other, the Germans put their weapons back to safe.

The two arrivals thumbed over their shoulders that the guards' shift had now ended. They swapped places. The two Germans walked away, slinging their weapons over their shoulders.

The two French guards unslung theirs and took up their position by the door. The new guards then took off the safety catches, and each shot their own departing target in the back.

One of the French mercs burst into the politician's room to stop him from calling for help. The other calmly walked over and shot their German colleagues in their heads as they lay on the corridor floor. There could be no witnesses.

The politician was hooded and frog-marched out of the hotel by the two-man relief team. The remaining two of the six-man team were in the hotel foyer, watching and ready for anyone foolish enough to interfere. None did.

Two Japanese 4x4s with engines running, each with a driver, waited outside the hotel entrance. All drove off down the main street without interference.

1. THE LAST STRAW

It was late on Friday. Actually it was just after midnight, so really Saturday, as Harry Logan walked the queue of people waiting to get into Whispers nightclub. There were three of them managing entries that evening.

Bob and Mike were on duty in front of the large doorway. They allowed customers to enter on the left-hand side and exit on the right; without overlap and confusion, especially at busy times.

They were your typical nightclub doormen, built to intimidate but not equipped with much else between the ears. Harry looked small next to them, even though he was a little over average height and stature. He wasn't overly muscled, but his physique was highly toned from years of army training and his motivation to keep fit.

He did, however, exhibit a powerful and confident presence. While not overtly intimidating, people tended to acquiesce to this pleasant spoken bouncer.

While new to this particular establishment, over the months since leaving the army he'd become experienced in this game. After all, there was little else an ex-serviceman without a recognised trade could do.

He could spot trouble a mile away and was always first on the scene to quell any problems before they escalated. When things occasionally got out of control, he dealt with the perpetrators without excessive force or violence. He'd left all that behind.

As always, Friday was busy. The queue was full of people who'd enjoyed many hours of cheap pub drinking before extending their evening into the nightclub scene. Harry's task for the evening was to patrol and control the line, ensuring there were no scuffles, queue jumping, or other nonsense from the many drunks lined up along the wall.

It was a cold and dry late winter night, with temperatures hovering around zero. There were no clouds this evening, yet only a few of the brightest stars could penetrate the city's light pollution.

All three bouncers wrapped up like Michelin men, unlike the waiting customers who chatted and chattered in their flimsy finery. He could never understand why young people would forgo common sense for what they deemed fashion. Even on this cold night, many of the young women in the queue wore flimsy, short dresses, with the thinnest and shortest of jackets; not forgetting the mandatory high heels.

'*Poor blighters,*' he thought.

He'd rather look boring and warm than those wearing fashionably cool clothes and being freezing cold. Ten to fifteen years ago, he was their age. Even then, he always dressed appropriately. Maybe, he was just too practical?

All was orderly as Harry walked back down the queue towards the main door. Approaching the front of the queue, a few metres further up the street, he could see a man escorting, or rather half-carrying, a rather limp young woman towards a taxi.

Another man had hailed it from the taxi line further up the street. He was waiting with the door already open.

Harry could see that both men were a little older than the club's usual clientele and wearing expensive designer gear.

'*Those two are not your average punter for this place?*'

He'd heard about this sort of thing happening but never witnessed it before. He didn't like the thought of anybody taking advantage of a woman. He wasn't raised like that, and it stuck.

Thinking all that, it could still be perfectly innocent. The guy could be the boyfriend who was escorting his partner home after she had drunk too much. Or, more than likely in this establishment, she'd taken something illicit.

Harry didn't want to leap to the obvious conclusion. It was, after all, his fourth night on the job. He didn't want to get a reputation for jumping the gun or interfering in others' affairs.

On the other side of the coin, his personal shitbag-monitoring-radar could be right.

11

He therefore tried the concerned citizen approach as he was walking towards them. "Is she OK? Can I help you?" Harry called out as innocently as possible to the man holding the woman.

"Nah, I'm good, ta," he replied without looking back while trying to quicken his pace to the waiting taxi.

He was having difficulty speeding up since the young woman severely hampered him.

"No problems, let me help," said Harry as he reached the couple, "I can see you're struggling there, mate."

He tried to reach out to help the girl. Instead of a thanks, Harry was met with a, "bugger off!" and a palm thrust before Harry's face.

The man quickly followed up with, "mind your own fucking business! Now piss off!"

"OK, OK fella, but 'fraid this is my business. She's a customer of the club who's not feeling well. We need to offer what help she needs. It's our duty as doormen," said Harry politely. It wasn't really true, but it seemed a good line to justify his intervention.

"Listen, mate. I honestly have to ask, could you please tell me who is she to you?"

"She's my fucking wife. Happy? Now fuck off!" Seeing Harry's reluctance to go anywhere, the man emphasised, "now! or else!"

Harry couldn't see a wedding ring on either of them. Then with all the innocence he could muster, he commented, "looks like she's lost her wedding ring. Shall we head back and report it to lost property?" It was a sarcastic comment. However, he said it with such innocence it went over the man's head.

"We can then take both your details and make sure we can return the ring if it's found. Anyway, it might be better she rests for a while, so whatever she's consumed wears off."

In the meantime, Mike, one of the bouncers on the door, shouted over to leave them and get back to the job. He finished with the reassuring final words. "I know these guys, they're OK."

Harry wasn't sure. Actually, he was sure.

The man's behaviour and body language were all wrong. If he was in this man's position, he wouldn't be so defensive. And, he could see this woman wasn't in any fit state to look after herself. Now he was close, Harry could see that she was only a girl, lucky to be eighteen.

Mike said he knew these guys, but he was over there and clearly wanted to stay clear for some reason. But Harry didn't know them!

As a newbie to the team, he was torn. On one side were his colleagues' reassurances and their experience and knowledge of the clientele. On the other side was his intuition and concern for the girl.

The other man who was standing by the taxi started to walk over, shouting. "Mind your own fucking business."

The taxi driver, not wanting to get involved with this lot, drove off. That further angered both men.

In the meantime, from the doorway, both Bob and Mike urged Harry to back off and get back; all was good. Harry was half-tempted to comply since his oppos seemed to know these two.

However, the decision was taken out of his hands! Any uncertainty Harry felt, vanished in an instant. The man who was by the taxi had now reached them.

Screaming a tirade of expletives, he lunged at Harry with a thin-bladed knife. Facing most other opponents, this man could have done severe damage to his victim. Unfortunately for the man, hand-to-hand fighting was bread-and-butter to Harry.

"Wrong move, mate," mumbled Harry. Without overt effort, he easily parried the attack. Using the man's momentum, he swung him past and onto the ground. The man landed with a sharp crack of bone on the paving stone. Harry smirked at the fallen man, "ouch, that's going to hurt tomorrow."

At that moment, another young woman ran over and shouted, "Amanda, there you are! I've been looking all over for you."

Then seeing the condition her friend was in, shouted at the man holding her, "what have you done to her?"

Harry looked over at his oppos for help, but they were busy doing anything else than pay attention to him or what was going on over there.

The other man pushed the girl he was half-carrying towards Harry, who reached forward and tried to catch her, to stop her from falling. Thinking Harry was off-balance with his hands full of a half-limp girl, he swung a wild kick at Harry's nether region.

Harry turned side-on, keeping the girl out of harm's way of the kick, as well as his marital parts.

The kick landed hard on Harry's upper leg. He winced in pain as it deadened his thigh muscle, causing him to collapse onto one knee. He managed to lay the girl down on the ground and out of the way, albeit not as gently as he could have, had he not lost the senses in his leg.

The man could see the girl's rescuer was incapacitated and decided to finish him off by kicking the kneeling Harry in the face.

Harry, now unencumbered by the girl, slid to the right, away from the oncoming attack. Using the base of both fists, he blocked the kick at the side of the man's knee. Still crouching, he spun round to meet the man still coming forward. Harry finished him off with a left punch to his exposed genitals.

The man's momentum carried him past Harry. He ended up collapsed in a ball on the ground, groaning in agony. He didn't know whether his crotch or badly damaged knee needed the most comfort.

It wasn't exactly a textbook manoeuvre, but it did the job.

"Serves you right, bastard." Harry couldn't help the angry comment.

It was all over in a few moments. Apart from those at the front of the queue, few realised, or more than likely didn't want to see what had happened.

Harry could now pay attention to the real victim here, the incapacitated girl.

The newcomer was now leaning over her friend, who was still pretty much out of it. She thanked Harry profusely and asked if he could help them leave. She told him that both their parents would kill them if they found out they were here.

This confirmed Harry's judgment of them being in their mid, possibly late teens and definitely underage for this place. He hailed one of the waiting taxis and stayed with them until the two were inside.

They quickly departed.

After several minutes, there was a wail of sirens, and a police car with two police officers arrived. They were quickly followed by an ambulance. The ambulance men tended to the two injured men. One of the police offices took verbal statements from the two injured men, while the other took Harry's. Another police car arrived soon after and those two police officers asked around for any witnesses.

Neither Mike nor Bob saw anything at all; surprisingly? They said they were too busy dealing with the queue. Those people at the front of the queue when the incident happened were already inside. So it was a waste of time trying to find them.

The man with the painful crotch and damaged knee accused Harry of attacking him and his friend for no reason. "He came at us like a crazy man."

The knife-wielder had sufficiently recovered from the bang to his head to support his friend's version of events. He did admit to using a knife, but purely in self-defence and only after Harry attacked them.

Harry was gob-smacked by their blatant lies and amazed that these two were even trying to blame him. "They're talking a load of rubbish since they know they're in deep shit."

He was sure of his ground and confident. Once all the evidence was checked, Harry knew he'd be in the clear and continue his work. "Please check the security camera?" Harry asked the policeman, pointing to the camera aimed in their direction.

"That'll show I was attacked after helping a young woman. She was actually a girl, probably sixteen or seventeen," said Harry in his defence.

Then a thought occurred to him. '*Bugger, how'd they get into the nightclub past us?*'

One officer went into the club and returned soon after, saying, "the security cameras aren't working. They've been off for a couple of days according to the owner."

Harry was shocked. "But officer, I checked them earlier today, they were working then."

"Well they're not working now, and those two are accusing you of GBH," retorted the policeman.

"I also asked those two over there," nodding in the direction of the two doormen, "and they are agreeing with the owner. No one seems to be corroborating your story, sir."

Soon after, a smartly dressed middle-aged man strode over and went to the two men. He was sporting one of those virility-inducing ponytails that grey-haired older men of a particular persuasion deployed. Harry knew Mr Bradley, the nightclub owner. He interviewed him a few days earlier.

Harry couldn't comprehend why the boss would say the CCTV wasn't working. It was part of the pre-evening checks that the boss insisted they do, and Harry was with him at the time.

After an exchange of words with the two injured men, the owner came over to the police standing with Harry and said, "I own of this place," he gestured to the nightclub.

He pointed at Harry. "This crazy needs to be charged with assaulting my two nephews. He was arguing with them earlier about money, and clearly, this was him finishing the argument."

Now it was all clear to Harry.

Bradley faced up to Harry and loud enough for all to hear, said, "you're fired. And we're gonna to sue you for injury, and ruining their clothes, and their dignity in front of all these people. And anything else we can think of." As an afterthought, he added. "And, you'll never work as a bouncer in this city again."

Then leaning further forward he quietly growled into Harry's ear, so no one else could hear, "yer a dead man walking, and as soon as yer out of the nick, I'm gonna stick ya myself."

Harry knew this man's reputation and realised he was in deep trouble.

A police officer asked the two men to come down to the police station to make a statement as soon as they were able.

The one who cracked his head was taken away by the ambulance to check for concussion; always a risk with a serious cranial blow. His brother accompanied him to also have his injuries investigated.

The police then asked Harry to come with them to the police station for further questioning and to make a statement.

As Harry was walking towards the first police car he looked over at his ex-colleagues for any sign of support. Mike looked over and held out his hands in a show of frustration and shook his head in disapproval, meaning that Harry should have backed off when they told him.

And that was that.

Harry was kept in the police station overnight, pending further investigation and evaluation reports. There was concern about his mental health from what people had said about him, and night-duty police officers were not trained in psychiatric assessments. All this would have to wait until the morning, along with the victim and witness statements.

Harry lay on his back, hands clasped behind his head, and sighed with resignation; it wasn't looking good at all.

He'd tried to do the right thing and just look what it had gotten him. He thought about his past and how he'd come to where he was now. His mind wandered back to when and where it all started, four years ago, in Nangarhar Province, Afghanistan.

2. THE NANGARHAR OPERATION

** *Four Years Earlier* **

The official story of how the politician's security team lost their ward was from an attack by a large group of heavily armed men. The two German security guards bravely lost their lives during the vicious gunfight.

The word on the street and in the cafes was different. The talk was about Albatross Tactical Security being involved in the death of their men.

The politician's kidnappers had to overcome an issue. They couldn't kill a highly respected and popular man without repercussions. The crop-changing strategy he and his government were promoting had to be discredited. There was no better person to do this than the politician himself.

The kidnappers planned to engage in a well-tried and successful solution that had served them so often in the past; holding an in-camera trial. The politician would explain how he was corrupted by western debauchery. He'd talk about conspiring with the invaders and their own government to destroy the livelihood of the poor, hard-pressed farmers.

His kidnap was a major blow to the Afghanistan government's and western policy in this region, and they needed to fix it. If the politician died, that would be bad, but manageable. However, if the kidnappers managed to get him to denounce the proposed agriculture plans, that would be disastrous.

The authorities had to reach him first!

Time was of the essence. However, the authorities had to exercise extreme caution. They had to ensure the rescue mission wasn't effected at the wrong place. Failed operations, especially when they involved unnecessary deaths, would turn an already sensitive political environment, hostile. The Taliban and others would love this as a side benefit.

Sergeant Harry Logan and his small team were sent to evaluate one of those few possible locations. Their highly secret and sensitive mission would be on-the-ground validation that the politician was indeed there; not a well-orchestrated smokescreen.

****

With the approaching dawn, the sun started to peep over the orange and brown distant hills of this part of Nangarhar province, throwing long shadows over the landscape. It was often around this time that routine humanitarian and local support operations commenced.

In the growing light, three armoured vehicles left the compound. The two lighter, fast support vehicles topped and tailed the largest (relatively slow) one. This configuration was typical of their UN work and nearby landing strip pickups. So there was unlikely to be any suspicion of covert activity.

Sergeant Harry Logan was in charge of the four-man team sitting in the largest, the Mastiff. In his early 30s, he was young for a sergeant; a testament to the high regard of his senior officers.

His platoon trusted him explicitly. They looked to him for guidance, sometimes even to the exclusion of those junior officers who didn't heed the advice of experience. Those young officers could be dangerous when ignoring the vast experience of their NCOs while on a mission.

Logan's parents had been missionaries. With them, he'd been travelling all his life, to everywhere their NGO sent them to help. They were good people, who instilled a deep sense of right and wrong into their two children.

His parents died doing what they loved.

He joined the army to satisfy his innate desire to travel.

His only sibling, a younger sister, Estelle, went into nursing; the caring gene from her parents went deep.

In civvy street, he'd be considered an individual contributor. While capable of managing a platoon of men, as was required of his sergeant's rank, he excelled when on specialised missions that required on-the-spot decision-making; without interfering junior officers. This Op called for his particular skill set.

His brief was to validate information received, on the possible whereabouts of a kidnapped local politician. If the politician was indeed there, they were to remain in situ. They'd then offer on-the-ground sniper and intelligence support to a rescue mission waiting to be dispatched.

With Logan was Corporal Jason 'Ratty' Williams, and together, they were a formidable sniper team. While Logan was an excellent shot, Ratty Williams had the eyes of a 'shithouse rat', hence his nickname. He was the regiment's top marksman.

Logan's ability as a spotter, to absorb the terrain, out-manoeuvre the target, plan and define the best sniper attack and defensive strategy, had saved their hides on many occasions. However, this was only possible with Ratty pulling the trigger with lethal accuracy.

As well as being the best of friends, Ratty married Logan's younger sister, Estelle, much to his delight since he'd introduced them. Logan and Ratty also shared and supported each other through the deep sadness that her death from cancer brought them a few years later.

Lance Corporal 'Gnasher' Taylor was their driver for this operation. His nickname came from how he ground his teeth in a grimace of pleasure as he drove in these conditions. He was a demon on these roadways, many of them not more than rock and sand-filled tracks. Sometimes one had to drive by the feel of the terrain, as did the locals, although few had Gnasher's feel-of-the-wheel.

There was nothing Gnasher enjoyed more than off-the-road and desert driving. For his downtime, he took 'dune-bashing' holidays to Oman and the UAE to hone his skills. He even won some local off-road driving competitions, much to the frustration of nationalistic officials and the respect of his fellow competitors.

The fourth man on the team was a well-trusted and known local Afghan. Everyone called him Nabi.

After changing vehicles, their next stop would be to visit the man who supplied this particular lead about their target's location and check his story. This man was Nabi's brother.

The three vehicles drove past the nearby town to the blank stares of many. Some smiled, and a few of the children waved.

The convoy stopped on the other side of the town and parked inside a small compound containing several buildings. The Mastiff's occupants exited into a large house.

Sergeant Logan always prepared for every eventuality. Behind closed doors, signal codes for the pick-up and other contingencies were confirmed and reconfirmed. They were to meet at noon the following day unless the recovery op was in progress.

"If we're not back by then and you've not heard from us, don't risk it," warned Logan. There was always the chance of an ambush if the Taliban knew there was a rescue mission en route. Worse still, this mission could be a setup to lure them into a trap.

"I and my superiors will be the judge of whether we should progress further, based on prevailing circumstances and Intel," said the young lieutenant formally and firmly.

"Of course, sir," was all Logan could say. He hoped the young officer wouldn't do anything rash if the worst happened.

The soldiers, minus four, and their officer re-entered their vehicles, and the convoy departed to execute their other and more overtly visible mission for the day.

Not long after, an old Toyota Corolla left the compound, with Logan's team inside.

All four were in local dress for the prevailing weather during their forthcoming Op. It was mid-autumn, with day temperatures often in the mid-twenties Celsius and at night times dropping to below fifteen. Their long tops and loose trousers were comfortable for the warm day ahead. Their jackets, plus a patu (a thick shawl), were ideal for the coming cold nights.

They drove the next part of their journey, approximately 50km, to Nabi's brother's solitary farmstead.

The small saloon car had to be nurtured across the rough roads while also avoiding prying eyes. It was an uneventful journey, albeit several times they went off-road when dust clouds from vehicles were visible in the distance.

Only a relatively short distance by western road conditions, it was almost noon when they arrived at the remote property. They approached with caution. The three passengers disembarked the small car some 100m from the house and checked the surroundings. Once they were satisfied that all was clear, Gnasher parked up in front of the lean-to garage, and the others joined him.

The four men walked up to the house, they were welcomed by a man standing at the front door, who loudly shouted Nabi's name. The two men enthusiastically bear-hugged each other.

"Rafi, these are my British Army friends," grunted Nabi, as he tried to extricate himself from the clenches of the other man. He pointed to each in turn, saying their names, "Logan, Ratty, and Gnasher."

"This is my brother, Abdul-Rafi."

"I am Rafi," he politely corrected Nabi.

"Yes, yes, yes, he prefers Rafi."

"Hi," said the three soldiers in unison.

"He speaks little English, so better I translate?"

Logan concurred with Nabi's suggestion.

Rafi excitedly shook the hand of each of his visitors as they entered the small house.

The main door directly accessed the living room. Two curtained doorways, partially concealing two bedrooms, sat in the far wall. At one end of the living room was a door to the kitchen. At the other end sat an open fireplace. The walls were whitewashed, and the whole house was spotlessly clean.

As was common, Rafi didn't introduce or even give the name of his wife to these newcomers. Sensitive to the customs of this country and region, they never inquired.

Nabi explained that the couple had two young children, one boy and one girl. Both were currently at school. The children wouldn't be coming home directly. Instead, they'd stay at their uncle's house until late evening, returning home only after the team had departed for their op.

"His children, they are very good, but they are young and cannot keep secret," Nabi translated for his brother, and they all laughed in agreement.

The couple couldn't do more for their guests, offering tea, juices, and local snacks on their arrival. When a plate was empty, it was immediately filled.

While Nabi and his brother respected the politician for the good work he'd done for his people, the large reward also contributed to their exuberant enthusiasm for this mission.

After lunch, Nabi explained, as best he could in his passable English, what his brother had seen and heard.

"Many trucks and people are coming to small, walled compound. It is owned by a local farmer and Rafi says he have Taliban contacts. Some people talking of a man imprisoned there. No one see his face, it is always covered. He has expensive shoes, not normal here."

There were a few more questions and answers to reconfirm a few points. Logan then radioed in his verbal report. It was confirmed that his team should proceed with the next phase of the mission as planned.

Nabi would be their guide since he knew the compound's whereabouts. His brother was staying at home with his wife and the children; once their uncle brought them back.

Logan and Ratty off-loaded and re-checked their weapons and equipment.

At the same time, Taylor went with Nabi and his brother into the lean-to. He wanted to investigate their local incognito transport for the next stage of their Op. The roads would be rougher, changing to tracks and sand. And the tough little Corolla was no longer going to cut it, even with Gnasher at the wheel.

Rafi proudly showed off his pride and joy, an old Japanese 4x4 truck. Taylor was horrified at its state. Every panel seemed to have multiple dents and scrapes.

Nabi explained, "this is excellent truck, owned by our father and now my brother."

"More like great grandfather," mumbled Taylor to himself.

He politely managed to keep a blank face as he looked around the weather-beaten, forty-plus-year-old vehicle.

On closer inspection, he could see that it was actually sound. When they started up the old V6, he was surprised to hear a clatter-free purr. Even better, the running gear was in amazingly good condition.

Taylor couldn't help commenting. "In the west, we have a phrase, 'style over substance' and here, it's clearly 'substance over style'."

Nabi and Rafi looked at him, wondering what he was talking about.

"Doesn't matter, just talking to myself about your excellent truck."

After all the checks, the team took a siesta. Each of the three soldiers took turns as a lookout until sunset. It was going to be a long night and they knew to grab as much downtime as they could, while they were able.

The wife never spoke to the team and said little otherwise. She kept herself to herself as she prepared a dinner of traditional Kabuli Palaw. It was as tasty as any they'd tried in and around their compound and outside on relationship-building activities.

Being proper guests, they finished the lot with nodding smiles and a thank you aimed at the cook. They were sure she blushed with pride behind her Niqab but still said nothing.

It was now late in the evening and time to leave before the children returned. The four of them said their goodbyes to Rafi and his wife, promising to be back soon.

As Logan climbed into the rear seat next to Ratty, he looked at the night sky. The forecast was for clear skies, but he still had to check. Cloud cover, or even worse, rain, would be a problem for the operation.

Without the light pollution of their base compound, out here in the desert, the sky was awash with small flickering LEDs, offering a stunning light show. He always marvelled at how the stars could light up the night sky and give out so much light when there was little or no other ground light. Of course he knew the reason, but it still gave him a sense of awe.

Still dressed in their Afghan attire, they set off. Nabi sat in the passenger seat giving directions. The truck creaked and rattled as it bounced along the dusty track through the valley. Its headlights were on for the first part of this trip.

Coinciding with the rising of the moon, they would drive without lights for the latter part of the journey. It was this part that required the specialist skills of Gnasher Taylor to keep them on track.

They weren't taking the fastest and most direct way to their target since they didn't want to meet anyone else en route and possibly have their location known.

As he nursed the vehicle along the poorly marked track, Taylor remarked, "I reckon it'll be almost two hours to drive the twenty klicks to parking up, as long as the track doesn't get any worse than this."

****

Their Op was simple, on paper anyway.

They would hide the vehicle where they knew there was cover, then hike a further three kilometres or so to the compound. They were there to watch, recce, and report only; at this time. If an extraction force was deployed, they were to offer sniper support.

First, they had to get there and verify.

As they approached their planned parking location, the terrain changed from a flat valley floor to a more rugged landscape with increasingly high hills, some with sharp cliff faces.

Interwoven with the rock-strewn narrowing valley floor was a network of channels and ravines called wadis. These wadis were dry most of the year. However, during times of rain, their vicious flash floods would carry away everything and anything in their path. First, there would be a trickle of water. Then a small stream would appear. Often as not, a wall of water, sometimes almost as high as the vertical wadi sides, would descend on any unsuspecting victim.

The team offloaded their equipment from the back of the truck. Logan and Ratty readied their gear for the hike. They kept themselves hidden from sight amongst rocks to avoid anyone catching a glimpse of their specialist weaponry.

Guided by Nabi under only moonlight, Taylor slowly reversed the vehicle down a narrow track, deep into a high-sided wadi. Facing forward in this location gave them a fast exit out of the wadi should an emergency require it.

No rains were forecast. So, hopefully their truck would be there on their return, not sucked tens of kilometres downstream. This was another reason for Logan's caution about the weather. Flash floods could happen at any time and without warning.

There was no warning!

An RPG -launched rocket roared down the wadi, hitting the truck head-on, blowing up their vehicle. Taylor and Nabi died instantly. It was an ambush. Whoever they were, had intimate knowledge of their plans or had somehow been following them.

Bullets firing from positions above Logan and Ratty started to kick up sand and bounce off the rocks around them.

From the relative safety of their cover, they returned intermittent rapid-fire in the general direction of the attackers, who were positioned above them. Logan needed their attackers to stay put while he assessed the situation. This tactic also reassured the attackers that they were up against limited weaponry and skills from only two people below them.

Both deployed their night sights. Ratty quickly readied 'Thumper', the love of his life. 'She' was an L115A3 long-range, bolt-action rifle that fired 338 Lapua Magnum shells with pin-point accuracy, at least in Ratty's hands.

Ratty could easily hit an orange at one kilometre. For him, hitting anything visible at this range of a hundred metres or so would be as simple as firing a shotgun in a coconut shy.

From the locations of the gunfire, it looked like there were at least 5 of them. With Logan spotting and both letting off bursts in return they identified their attacker's locations. Ratty picked off three in quick succession as they tried to respond.

The remaining attackers soon realised what they were up against, and no longer showed themselves. They now fired the occasional burst in their general direction, while staying concealed.

It was a stalemate, at least for the moment. Logan assumed the worst; the attackers would have reinforcements coming. This gunfight had to be closed down fast.

They'd been in similar situations before. It was now time for Logan to show off how fast he could run and weave, dodging the bullets. Logan ran, with Ratty letting off bursts of rapid covering fire from his automatic weapon.

Harry quietly got above the targets. From a crouching position, he fired a short volley into the back of the closest attacker. There was no finesse to the kill.

The other attacker heard the shooting and managed to return rapid-fire as he rolled fast to one side. Logan took three of those bullets. Fortunately, two were to his Kevlar vest. One missed the vest and hit flesh in his upper arm.

Logan shot back and disabled him, forcing him to drop his weapon. The attacker recovered and tried to grab his automatic rifle again.

Even though he was livid with anger at the death of a close comrade, Logan shouted in Pashto for the man to stop. He needed this one alive for interrogation. The Afghan ignored the command and was about to fire a killing burst when Logan fired a volley to his head and chest, killing the man instantly.

He heard a vehicle driving off in the distance. There were at least six attackers, and it wouldn't be long before more were on the way.

He shouted to Ratty that all was clear but heard nothing back. Fearing the worst, he sprint-stumbled down the steep hillside to his friend. He saw Ratty lying in a pool of blood.

He'd taken a bullet in the neck and was gushing blood. Logan tried to stem the bleeding, but it was futile. His friend had already lost a lot of blood. Even if they'd had a medic with them, the wound would still have been fatal.

Cradled in Logan's lap, Ratty choked out, "OK, now tell me, why you don't have a nickname like the rest of us?"

"I do, it's Logan."

"But, that's just your last name?"

"Yep, I blame my father." Logan grinned.

Ratty coughed as he tried to laugh. He died in Logan's arms.

The operation was over, and Harry needed to get back. Without knowing how the attackers knew about their actions and position, he couldn't risk eavesdroppers knowing he was alive. So, he delayed reporting-in until he was in a less exposed location.

He looked down into the wadi to what was left of Gnasher, Nabi, and the truck. He didn't need to go down and check; it was not a pretty sight, even from where he stood.

Logan decided to head back to Nabi's brother's house since it was out of the way, and more importantly, he knew how to get there. It was the safest place in this area, and it had transport. If the brother was involved, the attackers wouldn't have taken out Nabi in the first instance. Dawn was four hours off, and he'd an almost ten kilometre route-march over rough terrain; shorter than the twenty by road getting there.

First, he had to patch himself up as best he could to stem the bleeding. Retrieving the radio and the spotting scope from Ratty's Thumper, he departed fast. There was no time for burials or hiding equipment. The departing vehicle's occupant already knew full well what equipment they had.

****

It was a long, hard trek, not helped by significant blood loss. In the oncoming dark orange twilight of dawn, he could make out Rafi's house in the distance. So close, yet so far. He was exhausted and had to rest. But Logan knew that resting now meant not being found, and never again waking up. He had no option but to continue. He'd have until noon to get back to the convoy drop-off and pick-up point.

Logan was becoming weaker. As the dawn light grew, he saw the image of his dying friend in front of him, screaming at him, "stop being such a lazy shite, move yer arse!"

Logan pushed toward his friend, who never got closer, forcing one step in front of the other.

He tripped over a small stone, which he'd normally have ignored. However, in his state, it made him fall to his knees. He struggled to stand up but couldn't. So he crawled. The light suddenly disappeared behind a shadow, and he knew this was the end.

Then hands grabbed at him, and he tried unsuccessfully to force them off.

"Safe now."

Rafi pulled Logan to his feet and half-carried him the last hundred metres or so. His wife met them in the doorway, and they both helped him to lie down on the floor.

While pleased to see Logan, the couple also had a sadness about them.

28

Knowing that their loved one, Nabi, was not with this man, they knew he was never coming back.

Logan rested there on the floor for almost an hour. Even though he looked in a bad way, his injuries weren't life-threatening. In between bouts of lucidity, they helped him drink water and soup, re-pack his wound, and stop the bleeding. He now needed time to rest and rebuild fluids from what he'd lost en route.

Once he was sufficiently awake and coherent to have a clear conversation, Logan confirmed what they already knew; Nabi was dead. He tried to explain what happened, but the couple would have nothing of it. As an honoured and injured guest, their priority was to get him to eat and drink; to build up his strength.

Without going into detail, he explained as best he could that there was an ambush and Nabi's death was quick and painless. What gave them some relief from their anguish and anger, was that five of the killers were still out there, dead.

They rationalised this as being the will of Allah.

Logan envied them. At times like this, he wished he could have the same faith in the unknown that his parents and this kind and gentle couple enjoyed. Even though he'd a religious upbringing, that belief always evaded him.

The couple's two young children still slept and they didn't want them to have a view of Logan. "Young ones like to talk," said the husband in his stunted English. "Sleep under," he said pointing to the floor, "safe."

Logan looked, but couldn't see anything.

Nabi's brother opened a concealed trap door in the corner of the room, opposite the kitchen. A few wooden stairs reached to the bottom, four feet beneath them. It was a small space, ventilated, and surprisingly cool.

Big enough to hide all the family, this was obviously a bolt-hole ready for this eventuality. It held a large mattress made from canvas over old straw on one side with a few tins on the other.

Logan placed all his gear in the hole, away from the prying eyes of the children, then climbed down. Before Rafi closed the hatch, Logan said, "as soon as the children have gone to school, call me. I must immediately leave to meet my people."

Rafi nodded in acknowledgement.

Logan lay down on the hard, lumpy, yet so welcoming mattress and immediately fell into a grateful and deep sleep.

****

It seemed like only seconds had passed when he dreamt of hearing shouting and screaming. English voices shouted, "where is he!" He could hear children screaming but heard nothing from the couple.

Logan realised he wasn't asleep; the voices came from above. To his immense relief, his team had come to collect him.

He paused, his head now clearing. He questioned what he was hearing. This couldn't be his rescue team? He hadn't yet radioed in. Checking his watch, it was almost four hours until rendezvous.

Quietly collecting his gun, Logan approached the trapdoor, he could hear ripping and a voice lewdly drooling, "she's a pretty one, isn't she."

Rafi spewed out curses, and his wife screamed.

Logan then heard, "if you don't tell us where that bastard is, first we'll have some fun with her, and then those brats. And you can watch!"

Logan pulled his pistol and cracked open the trapdoor. He was shocked at the sight. The husband and wife had both been badly beaten.

The wife was on her back, with an Afghan man holding a bayonet, kneeling between her legs.

The other Afghan bent over Rafi and screamed into his face. He held Rafi by his hair in one hand, and in the other, he pointed a handgun at his head.

Logan quietly pushed open the trapdoor and slowly exited, keeping his pistol pointed in their direction. Once clearly visible, he shouted, "British army, these are friendlies."

The one with the handgun pointing at the husband saw and recognised Logan. He gave a friendly relieved smile, "Logan, you made it back, thank god!"

30

Logan relaxed for a moment, as the man pulled the gun away from Rafi's head. Then to his shock and horror, it ended up pointing at him.

As the attacker fired, Rafi pushed down on the gun hand causing the attacker to shoot Logan in the right lower leg.

Disabled, Logan collapsed to one side. That collapse saved him from the next, perfectly aimed, headshot; Logan's head was no longer there. As he fell and rolled to his non-injured side, Logan fired a double tap at the gunman, who collapsed, dead.

In the meantime, the other attacker was launching himself at Logan, bayonet in hand. He took a dead centre shot to the forehead. The dead attacker collapsed on Logan's wounded leg, who screamed in agony. Waves of nausea came over him, so he could hardly see.

Another attacker rushed into the room. Seeing Logan, he cried out, "bastard!" He levelled his weapon to shoot Logan, who was in no fit state to defend himself.

A shot resounded through the house, then another, and another. Rafi had picked up his attacker's handgun and shot the newcomer. He calmly walked over to the injured third man, while slowly and methodically firing into his body until the clip was empty.

A few minutes later, there was a roar from a powerful vehicle as it drove back toward where Logan had hiked.

The shot to Harry's leg meant he was unable to walk. He was later to find out that it had fractured his tibia. As the wife administered to the new wound, applied a splint, and re-packed the shoulder injury, the husband searched and stripped the bodies.

They weren't locals, which was no surprise to Logan after what had happened. Rafi found and lobbed their ID cards to Logan; they had Albatross Tactical Security identification.

Rafi extracted their cash, valuables, and anything useful. He looked in Logan's direction, pointing to the haul to check if he wanted his share. He shook his head as a no, and Nabi's brother smiled as he continued to rifle through their clothes.

Their weapons weren't army issue or even standard Albatross. Mercs often preferred to use their own choice of weapons on personal Ops; the attackers' weapons were even different from each other.

Logan knew that the fourth man who drove off would report what had happened. It was also safe to assume he'd also be from ATS (its common acronym), or at least working for them, and this visit was linked to the ambush that killed his team.

Logan was angry. Somewhere in ATS, people were responsible for killing his best friend, and he knew there was nothing he could ever do about it. Politics and big financial interests would prevent any repercussions.

The men were stripped and the couple started to remove the bodies from the house.

"What will you do with them?"

"Take wadi, animal eating," sneered the husband. "No one finds, soon, bones everywhere, many animals happy, full bellies." He rubbed his stomach smiling.

This trio would come to an unceremonious end from the wild animals of this area.

Rafi and his wife ungainly dumped the three naked bodies in the boot of the old Corolla, their arms and legs hanging out, dragging in the sand. He watched the car recede into the distance, the boot flapping up and down with every bump and undulation.

Logan couldn't control his laughter. A weird image of a large monster's mouth chomping on the humans came into his mind.

The closest wadi was about a kilometre away, and they'd soon be back. So, while they were away, Logan manufactured a makeshift crutch and engaged the two children to pack a few precious things to bring with them. The family was compromised and could no longer live there.

It was now pointless staying radio-silent. The fourth man knew what had happened. Soon, if not already, more people would be on their way. Logan radioed in, using the agreed emergency call sign. He requested an airlift evacuation for all of them, explaining his injuries and that opposing forces were coming for them.

"Give me five and I'll get back to you."

After the parents returned from their carrion feeding excursion, they packed their most valuable and transportable possessions into the small car. Everything else would have to be retrieved later, if ever.

Even though he'd only a smattering of Pashto, Logan couldn't help laughing at the disagreements between the parents and children. Unsurprisingly, what the boy and girl considered valuable possessions differed from their parents.

Before leaving, they burned the attackers' clothes.

All five immediately departed in the beaten-up old car. The couple sat in the front, Logan was stretched-out on the rear seat, and the two children were crammed into the rear footwells. It was also the safest place for them if bullets started flying.

Others would be coming fast in 4x4s, and the fleeing group needed to maximise whatever head start they had. And that might not be enough, even with a chopper on the way.

As they drove the old Corolla to the rendezvous, the radio crackled.

"Logan?"

He acknowledged with his call sign.

"No choppers available, repeat, no airlift. Proceed towards the rendezvous point. The convoy will now meet you en route."

Logan acknowledged. He was now worried. What were previously even odds to reach safety with an airlift were now low. If the attackers were close, they'd have no chance. He wished he could pray and believe it would do any good.

Even though they now took the shortest route back, it was still a long way on these roads. If these were decent roads, the group might have made good time. However, there were pockets of deep loose sand. If the car got stuck, there wouldn't be enough time to extract it. There was also the danger of rocks and other debris damaging the running gear.

"We will be met by my team who will protect us. We will soon be safe," Logan said with a forced smile. It might be there was no one coming after them, but that was most unlikely. They knew too much, and all would have to be silenced.

Rafi gave what he thought was a reassuring grin to Logan. "No problem. I excellent driver. I know road."

None of them really believed what both had said. However, they had no choice but to travel fast, balancing speed with caution.

With Logan's injuries, it was a painful journey across the badly rutted road-cum-track. Rafi had to ignore the stifled grunts of pain from his badly wounded passenger bouncing around in the back. He had to focus on his driving; for everyone's safety.

It wasn't long before Logan could see dust clouds behind them, which meant one or more vehicles were coming up fast.

The chase was on!

Soon after that first sighting, using Ratty's spotting scope, he could see two large 4x4s following them, catching up fast.

He radioed the convoy for their speed and position. From their stated location and doing a quick calculation, there wasn't enough time for the comparatively slow armoured convoy to reach them.

The convoy was in the same configuration as their drop-off. Leading the three vehicles was the fast 4-man Husky. Its vicious bite was a machine gun that could fire 50 Calibre rounds over 2km. Following the Husky was the larger and more heavily armoured Mastiff. Its teeth were a 7.62mm general-purpose machine gun. For this Op, it had the addition of a 40mm automatic grenade launcher. Taking up the rear was the nimble Foxhound.

All the vehicles had to stay together to maintain the convoy's integrity.

Logan knew that the relatively slow Mastiff, having a top speed of not much more than 50mph at the best of times, would hold up the convoy. He also knew to his dismay, the Mastiff, and therefore the convoy, would be even slower on these roads.

As the pursuing 4x4s closed in on them, Logan again radioed in their situation and vice versa. The convoy advised they were 30 minutes out from meeting up. Logan looked back. At their current speed, the 4x4s would be on them sometime before then.

Rafi sped up since it was a shit-or-bust situation. The poor car bounced and pitched over the rough surface.

At last, far ahead, they could make out a cloud of dust heading toward them. It was the rescuing convoy, he assumed, he hoped.

Looking behind with the spotting scope, Logan could see the now closer 4x4s were each full of men. The convoy was too far away and too slow. There was no chance of rescue, even at their increased speed, and no way to go faster.

The radio announced, "we're breaking with protocol to reach you in time."

"Sir, but…" Logan was now worried about the convoy as well. He knew what was about to happen.

To no one in particular, Logan muttered, "shit, they've got a gung-ho Rupert in charge. Poor sods."

"You cannot do what you're planning, it's suicide!" Logan called back, protesting.

"Shut it, Logan. Decision made!" was the abrupt response from the officer in charge.

At that, the two smaller and faster vehicles, each able to reach speeds of 70mph, even on these roads, quickly accelerated away from the heavier Mastiff. This was a dangerous decision. The commander was taking a calculated risk that those following the Corolla didn't have time to prepare for an ambush that would have devastated the broken-up convoy.

The following 4x4s were now less than 500m from the Corolla. Logan could see men in both pursuing vehicles standing through the sunroofs, all in Afghan attire. Their automatic weapons trained on the little Toyota; they waited.

The Foxhound drew away from the Husky. With luck, the faster vehicle might reach the Corolla in time.

However, there was a big problem with this plan. Even if the Foxhound could reach the little Corolla before the following vehicles, its four occupants would be out-gunned by those in the two 4x4s.

What was earlier a safe convoy of three became an exposed straggling line of independent vehicles, heading to an unlikely rescue; and possible ambush.

The rescuers couldn't open fire on the following vehicle since this would be construed as aggression towards 'innocent' road users.

The convoy commander was taking an immense risk.

Logan identified the leader of the attackers, who was becoming increasingly agitated. It was obvious to him and everyone else that the Foxhound might make it in time to rescue the Toyota's occupants. As the Corolla came within range, he shouted in Pashto, "fire on the car, but don't kill them all."

Bullets pelted the small car and blew both rear tyres. The Corolla now struggled to move at all. Rafi fought with the steering wheel, trying to drive as fast as the car could. He and his wife started to pray, and the children cried; it was now all over for the occupants.

The leader of the attackers grinned widely, showing off his brown, tobacco-stained teeth. Disabling the Corolla meant they'd get there first. At best there'd be a stand-off. At worst, they'd use the hostages to get away.

Jubilant cheers and war cries emanated from the following cars' occupants. The attackers had won! Their prey was within their grasp, and the rescuers had given up.

Opening fire on the old Corolla was the attackers' fatal mistake!

The Husky and the Mastiff were quickly ready and in place. They were no longer aggressors but defenders in response to an attack.

Firing from different sides of the road to avoid hitting the old Toyota and the Foxhound, they pounded the following vehicles with heavy-calibre gunfire and grenades.

Within a few seconds, it was all over. There was little left of the two 4x4s and their occupants.

When the Mastiff arrived, a medic checked none of the others were wounded before starting work on Logan.

Major Anderson came over, "well Logan, you do like to have your fun, don't you? We cut it a bit fine, didn't we, eh?" he grinned.

"Sorry sir, I didn't realise you were in charge of the convoy. Otherwise, I'd not have…" Logan didn't finish his sentence.

He was cut off by another, "shut it, Logan."

"Yes, sir," said Logan with a beaming grin. "Thank you, sir. You saved all our lives by breaking formation."

The major laughed. "Bollocks, I learned this from your report on last year's hospital extraction. Fast thinking and a brilliant strategy from a mere sergeant. Made the insurgents think they'd won. All I did was follow your lead. I learned this tactic from you, old boy."

"Anyway, who out here's going to argue with me like you then did with Lieutenant Smythe?"

Logan remembered the thanks from the people rescued that day. Soon after the euphoria of that rescue, the official dressing down from his commanding officer followed. Logan had refused to follow a superior officer's command, even though it saved lives.

He could have been court-martialled. However, that incident was highly visible. If the details came out, it would have been embarrassing to the company command.

The following week, Lieutenant Smythe was reassigned.

A check on what remained of the two 4x4s' occupants showed no survivors or useful ID.

There'd be people looking for them, so there was no point in further delays. The convoy headed back to base.

****

In the back of the Mastiff, the parents played with the children. They were doing their best to occupy them and keep their minds off what had happened during the last few hours.

Logan eyed the four of them, admiring the resilience of these children. The kids were doing remarkably well despite everything that happened.

On their way back, some distance ahead, they saw a newly erected checkpoint blocking the road. The major turned round to the parents and children and held his finger to his mouth, saying, "shhh." The parents hugged the children, who quickly and thankfully became quiet.

Approaching the checkpoint, they saw it was manned by armed local militia and personnel dressed in ATS uniforms. As they drew up in front of the barrier, Major Anderson asked, with a display of concern, "this checkpoint is new. Wasn't here earlier. Anything we need to worry about?"

"Insurgents sir. Attacked a compound and killed a prominent politician. Have you seen a white Toyota Corolla?"

"Seen nothing at all on the road. All quiet."

"Thank you, sir."

Carry on," the major said to his driver.

****

En route to base, the major joined Logan, who lay on a stretcher in the Mastiff. Logan could give Major Anderson a short verbal de-brief but only the non-controversial details.

Logan realised there were political ramifications in the evidence he had against ATS and didn't want to drag the major into it. So he asked, "respectfully sir, the rest is highly sensitive. Any chance I only de-brief the C.O.? Really sorry sir, but I can't say anything more. People could get hurt."

Anderson knew and respected this sergeant enough to support and accept his request. Having experienced recent events, Anderson realised the Intel from this Op was likely to be above his rank and responsibility in any case.

On arrival at the compound, Logan was taken to the field hospital, where they operated on his fractured tibia. His shoulder wound was clean and only needed stitches.

"Do as you're told, and none of your macho bollocks, and you'll be fit for full active duty in two to three months," said the female surgeon after the operation. "You need rest and physio."

Rafi and his family were given into the care of a social and re-allocation team for those situations where Afghan nationals were in danger. Their case was fast-tracked. The children had gone through enough already. Saving Logan's life and supporting the efforts of their government and the allies also helped their case.

Once Logan had come around from his operations, the doctor asked if he was able to do a private debrief. Logan enthusiastically agreed. He had a burning need to talk about the failed mission. In particular, he wanted to explain the involvement of ATS and possible Taliban collusion. This assumed he could speak with the right people; he was.

The major had passed on Logan's message. The two visitors comprised Lieutenant Colonel Parks ('Parkie' behind his back) and another man he knew to be the base spook.

No one knew the spook's name or what his duties were. Logan had seen him coming and going on his own and occasionally saw him on joint ops with the 'balaclava brigade', as Logan called them. As was tradition, the spook needed a nickname, and the one given to him by the company was Luke, as in 'Luke-the-Spook'. Not a particularly inventive name, but it served its purpose.

Parkie vouched for 'Luke' as being 100% reliable and trustworthy. He left the two of them to talk alone.

Logan then delivered a full and detailed account of what happened.

Part of the way through Logan's story, Luke interrupted. "When you compile your report, I trust that the involvement and your suspicions of Albatross Tactical Security will be left out?"

"As you request, sir." Logan continued to explain what had happened.

Luke took a great deal of interest in the story, asking many detailed questions. Surprisingly, Luke asked a lot about Logan's interpretation of events and his suspicions.

"It doesn't take a rocket scientist to work out what happened. And also, how come ATS people were so quick in getting to Nabi's brother's house," were a couple of unprompted comments that Logan offered.

"I've seen the reports from the others involved. You showed a high level of resourcefulness in getting back. Interesting observations. Well done chap."

He then left.

During this and follow-up interviews, the spook made detailed notes, none of which appeared in the official files.

On his final debriefing session before leaving, Luke commented, "looking at your files, you seem to be in demand for Covert Ops, also by the special services teams. Always in a supporting role, and often in more danger than the rest of them."

Not knowing where this discussion was going, Logan could only respond with, "it's the job, sir." He waited for the spook to get to the point that was eventually coming; hopefully.

"Yet you're not with them officially. You applied to these sections and were rejected, even though you met all the physical and technical tests for entry. Do you know why?" asked the spook.

"Dunno, sir?"

"Speak freely man. What we discuss, stays between the two of us. I expect the same from your side as well."

"OK. I know my reputation precedes me. Don't like what they consider mavericks, but what I consider a soldier using his head."

"There are conflicting reports about you. Some say you're an unknown quantity and dangerous."

Logan thought about how he should respond. "Some Ruperts are good, like Major Anderson." Since this man was clearly not an officer, it seemed reasonable to refer to officers as 'Ruperts'. "The good ones know when and who to ask for advice and support. They use the experience of the people around them. They and their command are the most likely to survive the shit around here."

"Then there are the arrogant arseholes. While they may or may not survive, they often kill their men." He would have liked to add 'criminally negligent', but that was probably going too far.

"I've upset a few of these idiots by saving their lives when I had to ignore, sometimes overrule, commands. I expect there's a mixed bag of reports about me, which makes people nervous."

Logan mimicked a posh accent, "issues following the chain of command, doesn't know his place." Then back in his normal voice, continued, "or such-like? Am I correct?"

"Yep, pretty much so," said the spook, looking at a file. "It says here, 'not always a team player and when lives are on the line, he'll follow his instincts and not orders. He's a dangerous man to have in the team'."

"And here's another one, 'this solder is sharp and a strategic thinker. I've learned to listen and follow his advice, even though only a corporal. His quick thinking saved lives'."

"As I said, there are some good ones out there," retorted Logan to a thoughtful spook, "but not all."

Luke left once he had everything he wanted and made the promise they'd talk again.

Rafi and his family visited Logan the following day to say goodbye. They were being re-settled, and no one was supposed to know where, not even them, until they arrived. The re-settlement team then took them away to their new life and new IDs. Logan never saw or heard from them again.

Ratty's body, Thumper, and the remains of Gnasher and Nabi were recovered. Ratty's body's repatriation was also Logan's plane. Thankfully, Logan was well enough, albeit on crutches, to attend his best friend's full military funeral.

****

The compound doctors were correct; his physical recovery did take over two months.

Emotionally, it was a different matter. Nothing more was said on the ATS subject. During his recuperation, Logan also developed a burning rage and hatred for everything ATS. Since he couldn't talk about it, his anger grew like a cancer, eating him from within.

However, he did learn one thing; ATS was extremely well-connected, with a reputation for having a long memory.

Once fully recovered and signed off fit, Logan was refused active duty. Could it be his psych. eval? He never knew.

He was deployed to the Logistics Corps back in Afghanistan. Awaiting the flight to take off to his new posting, Luke appeared and came over.

"Mind if I sit?" he gestured to the seat next to Logan.

Logan gave the spook a questioning look, merely offering a shake of his head as an uncertain affirmative. He always wondered why the promise of a further discussion after the debriefing sessions never materialised. And here he was.

The two never spoke until they were airborne. Over the loud noise of the military aircraft's engines, Luke turned to Logan and spoke directly into his ear.

"Want to hurt ATS and those militia groups responsible for the shit you went through? And I mean, hurt them badly. You might even get a shot at the 4th man and the person running the show."

Logan immediately responded, "how?" There was no hesitance to Logan's enthusiastic response. Luke knew Logan was recruited so continued.

"We've been after some elements in ATS for a while now. We have certain evidence that they've been working with the Taliban, various militia, and growers. They've been using their connections in the drugs trade to build a production business there."

Logan gave a curt reply, "doesn't what happened on my last Op give you enough ammunition to go after them?" Then with frustration, "what more evidence do you lot need?"

"I don't need more. If up to me, I'd close down the whole operation. But it's not up to me. I'm a soldier, just like you, but I fight a different type of war. Unlike you, I, and my masters have few tools at our disposal."

"We need to do a bit of invasive surgery on ATS, also their friends and allies. It has troublesome sores to be drained of pus before the whole body gets gangrene; excuse the medical analogy."

"Why are you telling me this?"

Without answering the question, Luke continued. "We need to lance a few septic boils; that requires a precision scalpel. This is a one-man operation, and you fit that bill. You'll make our incisions but your way. Of course, you'll need specialist training, which I'm sure you'll walk. However, if you fail, you'll be back on active duty."

It now dawned on him why they rejected his active duty request.

"So, you want me to kill a few people in revenge for them killing my best mate?"

"If you want to put it that way, that about sums it up."

"Then, why not just say that! Y-E-S, yes. I'm in."

And that started the next chapter in Logan's life.

3. THE OFFER

❋❋ *Present Day* ❋❋

At 5 am the morning after the nightclub incident, Harry Logan was rudely awakened by a thump on his police station cell door. Moments later, it opened, and inside walked a smartly attired man. He wore a dark pinstripe suit and had the shiniest shoes he'd seen since leaving the army. He looked in his forties and had sprinklings of grey in his dark hair.

The man sat down on the bed next to Harry and nodded to the policeman, who then closed the door and left.

Harry said nothing but simply waited for what the man had to say.

"So, ex-Sergeant Harry Logan, you've gotten yourself into some bother. All the evidence the police have contradicts everything you say. No one believes you, and you've nothing to support your side of the story. Seems you're stuffed, to use the vernacular."

He spoke with what Harry could imagine was a posh private school-educated accent, similar to many of the Ruperts back in his army days. Yes, come to think of it, he did have the look of a Rupert.

Harry nodded a yes. Assuming this was part of the legal process, he asked, "are you my lawyer? I've not been involved with this sort of thing before, so don't know how these things work."

Then thinking about it, he followed up with, "isn't it early for lawyers to be visiting clients?"

"No, no, my boy. Not a lawyer," the man laughed. "I'm far better than any lawyer for what you need right now. I can prove your innocence, and you can walk out of here a free man without a tarnish on that illustrious military career of yours."

"How can you do this when the police can't?" responded an incredulous Harry.

"Simple, we are not the overworked police dealing with all last night's drunken festivities. So they never investigated further. And, why would they, eh? Why waste their time, using up valuable manpower on a slam-dunk case like yours? Yours is yet another case closed, that helps them achieve their arrest targets."

"So, why are you helping me; what's in it for you?"

Then it clicked. He challenged, "what do you want from me in return?"

We know you, Mr Logan. You're one of us, well used to be. We like to look after our own." He had the nicest of smiles. If Harry hadn't known better, he'd have believed him.

"So, while you have been lounging in this fine establishment we've been busy bees on your behalf." His manner was too jovial for this time of the morning, especially after what had happened a few hours ago to Harry.

The man continued his story since he seemed to like the drama. "Basically, we've found the girls, and they confirmed your story. We have mobile footage from a couple of the people at the front of the queue and their supporting evidence. Saying that, they won't stand up in court against those two men; too frightened of repercussions. The nightclub owner is a rather nasty little man."

He let that sink in for a moment. "We can prove that the two guys were up to no good with that poor girl. All were lying to the police, including their uncle and your other bouncer friends. With all that evidence, you can walk now. Not a chink in that perfect character of yours."

Harry was naturally suspicious. The police found nothing, yet during the night, this man (and probably others) went out to collate evidence for no apparent reason. If what he was saying was true, a quid-pro-quo was coming.

"OK, what's the deal, and how can I trust you?" was Harry's obvious next question.

The man held up his index finger as a sign for Harry to hold fire with any further questions. After dialling a number on his mobile phone, he passed it to Harry without saying a word.

"Hi Harry," said the man on the other end. "We've missed you since you left the army and our little gang."

Harry immediately recognised the familiar voice of Luke-The-Spook, with whom he subsequently worked after his injuries.

"Listen, the man with you can be trusted. He's a genuine offer to get you out of all this, and you'll end up a rich man in the process."

Before Harry could ask anything further, he hung up. Harry had worked with Luke for four years and trusted him.

'Well, as much as any of that lot could be.' He inwardly corrected himself.

While with the Army's Logistics Division, Harry enjoyed a parallel secondment, working with Luke. At that time. Harry was single-mindedly bent on retaliation. The spook and his masters capitalised on those feelings of anger, frustration, and revenge.

Harry was angry at himself for not killing the remaining two attackers more quickly, which could have prevented his friend's death.

However, he was angrier with ATS and the 4th man that got away from the attack on Nabi's family. Then there was rage at those others behind the attack on Logan's team and whoever else colluded with the whole damned mess.

At that time, he was a time bomb waiting to explode. The security services capitalised on those feelings and channelled those emotions to their advantage.

Over the following four years, Harry became the highly trained and skilled scalpel that the likes of Luke and others wielded. He excelled in these fully deniable solo operational roles.

However, time passed, and Harry healed. He needed out of the never-ending cycle of suspicion, intrigue, and killing. There was always the promise of the next mission getting him closer to those responsible, but it never came. It was time to leave the army and put all that pain behind him.

And for a few months, he'd succeeded, until now.

Harry, resigned to what was about to come, then said to the man, "OK, I'm all ears."

The man explained the Op to Harry, who listened without question.

When the man had finished, Harry responded. "I'm no longer your pet monkey and I'm not going to kill on demand again. I've left that behind."

"We are not asking you to kill anyone. This is merely a job that requires your unique talents. And as a contractor, and since no longer in the employ of Her Majesty's Government, you'll be paid handsomely for your services."

Harry stared at the man sitting next to him. He knew this was yet another game they were playing with him, but he had no choice.

"If I say yes, what happens?"

"In 15 minutes, you walk out of here a free man, with all charges dropped. Half the money will be deposited in a Swiss bank account, and I'll give you a contact number for a person who'll be your controller for this operation. You must call that number today."

He handed Harry a telephone. "This is a non-traceable phone. Call the number that is plumbed in and take instructions. It's as easy as that."

"So what if I let you clear me of all this nonsense, take the money, then tell you I've changed my mind?"

"That would be silly indeed, haven't you learned anything about us from these past four years?" responded the man.

"Your Mr Bradley, as you know, is a man of dubious pedigree. He WILL find you with our help. He WILL hurt you, then he WILL kill you, and he'll walk away without any consequences befalling him or his people. And no one will care."

"In parallel, ATS will receive information on you that you would not like them to have. You might survive one, but not both. Do we have an agreement?"

Harry, resigned to what was happening to him, shook his head in the affirmative. There was nothing else he could do.

Fifteen minutes after the suit left, the charges were dropped. Harry walked into the cold, dark morning air. He was free, albeit still a hunted man.

He called the number, took instructions, and made plans to live and hide in open sight.

4. SAFE LANDINGS

Harry Logan woke up from a rough prodding in his back with something hard. There was a time when an abrupt awakening would have brought him to instantaneous action. These days, bundled up like a bag of old washing made that reaction impossible. His outside layer was a well-worn sleeping bag cum straight-jacket that limited movement.

It was late winter, the nights were cold, and street-living at this time of the year required being well-wrapped up in layers. As well as protection from the weather, all this covering offered some protection from the like of drunken arseholes who felt the urge to victimise and abuse vulnerable homeless people. The downside was his inability to self-defence.

His immediate reaction was to cover up as best he could while squirming to see who was enjoying the moment and prepare for likely trouble. He carefully turned around and looked up to see what was going on.

The low morning sun streamed through the myriad of shattered windows and cast a shadow over him from the looming figure. Once his eyes adjusted to the light, he saw a man using a large baseball bat for the prodding.

Baseball bat man had the look of another street dweller. His dirty, old, undersized greatcoat was partially held closed by a belt that was fighting to retain a body long gone to seed; if it had ever flowered, which looked unlikely. Underneath, looked to be several layers of various clothing to keep out the biting cold. Below, hung a pair of filthy, baggy trousers. He was of medium height, with an overgrown stubble covering an under washed face. His head was bald on the top, like a tonsure. What hair remained was shoulder-length and lank.

'*A vision only a mother could love,*' the man on the ground thought to himself as he looked up at the man wielding the bat.

Harry could now see other people hovering in the background; his hangers-on. Two more confident ones hung around close enough to offer verbal support to baseball bat man, but not too close. These two were nervous about any potential physical response from Harry. They needn't have worried. He knew there was no point in trying anything but to go with the flow.

Behind them, Harry could see a couple of others with an even more hesitant supportiveness about them. They clearly didn't want to get directly involved but had to be seen to be in on the action. One was a rather scrawny girl of unknown age. She could have been pretty at one time, but life on the street had taken its heavy toll on her frail body. The other was a small, weedy-looking young man.

Harry looked around in the morning light. There were many others around. Some were still sleeping, and others glanced over from their resting places but not too intently. They just watched in a sort of concerned yet resigned way.

Realising his prone victim was neither in any state nor willing to defend or protect himself, bat man's confidence rose. He leaned forward and explored his victim's ribs with a shabby pair of flappy-soled boots. Leaning down, and through a mouth half-full of tobacco-stained and rotten teeth, he hissed at his prone victim, "this is my turf."

'*The breath, my god his breath!*' Harry cringed, almost retching, as he lay there on the ground. This man had the breath of a rotten fish stuffed down a wrestler's jockstrap. Bat man didn't need the boots or the baseball bat to inflict pain; breathing on someone would have been suffering enough!

Standing back up again, and for all to hear, the man with the baseball bat half shouted, half sneered, "piss off, or pay! You have to pay to live here." He gestured to the building they were in; now a derelict shell of a once-proud member of the UK industry.

Since his get-out-of-jail-free card, Harry had been living on the street. During that time, he'd experienced many instances of the weaker being abused by the stronger. Often it was a demand for money or possessions, sometimes simple threats, and other times plain nastiness and bullying. But never before had he a demand for payment to live on the street; apart from some of the hostels, of course. But, that's a different matter.

Last night, the shelter of this old warehouse gave him the best sleep he'd had during the last few weeks. If it's not the weather, it's the police, the wardens, security, thugs, and others, all trying to sap what little self-respect people living on the street have.

It's so hard to find somewhere to sleep without fear or interference, especially if you want to avoid the shelters. And, many in his position had a rational, sometimes irrational, fear of authority or being recognised; for whatever might be their many reasons.

He looked at the man hovering over him, and replied, "I've only got a few quid."

"Hand it over, all of it," hissed the man over him.

Harry fumbled in his sleeping back and pulled out an old cloth containing his meagre wealth. Baseball bat man grabbed the lot.

"How do I eat?" the man on the ground asked loudly, not wanting this foul breathed-man to come too close to hear.

The man placed a foot on the prone man's chest. "Get off yer arse and get begging, or whatever you fucking do. I'm generous, and I only take half your money for livin' 'ere," he laughed.

"If you're back here tonight, don't think about cheating me out of what I's owed. Woody here'd love the opportunity of getting t' know ya better," he threatened, swinging his bat menacingly. "I knows everything what happens in my manor. We're a happy family here," he said smilingly and gestured around with his stick to the people who watched on with feigned disinterest.

Now he'd finished with Harry, he strutted off to his quarters, a concoction of large boxes made into a den. It didn't look much. However, sheltered from the worst of the elements by the building, all that cardboard was a great insulator against the cold.

"Oi," he shouted to the scrawny girl who was on the periphery of the altercation.

She looked down in a resigned sort of way and followed him into his place. The noises emanating from the boxes were not of her pleasure. Baseball bat man's two lackeys smirked at each other knowingly.

With the excitement over, those who'd looked on went back to whatever they were doing, or not. The newcomer could now take in his surroundings.

It was night when Harry arrived. Now, in the early morning light of a new day, he could now properly check out the environment he couldn't view last night. Looking around, this was a massive building. It must have been over a hundred metres long and almost fifty wide.

In its heyday, it could have been a factory or warehouse, perhaps dating back to mid last century, or earlier. However, Harry was no historian, so didn't dwell on that thought.

Starting halfway up each of the graffiti covered side walls was a row of tall windows, most of which had broken panes of glass. Each side of the apex of the roof contained more windows, many fortunately unbroken. Unnoticeable from the outside, they weren't a target for the kids who enjoyed breaking windows, especially when they knew homeless people slept rough inside.

As a result, many potential dry places offered shelter from the worst of the elements. However, these would depend on the direction of the wind blowing in the rain.

Two rows of pillars supported the roof. Each pillar had a concrete base with steel on top. They rose to a web of interlocking large rusty steel girders. All supported a roof that was possibly twenty metres high. It was built in the period when over-engineering was the norm, resulting in a structure that was safe and sound.

It would hopefully protect the street dwellers for many years to come unless greedy developers became involved. Harry was surprised it hadn't already gone under the wrecking ball.

There were high-level gangways around the side; of dubious safety. On one side, there was a raised platform under which bat man had his boudoir; once possibly supporting the foreman's offices. Dotted around were rusty steel barrels, piping, and other general items of a bygone industrial era.

This building was a good find, validated by the many others who had the same idea. Several other large cardboard shelters clustered on the same dry and sheltered side as bat man's lodgings. Harry assumed the elite of this troop enjoyed this area. The rest of the building gave haven to many other people, wrapped as best they could to avoid the cold and wet late winter nights.

After a while, baseball bat man came out. He stared a warning to the newcomer. Then, with his lackeys, he headed off to do whatever they got up to.

5. AN EDUCATION

The small, thin guy went to the 'luxury' boxed home from where baseball bat man had emerged. He reappeared shortly after and looked in the direction of Harry. The small man stared for a few moments deep in thought, then came over and sat near the newcomer. It wasn't too close to invade the newcomer's space or be strangely uncomfortable, but close enough to suggest he was happy to talk.

After a few moments of wondering if this was a good idea, the thin man looked over to the new guy, who smiled back in assent.

The thin man slid a little closer and said, "Hi, I'm Tom. The girl over there who went in with Fish-Breath is my sister, Jess."

"I'm Harry," said the newcomer who'd been the focus of everyone's recent attention.

"Fish-Breath? So, why Fish-Breath?"

Harry quickly realised his daft question. He remembered the foul smell that engulfed him when being threatened close-up by the dirty slob. Holding his nose and pretending to be sick, he grinned at Tom. "Oops, forget I asked that daft question."

They both laughed. And after that initial bonding and joking, Tom's confidence grew.

"Fish-Breath and his mates like to call me Weasel," said the small man. "He loves to slag me off in front of everyone, particularly in front of my sister. He'd love it if I left, but I'm staying put, no matter what."

There was an air of determination from this man, despite his lack of physical presence.

"So, why don't the two of you up and go when he's not around?" asked Harry.

51

Tom gestured toward the boxes from where Fish-Breath exited and where the girl still was. "She's a druggie, needs her fix, and he supplies it. What she goes through in there is the lesser evil compared to when I found her."

Tom sighed and was silent for a few moments, then continued. "He's a shit, but after all the drugs he's taken his libido's all but knackered. So her services are not in great demand. Saying that, showing off his prowess earlier to you in front of people here gave him a thrill that he needed to satisfy, hence Jess being summoned."

"Sorry," was all Harry could think of saying.

Tom quickly responded. "No, no, I'm not blaming you. It's just the way it is, and the way things are around here. If not you, there'd be some other reason. It least that's the last she'll have to go through for a few days, if not longer."

Tom perked up, saying, "anyway, he's only the one bastard, and that's better than she had before. So, she does what she needs to. In return, she gets protection and access to cleaner stuff than he sells around."

As an afterthought, "she's addicted to anything she can get."

Harry said nothing, preferring to let the man speak and get whatever off his chest he needed to. He needed information on how things worked there so he could survive. Indirectly, this man was supplying just that.

"What else I can do?" the small man sighed. "Look at me! I'm not in a position to protect her. But, I hang around to do what little I can."

Tom sat in silence for a while, clearly trying to decide if Harry was OK.

Harry looked over this small, yet brave man. If what he said was true, he admired his tenacity. "You're a good man to do what you do. She must be thankful to have you around."

Tom smiled a combined sigh and thanks in return. Eventually deciding that Harry was OK, he explained their background. For some reason, Harry looked like someone who'd listen.

He told Harry that Jess was taken into care and eventually ran away from the care system that let her down. Tom blamed himself for not doing more to protect her at their home since he was the older brother. Now, she'd no home, no parents, and no way to safely get back into the system. Tom felt it was down to him to offer what meagre support he could.

"When they took her away, splitting us up, I stayed with my mother to look after her. I thought Jess'd be safe in care, but they screwed her up proper, in every way. I didn't know until she ran away and disappeared onto the streets where no one could find her. I vowed if I found her, I'd never leave her again. So, here we are, stuck with this lot," Tom shrugged with resignation.

They'd survived a lot together. She was all he had, and vice versa. The only way Tom could help her was to be with her on the streets and do his best, which he knew wasn't a lot.

Harry realised that Tom had been bottling it all up for a while. Spewing this out to a complete stranger somehow offered a modicum of therapy.

Harry could do nothing more than offer a sympathetic ear. It was none of his business and something in which he couldn't get involved.

Tom then said, "Fish-Breath's name is Albert James Wilson. Most people call him 'the Bastard' because that's what he is. But he's right. Living here does give us protection from the outside. He knows very bad people, and no one bothers us here."

Tom explained that Albert had been on the street for years. Some of the older people remember him appearing. He initially ran drugs for some of the gangs but started to take too much himself. Apparently, he'd had a type of schizophrenic episode. People suggested it was because of too many drugs for too long; it wasn't only weed he enjoyed at that time. Just like Jess nowadays, he took anything and everything he could then lay his hands on.

"He still hears voices, and at those times when he hears them, I try to keep Jess away. He sometimes goes mental!"

Harry knew that drugs could initiate these and many other issues. He'd seen it so often from his parents' missionary work and later on tour in the army, both inside and outside the military compounds.

One of the first things that medics and Ruperts reinforced on every new tour, especially in Afghanistan, was the abundance of drugs and the dangers of using them. For many people, even the likes of Cannabis, which many consider harmless, is dangerous and can bring on schizophrenic episodes and other reactions, especially in younger people.

"So, I'm assuming our Albert still deals or runs for the gangs?" Harry asked.

"He thinks he's a dealer, but the main man around this 'hood is Moses. Fish-Breath's nothing more than a pusher."

Tom explained that Moses' real name is Jeremiah Williams. Through Albert, he'd found another small, but still good enough, market to sell the worst of his product.

"Moses cuts drugs with all sorts of 'shit,' so they become affordable. Fish-breath then cuts it further and sells it even cheaper to that lot." He waved his hand at the people around them. "And to loads of others living on the street who come around."

Tom told him that people had been ill from the bad drugs, and some had even died. Jess had also been very sick once and taken to hospital; that was from Moses direct. So, whatever additional chemicals Albert cut into the drugs would be worse.

"Moses has a rep. on the street for his bad gear, but who's going to complain if the drugs are affordable? And who amongst this lot is going complain about Albert?" said a frustrated Tom.

"So why the nickname Moses?" Harry asked.

"He keeps on spouting his four commandments; the name stuck.

You shalt only buy from him.

Keep your gob shut.

He's THE boss.

Once in, you're only out when dead."

"So, if Moses is only a local dealer, who's his supplier?"

Tom replied that Moses is a runner-cum-dealer for the main drug gang that sells in this area. It was they who were the real power around here.

"If ever you meet Moses be careful. He's evil and full of his own shit. He always carries a gun tucked in his back for the rep. and the fear factor. But he loves his stiletto and cutting people. He's awesome with that knife."

Tom made knifing gestures as he spoke of Moses' knife prowess.

"Moses is always with his two minders, they're called Jeff and Eddie, a very dangerous pair. No one messes with them."

Tom further expounded on these minders. "Jeff's Eddie's uncle. Eddie's a nutter, a crazy who enjoys hurting people. Jeff's a real hard man, but straight. He does his best to keep a lid on his nephew. He's your typical minder, only hurting when told or needed. Theirs is a strange relationship."

Tom was either too scared or didn't know anything more to elaborate about Moses and his men.

However, he did explain the financial dynamics between Albert and the two siblings. Since Jess was with Albert, Tom wasn't required to pay to live in the area.

However, everyone else had to pay half of any money they earned or whatever Albert decided was appropriate on the day. Failure to hand over money often meant a painful introduction to Woody.

Tom asked how Harry got here, not this location, but his circumstances. "You're not the typical bloke we get around here. You're too normal, educated, and it doesn't look like you're mental. No drugs by the looks of you?"

Harry looked long and hard at Tom. He wasn't too sure how much he could or should tell this man.

Tom tried to reassure Harry. "If you're hiding, I get it. Look around, loads of them here are in the same boat. Some of the poor sods can't even remember what they were hiding from."

Harry decided that he needed to give something of himself in return. So, he gave the potted version of his story, at least what he was at liberty to say.

"I was discharged from the army a few months ago," started Harry. "I spent my last few years as a staff sergeant working in their logistics. We NCOs did all the work and made all the decisions. The Ruperts did bugger all, except take credit for successes and passed the buck for failures."

"Before that, I was on active duty in Afghanistan. My unit was attacked, and I got this." He showed the long scar on his right lower leg and mentioned some of the many others he sported around his body.

"No longer fit for purpose; that was the end of my front-line duty," he said with visible bitterness. "That mission was the start of all my problems."

"When I was well enough, I was given a desk job for the remaining years of my enlistment. The army logistics division plan, manages, and distributes all the army needs to wage war. If our lot screws up, my mates out there don't get what they need. I wasn't having that."

He then lied, "It was the most boring and stressful years of my life."

Harry hated himself for what he did latterly but kept those black thoughts to himself.

'It started as the most righteous time of my life, then everything slowly turned to shit!'

Harry pulled himself out of his morbid thoughts and continued with a forced grin, "I pissed off a lot of people when I complained, chased, and harassed to protect our boys out there. It was bad enough with some of the garbage kit they did have without my lot screwing up."

"So I left to start a new life with the woman I loved, who'd waited for me. I thought civvy street life was going to be wonderful after my army days."

Harry's face became angry as he recounted with bitterness, "on the way home from being discharged, I got an SMS from my fiancée. She dumped me."

Tom could see a growing sadness about this man as he continued. "She said I'd changed. I was no longer the man she agreed to marry; I was a stranger."

"That was a killing blow since I left the army for her. She said the army killed the man she loved. Then to twist the knife in further, when I got back, not only had she buggered off, I was left with massive debts, all in my name. Over the years, I stupidly sent her money to manage everything while I was away."

Tom looked at Harry questioningly.

"Yes, before you ask, she was right. I'd changed. I was a different man, an angry and confused man; I still am."

Harry continued his narrative. "I cleared what I could with my discharge money and from selling my flat. My pension's in hock, so no money coming in. I had to try and work off the rest. I was then living in various bed-sits, doing what security jobs I could get while being 'transient', as they call it."

"So, all I could get was the worst cash-in-hand jobs, no questions asked." Harry's anger and hurt showed as he talked about the decline in his life after the safety and security of the army.

"On top of all that, I hurt a couple of poncy rich gob-shites outside a nightclub. They were taking a young girl away. She'd either taken something or was too drunk to defend herself."

"I was banged up, then eventually released without charge once the girl and her friend explained what had happened. However, the word was out not to employ me; I'm tarred as a nutter."

"It gets worse. The nightclub owner is looking for me; the two gob-shites were nephews of the owner. Now, he IS a nutter."

"So, here I am; no money, overdue rent, no home, no friends, no family, and marked. I'd been on the street for a few weeks before I found this place. I thought I'd struck lucky here until Albert arrived."

There was silence again for a while between them. Both stared out across the warehouse.

Tom smiled and broke the silence with, "ah, thought you looked like a newbie." And then with a concerned face, he advised, "you either need to leave or get out there and get some money today."

Harry nodded in understanding and appreciation of the sentiment. Feeling that he could trust Tom, he replied, "I've some money hidden that'd keep Albert happy for a couple of days."

Tom smiled in return. He wasn't going to say anything.

"Hungry?" Tom asked.

"Absolutely."

"Wait here." Tom stood up and wandered off outside.

The sun was showing noon when Tom returned carrying an armful of things. He called over to Jess while he sat with Harry.

Tom had brought a load of old sandwiches and out-of-date food. Seeing all those edibles, Harry realised that he wasn't merely hungry, but famished. He'd not eaten since the previous afternoon.

Harry could see the signs of severe addiction in Jess as she walked over and sat opposite. She was very thin and frail-looking, with wide pupils. He could make out needle marks on her arms as her sleeves rose when she reached out for food.

What was even sadder to see on such a young woman was the cut marks on

57

her wrists, which he took as self-harming. As Harry stared, she covered her arms up with embarrassment. Then she forced out a smile as if all was good.

Now they were all sitting close, he clearly saw her features. This young woman could easily have been on the cover of a magazine.

'*Bloody shame, to end up like this,*' he silently thought.

The three of them enjoyed a veritable feast. Where Tom got all that food, he could only guess. Tom was indeed a useful find, and Harry thanked him profusely.

****

Albert and his two lackeys arrived as evening descended. Jess was over near the entrance, eagerly waiting for him. Harry realised her enthusiasm wasn't for Albert but for the small packet of powder he passed to her as he walked by. She rushed inside Albert's boxes.

Harry looked at Tom, who merely shrugged his shoulders as a sign that this was the way things were.

Albert plus his cronies sat by his abode and waited. People came over to him and started handing over their payment; mostly coins, a few from each person. It was clearly adding up, to Albert's visible delight.

One elderly-looking woman received a nasty slap to her face, launching her backward and to the ground. Albert reached down and grabbed her by the scruff of her coat while the other two checked all her pockets and bags. They took every last coin.

Albert gave Harry a warning look.

Realising it was his turn, Harry went over and handed over some coins, hoping they'd be sufficient. Albert grunted in acceptance. With a shake of his head, he instructed Harry to depart.

Over the next few days, Tom and Jess took Harry to some of their favourite places to beg. They taught him how best to garner sympathy from the people hurrying by. Jess was elfin-faced and ever so thin. She could put on an emaciated, pathetic look that drove into the heart of anyone that stopped.

Jess and Tom were even better as a double act, playing the little-lost-boy-and-girl card. They were well-rehearsed artists of the process. Their best results were when they enticed people into a conversation. The beggars then turned into real people. When their targets were hooked, they found it tough to refuse to donate some cash to the siblings.

On the rare occasions when Jess cleaned up, her hidden beauty peeped out. And those were rare indeed. She didn't like people to see her physical beauty. This advantage for many was the curse that brought her to this situation. She hated her looks.

Tom despised his small and weak frame but not because he disliked his appearance. It was his lack of physical stature that prevented him from protecting the people for whom he cared.

When Albert wasn't around, the three talked, sometimes laughed, and became close. When in a common circumstance like this, it's good to have people. Harry needed them. They helped him learn about what was happening here, the 'hood, how to fit in, and most importantly, how to stay safe.

In the army, there were defined rules of engagement and how to interact with others. They were explained, trained, and instilled. On the street, without help, it was painfully acquired guesswork.

Harry began to feel a whole lot more relaxed. He wondered how long this might last before his past caught up with him. Or, perhaps Albert might have a bad day and decide that Harry needed a lesson; for some reason?

The food was not gourmet, and the ablution facilities were not at the Ritz level. However, with sufficient money to keep Albert and his men at bay, life was as good as any time he'd experienced.

'A good find indeed,' he mused.

6. THE WORM TURNS

It had been a miserable day begging on the street. The heavy rain and driving wind always meant poor pickings for those that relied on the goodwill of others. The potential donors of cash rushed past. They were only interested in getting to where they wanted as quickly as possible, avoiding the discomfort of the bad weather.

These people rarely hung around in the pouring rain. No way were they going to rummage in their pockets or purses for a few coins for the likes of those living on the street, the people who needed it the most. The meagre coins Harry received that day barely paid for the sandwich and cuppa he felt he'd earned.

Harry was cold and wet when he arrived back at the warehouse. Albert was also not having a good day; it showed in this mood. Today's rents were down, and he struggled to make enough from those around to feed his and his lackeys' habits.

"None of you fuckers appreciates what I does to keep yer'all safe!" he moaned.

Few were brave enough to withhold any money. Most handed over all the few coins they'd managed to take on this day. They knew from painful experience that going hungry was better than a discussion with Woody. Some only received a slap for not having money to hand over. Unfortunately, for others who were not in favour or less able to defend themselves, Woody swung, and landed painfully.

It wasn't pleasant to watch the goings-on near Albert's area. Harry could only observe and keep his own counsel, as did most around here.

Harry knew he resided in the not-in-favour category, so he stayed where he was.

Tom nudged Harry to go and join the queue.

"Got nothing to hand over."

"Why didn't you tell me earlier?" Tom whispered. "Jess and I could have done our double act to help. We'd have gotten something to give him."

Harry said or did nothing in response. He just looked straight ahead.

Tom again whispered, "you'll have to go over and take whatever he hands out. Better you go to him. If he comes to you, it'll be worse. He knows it's been tough out there. He's not stupid, well, not that stupid."

"I have nothing," said Harry. "If I go over there, he'll make an example of me. I know it. Maybe he'll ignore me this time. Better I stay here and see what happens."

Harry hung out of sight, waiting to see what might happen, or not.

When Albert finished with the others, he and his two lackeys looked over to Harry, expectantly.

Harry didn't move and avoided their gaze. Tom looked pleadingly at him, nudging him again to get up and go over and plead his case. Harry sat still, looking into space.

Albert came over with his boys and said, "I don't come to you. You come to me, so all of it!" he growled.

Without any response or acknowledgement from Harry, he went right up to Harry's face and loudly pronounced, "all of it!" The smell of Albert's breath again almost made him throw up.

Harry got up hesitantly and nervously. He lunged forward and head-butted Albert. In his experience, a simple yet conclusive show of force was often the quickest way to end a dispute.

Albert went down, shocked and dazed, with a smashed, bleeding nose. For a moment, his thinking was disabled. He sat there, temporarily immobile, while the blood and snot dripped from his smashed nose.

Recovering his thoughts, he spluttered to his two lackeys, "get the fucker!"

They were uncertain about what to do. One thing they quickly realised, this man no longer looked a victim. Harry's defiant, I-dare-you-to-defend-your-boss look made them realise that any retaliation would be an unhealthy choice for them.

Harry had needed Albert to come over to him, to emphasise the point he'd made. Tom had to be kept in the dark.

"No one invades my space, especially when you have the breath and face of a rotten corpse," Harry spat the words quietly to Albert.

To the lackeys, he ordered, while pointing to Albert, "go away and take that snivelling heap of cow manure with you!"

They looked at each other, uncertain of what to do next. Eventually, with a resigned look, they helped Albert up and took him back to his hovel.

Albert sat down in front of his abode with a dirty, and now red, cloth held over his nose. He stared menacingly at the man who dared to hit him. Harry could hear Albert admonishing his lackeys for their lack of support, threatening to replace them.

Jess knew she needed to keep in with Albert. She went over and bent down to see how he was. From her body language, Harry could see that she was trying to help and administer to his injuries.

Albert slapped her so violently that she fell back, landing in a sobbing heap.

Tom knew this was no time to go over and help her; it would only make matters worse. All he could do would be to pick up the pieces later. Instead, he gave Harry an accusing, now-look-what-you've-done look.

Harry, both ashamed and distressed at what had happened to Jess, couldn't hold his new friend's gaze and looked away. He had to take this course of action, but he didn't expect these consequences. How could he have foreseen this? Although he desperately wanted to go over to Jess and admonish Albert until his knuckles were raw, he couldn't. Head-butting Albert was more than far enough at this juncture, even perhaps too far for his purposes.

After a short time, Albert got up and glared at Harry, who, in return, merely blanked him. Gesturing to his two men-at-arms to come with him, the three left.

Once they'd gone, Tom went over to Jess to see how she was. After giving them some moments, Harry went over to both and said, "Jess, I'm sorry what he did to you. I didn't expect that to happen."

Wiping a bloody lip, she quietly mouthed while sobbing, "it's OK."

Then to Tom, a more upbeat Harry suggested, "you might as well have the penthouse with your sister. Albert won't come back to get the same again, well, not for a while anyway."

Tom gave him an uncertain and unbelieving look.

"Listen," said Harry reassuringly, trying to reason with a terrified Tom. "I've seen bullies before, and they eventually back off when up against someone who fights back."

Tom looked worried. He challenged Harry. "You don't know him, he'll be back. Fish Breath will want revenge, and he won't be alone. Are you going to stop all of them?"

Harry said nothing.

"I thought not," he accused Harry. "I know him, he's crazy. Those voices of his will tell him to come back because he wants to."

Tom was now crying, not for himself, but for his sister. "We can't stay near you. He'll take it out on Jess again and he'll hurt her. I know it! He's done it before."

"I don't care what happens to me, but if I'm not around, what will happen to her?" Then with a final exasperated sigh, "look what you've done to us, to her!"

No reassurances could overcome Tom's too deeply ingrained fear, to believe it could be over. Harry also knew there would be consequences but kept those thoughts to himself.

Everyone knew Albert would return, but only when he'd proper help. It might take days, even weeks, but the expected retribution would happen in due course once he could persuade his suppliers. They'll lose money while Albert wasn't here selling. Albert's side of this business was small-fry, so Harry expected it would be later than sooner. He'd just have to wait it out.

Tom then turned his attention to see how Jess was.

All around were suddenly keeping their distance and avoiding Harry's gaze. Clearly, he'd contracted the plague. He felt sorry for the others around here who'd never had the confidence to deal with people like these.

Harry had been in the thick of it everywhere he went, in and out of the army. He knew bullies and hated them. He was bullied in his various schools as the short-term outsider, then in the army as the namby-pamby missionary boy.

'*It only stops when you stand up to them,*' he thought to himself, and as an afterthought, '*but it can be a painful and bloody process.*'

In the meantime and he needed to prepare. It was late, he was tired, and tomorrow was another day to plan with a fresh mind.

7. REVENGE

Harry settled down for the night. Like any house or flat in which he had slept, there were always those household creaks, clunks, whistling, and other noises that one's brain tunes out. He was used to sleeping out on army Ops, filtering out those night-time ambient noises. By now, he was used to the background noises of the docks, roads, and factories nearby; and he slept soundly.

Too soundly!

In the middle of the night, he was awakened by a hard kick to his groin. Stuck in the confines of his sleeping bag, his straight jacket, it would be tough to defend himself.

In the faint light emanating from the distant port works and streets, he saw Albert swaying and smiling above him with that half-toothed grin. Albert was full of confidence, looking down at Harry while slapping Woody in the palm of his other hand.

Harry underestimated Albert. He knew he'd return since this was too good a number not to fight for. Unfortunately, what Harry expected to be at least days before Albert's ugly face reappeared, had surprisingly taken mere hours.

Tom warned him, and he didn't listen. The others who shied clear of the situation also knew better. Harry cursed his arrogance and stupidity. Harry realised he'd acted like a newbie Rupert and badly misjudged the situation. He should have listened to Tom, the experienced sergeant here.

Coming to his senses, Harry discovered why Albert was so full of confidence. In the dim light, he could see a new group of characters with Albert. Obviously, this was Moses and some of his crew. For some reason, they'd dropped everything to come and support him.

Harry couldn't reconcile why they'd done that for such a low-life.

Again, he expected this to happen, but much later. By then, he'd have made sure he was better prepared. Damn! Damn! He should have better explored Moses' and Albert's relationship dynamics. And he should have listened!

Before Harry could do or say anything, Albert's Woody struck him on the side of his head. Harry was out for a few moments and woke up to a barrage of kicks from Albert's two cronies and Woody 'kisses' from a now very brave Albert. All he could do was curl up in a ball with his back to the wall and hope for the best.

Through his arms crossed in front of his head, Harry could see one of the new crew put a restraining hand on Albert's arm, telling him enough. He assumed this was Jeff from what Tom had said about Moses' guys.

Moses was laughing while walking back and forth in front of Harry, sporadically managing to get one of his own kicks in. He was delighting in the spectacle and cursed his minder for interfering in the show.

"Sorry boss, just wanted to protect you. If this tramp gets killed here, the filth'll be around asking questions. And I was thinking that you don't want to be involved with that shit."

He nodded in Albert's direction, "does helping that low-life really justify the heat?"

Moses took time to think. From what Harry had heard, Moses was not the sharpest knife in the cutlery drawer. Being strung out further slowed his decision-making process. However, what he lacked in intelligence, he more than made up for in street cunning and viciousness.

Fortunately for Harry, Moses had enough awareness to see sense. He leaned down and grabbed Harry with a drug-induced trembling hand. Moses whispered threateningly, "no one sells drugs in my hood without my permission. I supply here, and Albert's my man, and you don't mess with my men. Sell again here, you're dead!" he hissed.

Harry cursed himself for not thinking about this. It should have been obvious that Albert would have told any lie to get Moses' attention. And the best one to get his attention fast would be Harry dealing on his patch. He couldn't believe he'd been out-manoeuvred by the likes of Albert!

Harry knew he'd no chance to respond. As the blows commenced again, he could only cover up and ride them as best he could.

"Smack'im good, but don't kill the bastard, he's right," said Moses nodding in the direction of Harry's reluctant defender.

Conversation over, the beating continued until Albert was sufficiently pleased with himself, and satisfied that he'd made the point to those around. He was still the boss in this mini-fiefdom. He was also exhausted from the effort he exerted on Harry.

"Dump him away from here, in the river's good, and on the other side of the harbour," sneered Moses.

Albert's two minders each grabbed an arm, pulled Harry's limp body from his sleeping bag, then dragged him off.

Reaching the harbour wall, they removed his coat and boots. He was wearing nothing else of value. They searched his pockets and found over forty pounds in small notes and coins. They looked at each other, wondering why this man refused to pay Albert a few pounds and avoid all this trouble. Their greed overcame further thoughts and questions, and they split the money that Albert would never see.

8. LIES AND MORE LIES

It wasn't until lunchtime before Harry started to come around. He was in and out of consciousness over the next few hours until regaining enough of his senses to know where he was. Harry lay for the rest of the day in the hospital bed as the memory of what happened started to come back.

"Thank you, NHS," he mumbled.

A nurse came over when she heard him speak and realised he was pretty much fully conscious. She smiled and pronounced, "my word, you've been in the wars. I hear you fell in the river, but unfortunately, the tide was out, hence the injuries. Is that right? Seems a lot of bruises for a fall?"

He nodded in vague agreement and then asked, "where'd you hear that?" His jaw and face hurt as he spoke. He could feel the cuts, some with stitches. His face was sore all over.

"The ambulance team said it was a smallish man and a rather sickly-looking girl."

He mouthed a painful acknowledgement.

Soon after, two policemen arrived. The police had already interviewed the ambulance team and refuge, but they couldn't offer any clarity. They hoped Harry might shed more light on what happened to him. "Want to tell us who beat you up?"

Harry was very vague, pretending not to remember too much. "I was walking along the bank. It was dark. I must have tripped, or slipped, or something. I remember falling, and that's all. It's all a blank until I woke up here."

The younger policeman wasn't happy with the story he got from Harry. He pressed further, "are you trying to tell us that you got those bruises all over your body from a fall? You've no shoes and no coat on a cold night. We know something or rather someone happened to you."

"Sorry, officer. I just fell. Dunno what happened to my clothes."

"Do we look stupid?"

Harry inwardly smiled as he thought, '*do you really want a reply?*'

Instead, he spoke out loud, "there's nothing more, sorry. It's all a vague memory, it was late and dark, and I slipped. Thank god someone found me."

"They said they were friends. Who were they?"

Harry didn't want them going to the warehouse and putting Tom and Jess in the spotlight for the mess he'd created. "There was no one else around. I don't know who they might be. From the description the nurse gave me, could be anyone. Sorry, but I can't be of any more help. It's really sore to talk."

The older policeman then took over and overly enthusiastically confirmed it was a fall. With a wave of his hand, he beckoned the younger officer to leave the room with him.

The younger one verbally pushed back. "There's been a serious assault here. Got a few more questions to ask him."

"Let's talk outside," said the older officer.

The unhappy younger policeman, under protest, complied and followed him out of the room.

Thinking Harry was out of earshot, or perhaps didn't care if over-heard, the older constable said to the younger, "whatever you think, this was an accident; it's No Further Action. And that means no paperwork and time-wasting."

"But he's taking the piss. It's obvious to anyone that he's been given a good doing-over. And we're supposed to accept all that bollocks he's spouted out?"

"It's N-F-A," the older policeman this time spelled out the acronym very slowly to make a point. "And that's the end of it as far as we should be concerned."

The younger PC tried to respond but was cut off.

"Stop! I've been around this loop before."

Then in a more conciliatory tone, the older policeman explained why this course of no-action was right. "It's not that I don't want to find out what happened. Yes, I agree it's a serious assault. And if we push this, Skip will have to get CID involved. Then all of us will go round in circles investigating a crime no one cares or will talk about." He gestured in Harry's direction. "Not even him."

"We've got cases right now that need our help where we can make a difference, or at least make some headway, perhaps even solve. Sorry lad, this is going nowhere. We have to prioritise."

The younger capitulated to experience and the reference to their sergeant not being happy. The two policemen came back in and went through the formalities. The case was officially closed as an accident.

The medical staff thoroughly checked him out. They ran tests to ensure was no damage to internal organs and checked nothing else had been broken.

A consultant visited after the results were back from all the tests. "So, a fall was it?" he said, looking at the charts, x-rays, and other documents.

Harry nodded yes.

"Wow, that was some mountain you bounced down," the doctor said with a big grin, "and we'll leave it at that."

He then explained to Harry that he was lucky and highlighted the main injuries. "You've concussion, several broken ribs, most others badly bruised. There are cuts on exposed areas, and we've done a bit of sewing on the deeper ones." He also commented on the colourful mosaic of red, purple, and black bruises all over Harry's body.

The consultant was initially worried about kidney damage but was now more confident all was fine, or at least would be, after time. "So, it looks like we'll be having your presence for a few more days. Need to run a few more tests, a few more pees, etc. OK?"

Harry uttered a grateful, "thank you," for their help.

"Anywhere you need to be, anyone you need to contact?"

Harry's head shook a no.

"Are you an athlete? I can see to have the physique of one, even though you're in your mid thirties. Listen, I've worked with ex-athletes," he continued. "Once age catches up with them, and their career is over, they can

70

have problems adjusting. I know you've been homeless recently. So what caused that? I know people who can help you get back on your feet. Do you want me to make a few calls?"

"Thanks for the concern, but really, all's good."

'If only you knew half the truth about me, you might not be so happy to help.'

"OK, understood. I've got a favour to ask. Your body's injuries would be a great training ground for junior staff." With a smirk, he added, "your injuries so resemble those from a severe beating with hard objects and footwear, it would be good for them to see and learn. So, I hope you don't mind if I bring around a couple of the youngsters to explain your injuries and examine you as they heal."

Harry forced a smile of agreement. He was happy to do what little he could to repay them.

His first visit to the toilet was a shock. While washing his hands, he didn't recognise the man who looked back at him in the mirror. The reflection was a swollen, bruised, and cut face that would have made Charles Laughton's Hunchback, Quasimodo, appear attractive. Harry never had a pretty-boy appearance, and the scars left after his beating weren't going to improve matters.

The consultant was, at best, economic with the truth. The reality was many visits from senior staff, explaining to their numerous juniors the various bruises and how one could identify the results of a severe beating versus a fall. Harry accepted the attention graciously, knowing he was repaying the NHS by training all these junior staff members with his body's injuries.

Having seen the effects of concussion, Harry knew the dangers and the score. From the doctors' warnings, he knew to stay put. The NHS' hospitality for those peaceful nights and well-fed days was going to end all too soon. And one good thing about his hospital stay was being able to plan his next moves and the various contingencies.

On the fifth morning it was time to leave a clean bed, hot food, and drinks. It was time to get back to the out-of-date sandwiches. As he discharged himself, a junior came over and said, "you'll need a couple of weeks of taking it easy. Do you have anywhere to rest and recover after here?"

Harry looked at the doctor for a few moments while sarcastically thinking that

71

he'd book himself into a private rehab centre by the sea!

Harry immediately felt ashamed of his thoughts about a well-meaning professional; the doctor was only thinking about the best for his patient. Instead, he replied, "I'll be fine. I've lots of friends where I'm going, don't worry."

The staff and the social services team were great. His old clothes never reappeared. He assumed they'd never survived the hard washing that might see them clean. In their place were clean underwear, heavy-duty working shirts and trousers, a thick cardigan, a substantial long coat, and a sturdy canvas bag. All were second, or even third-hand. They were sturdy and warm for the cold days and nights ahead. An old army surplus sleeping bag also materialized.

He thanked them profusely.

As Harry took his leave from all the staff, the consultant said, "you've had a concussion from that nasty fall, whatever you call it. You really cannot afford a 'fall' like that again; the next one could kill you. Remember, no heavy or rough physical activity, at all, for at least a couple of weeks, and ideally a lot longer."

Harry smiled and said jokingly, "I'll cancel my gym membership."

As he walked away, the older doctor said to one of the juniors, "nothing we can do here Peter, there's a good chance we'll see him again one way or another."

"You think so?" responded the younger. "Don't know what you mean by one way or another?"

The consultant looked at Harry turn off the corridor towards the exit. "Yep, it'll be either here or perhaps in the mortuary. I did some work in the field with street dwellers. He is heading back to whatever caused his injuries. Wherever and whatever he's heading into, he's not in any state to survive."

The consultant hated the phrase 'Down-and-Outs,' since it smacked of terminal failure for all of them. He knew that with the right physical, emotional, psychiatric, and social help, many could make it into what most people consider normal life. There just had to be the will. At least he was happy in the knowledge of the people he helped and the results of his work with them in his younger, more resilient days.

9. RETRIBUTION

Harry had to find and thank Tom and Jess. They saved his life, and he owed them at least that. He brought this on himself. But worse, he put Tom and, in particular, Jess at risk. And he was thankful that despite what he'd instigated, they had done the right thing by him; and at great risk to themselves.

What should have been a ninety-minute gentle stroll from the hospital took over two hours before he arrived at the old warehouse. The walk had exhausted him.

So, he sat and rested in the area that used to be occupied by his plastic sheet, sleeping bag, cardboard, and holdall. All he had, had obviously been purloined; no one expected him back.

Albert and Co were nowhere to be seen. There was no sign of Tom and Jess. He thought about asking around. While a few residents glanced in his direction, none dared to acknowledge his presence, let alone come over. Mr Plague had returned.

Albert must have seen him there, or someone had got word to him of Harry's presence. When Albert arrived later that afternoon, he wasn't alone. Moses and Co were again with him. Now that Harry wasn't bundled up and vulnerable as before, Albert held back. It was Moses who came over with his two bodyguards. Harry knew that these two were not the useless hangers-on that followed Albert around.

In the full light of the day, he could now clearly see the three newcomers. Moses was the smallest of the three. He was skinny, with sharp facial features and tiny, sunken black eyes. His face had the clean straight scarring typical of someone involved in knife fights.

Moses' two minders were much the same height, a little less than six feet. What Harry took to be Jeff was broad, muscular, and probably in his forties. He'd the watchful look and demeanour of an experienced minder, probably ex-forces.

The other was slim, younger, and likely in his late 20s. He was what some would call a 'pretty boy', not the look of a minder. Harry saw an eager nastiness in his eyes in anticipation of the forthcoming spectacle.

Harry slowly stood up, his body creaking and aching with the effort. He hoped his pain didn't show to those standing before him. He was ill-prepared for any physical activity and let alone a brawl. He remembered the doctor's advice, "you have to take things easy."

"Welcome back. Bit sore, eh? Well, you're not goin' to be sore no more," said Moses sarcastically.

"So you want to go clubbing again with Albert 'ere?" He laughed at his attempt at humour. The others smiled when he looked in their direction.

Moses was not as on edge as the last time they'd met, but there was still the latent glaze of a heavy user in his eyes.

"I've got nowhere else to go," said Harry in a frightened and conciliatory tone.

"Mr Moses, I'm really sorry. I didn't mean to hurt Albert. I was scared what he would do to me if I couldn't pay that day. Honest, I wasn't selling drugs. You can ask anyone?"

Moses sneered. "I don't give a fuck. You were told to stay the fuck out of the hood and now you's back. You fucked with one of my boys, dat means you messed with me. You got off lightly and alive, then," he emphasised the 'then.' "Ain't happenin' again!"

He glowered at Jeff, who'd earlier suggested Harry shouldn't be killed. Jeff looked back in acknowledgement but kept his counsel, staring downwards.

Harry heard a click. In Moses' now steadier right hand appeared a nasty stiletto. The long thin blade glinted in the light. Harry cowered, crouched, and turned to the right, trying to protect himself from the threatening blade.

Albert, standing behind Moses, did a little dance of anticipation but kept well back.

Moses played with his victim, swinging the blade back and forth. "I'm gonna cut you like...," he couldn't think of a suitable simile, so left the 'like' hanging there.

In the background, he could hear Albert repeating, "do 'im, do 'im, do 'im."

"Shut the fuck up!"

Albert continued his dance of anticipation but now in silence.

Then leaning in close, Moses said menacingly, "here's what we do to street trash like you that don't take no notice of me." He enjoyed the foreplay with this garbage, and now it was time for the hurting to start. He lunged at Harry to make the first of what he thought would be many stabs and slices.

Or so he thought.

In one swift combined movement, Harry uncoiled, spinning forwards and upwards. His left arm shot out to the left with a block, forcing the knife hand out of immediate danger. At the same time his right hand knuckled Moses in his exposed throat, smashing his windpipe.

With a look of shock and fear, Moses gagged and sagged to the ground. He knelt there, gasping for breath, staring upwards, shocked at what had just happened. Harry stepped to the side of the small man who knelt there. As he'd practiced so many times, he wrapped one arm around the small man's neck, then with the other, jerked and pulled, breaking his neck. Moses crumpled to the ground, dead.

Harry was neither tall, nor overly muscle-bound. However, what he lacked in brute strength was more than compensated by the technique that came naturally from years of specialist close-combat training.

As brief as it was, the exertion took its toll on Harry's aching body, and he felt a wave of dizziness coming over him. Thankfully, it quickly passed, and he hoped no one noticed. After their beating, the game he now played put him on dangerous ground. If, they realised how weak he was or called his bluff, it would be the end.

The two minders were stupefied. They looked at Moses aghast and then at Harry. The whole thing took a few seconds. Albert recovered first, and shouted at them from even further back, "go on you two, do 'im!"

The younger one was about to make a lunge but was checked by the elder.

As Moses collapsed to the ground, Harry had removed his knife from his lifeless hands. The older minder eyed the vicious blade.

The man who was about to die a slow, painful death quickly moved in close to the now unemployed minders. The tables had turned. Now, it was they who felt at risk of the same fate. Jeff was experienced and knew what they were now dealing with; someone who could very efficiently handle himself.

Not knowing if they were armed, Harry knew it was best to get close. He held the stiletto to the younger man's throat. From what Tom had mentioned, the older minder looked after the younger. This was the way to control both of them.

Harry told Jeff to take off his jacket, lift his shirt, and slowly spin around. At the same time, he patted Eddie down for guns and knives and found nothing. He pushed Eddie towards Jeff. While the two of them were off-balance, Harry quickly stepped back and bent down to search for the gun that Moses invariably kept tucked into the back of his trousers; he prayed it was there.

It was!

Again he silently thanked Tom for that information as he removed it from the dead body. Even that small act of bending down, sent clouds over his eyes. Thankfully they soon cleared.

Seeing a potential opportunity with Harry bending over Moses, Eddie recovered first and nudged forward to make a move. He decided not to finish the action with the gun pointing in his direction.

"You're out of a job," he said to both minders. "Now, back off!"

Albert and Co also shuffled back out of harm's way. Jeff and Eddie reluctantly moved backward, albeit as little as possible.

Harry was impressed by Moses' choice of handgun, a semi-automatic Sig Sauer P938. It was light at sixteen ounces; a lethal sub-compact pistol. It was actually one of Harry's preferred secondary weapons.

By the gun's weight and balance Harry was sure it was loaded. Since this bunch of losers were out of reach, he had to check.

A quick flick of the magazine release on the left-hand side and an almost instantaneous check confirmed the extended magazine of seven bullets was full. It was more than enough to deal with those standing before him. Well-versed in the process, he then checked the action and chambered a round while cocking it.

They watched in awe at the speed he verified the gun's operation. While frustrated, they had no chance to pounce.

"I'm Harry, pleased to meet you. As you can see, I was pissed off with your boss," nodding towards Moses' body. "Don't you two piss me off as well."

He could see that the older of the two was less impetuous than the younger and likely to be more sensible and responsive. "Name," he said to the older minder, even though he knew who each were. Extracting little pieces of information from them was the start of breaking down their resistance to further questioning and orders.

"Jeff," said the older one. Then nodding in the direction of the younger one, "and this is Eddie."

Still pointing the gun in their direction, Harry stepped back a little from Moses. He told Jeff, "empty Moses' pockets and put everything there," pointing to an old wooden barrel. Harry was not in any shape to do any more crouching and standing up. He covered Eddie with the gun but was mindful of the older one.

Jeff extracted a thick wallet, a nasty-looking knuckle-duster, a set of house keys, a large number of small packets of powder, a mobile phone, and from his inside pocket, a thick envelope.

Once finished, Harry told Jeff to step back and join his nephew. Keeping a watchful eye on the two minders, he checked the wallet. Inside were several credit cards, a lot of cash in large denominations, Moses' driving licence, and other IDs. He pocketed the lot.

Harry beamed with delight as he checked the contents of the envelope. It was thick with £50s.

As Harry placed it in his coat, Eddie piped up indignantly, "that ain't yours, that's money Moses owes Dexter. You're fuckin' dead if you walk away with that. Dexter ain't no pussy like Moses."

"I'm dead anyway," Harry responded, smiling. "Might as well enjoy my passing."

He picked up what looked to be house keys. Waving them at the unemployed minders, he demanded, "address?"

"That's ours and Moses' gaff!" again piped up Eddie.

"Well, he's not needing it now and you're now officially homeless," he replied. Then gesturing to the warehouse surroundings and the people who were making sure that they were not seeing what was going on around them, suggested, "please come and join the club, you'd be most welcome."

"Address!" he repeated menacingly, emphasising the gun that pointed in their direction. Jeff gave the information. Harry already knew this from Moses' ID but was again checking to keep them honest. Giving up this additional information was a further chink in their resistance. ·

"That's a shame," said Harry looking at Moses.

Before the duo could ask why Harry suddenly felt sorry for Moses, he followed up with, "good gear that scrawny git's wearing, shame it won't fit me."

Harry crushed Moses' mobile phone underfoot and kicked it away. He told Jeff and Eddie to empty their pockets onto the same barrel.

"Fuck off," said the younger.

His response prompted Harry to step forward and deliver a hammer blow to Eddie's jaw with the pistol butt. He remembered to do this with the safety on. Harry was waiting for an excuse to strike at least one of them. He needed to emphasise his control over the situation. Eddie gave him that opportunity.

Being hit by a gun butt hurts badly. It's got the weight of holding a bag of coins in a fist but without the risk of damaging one's fingers and knuckles. And to make matters worse, the solid edges could rip flesh if struck hard enough. And they did exactly that.

The young man staggered back, falling with the shock and impact. Squealing in pain, he shouted, "you fuckin' cut me." He could feel the blood oozing through his fingers from a nasty bleeding gash; his appearance being more concerning than the blow.

"That'll add character to your face. Next time you'll do what I tell you."

"Now, empty your fuckin' pockets!" said Harry raising his voice. Then gesturing to the filthy ground, he couldn't help himself following up with, "and stop bleeding on my nice floor."

They then both duly complied; another chink of compliance.

Jeff and Eddie stared daggers at him as they placed all the contents of their pockets on the barrel.

'If looks could kill,' Harry thought to himself.

Once they'd finished, he motioned them backward with a wave of the gun. Rifling through their wallets, he extracted all the cash to their obvious frustration and anger.

"Let's call it criminal injury compensation," justified Harry.

He half-expected a lunge from the more fool-hardy younger one, but it never came. Jeff had positioned himself to stop his nephew but it wasn't necessary. Eddie had learned his lesson; for the moment anyway.

Picking up a BMW car key that Jeff had removed from one of his own pockets, Harry demanded, "what and where?"

Jeff wanted this charade to end as soon as possible. Therefore, he was as brief in his responses as he was outwardly compliant. He wanted to get away and return with more bodies and weapons. So, the older minder quickly piped up, "old red 525, round the back, dunno the reg. It was Moses'. I'm only the driver today."

Harry smiled at the realisation that Moses was not a big player. People in this trade liked to show off their wealth, and this sort of car spelled bottom rung. While there would be severe repercussions, he didn't expect it would be from anyone much more dangerous than these two.

Saying that, he apparently had Dexter's money, so perhaps there might be some consequences after all. He had to close this down and leave fast after they left.

Harry crushed their mobiles underfoot. He let the two ex-minders take back what he left on the barrel, including their keys to Moses' house.

Turning to a shocked and speechless Albert, he growled, "in the words of the newly deceased 'prophet' Moses, what do we do to street trash like you?"

Albert quickly departed, his men close on his heels.

Pointing the gun at Moses, he said to the two minders, "I suggest you get rid of the real trash here. Dump him in the river with the rest of the rubbish. It will save us all a lot of heat. And this time, make sure the water's in and going out. I want his body washed away from here. Any problem?"

There was a pause.

"All good?" he repeated, a little louder this time.

They were learning to take heed and nodded in understanding. Moses was picked up and dragged away.

No one expected police involvement since there was too much to be explained by all. And the onlookers? Well, what happens on the street stays on the street. It's safest to mind one's own business. Most, if not all, of the people here, lived in this environment to avoid attention. So, it was unlikely any alarms would be raised from their direction. However, he'd have to wait and see.

However, the recently departed Albert niggled in the back of Harry's mind.

Not long after they'd gone, Tom and Jess appeared. Harry could see their embarrassment at their lack of support and keeping their distance. Seeing the siblings' uncertainty, Harry strode over, hugged them both, and thanked them profusely for saving his life.

"Listen you two, I know you took a big risk by taking me to safety." Grinning, he added, "it must have been hard work; you're stronger than you look. Honestly, I don't know how to thank you enough." Tom and Jess beamed in appreciation that there were no hard feelings.

Harry handed Tom most of the sachets he'd taken from Moses.

He kept a couple for contingencies. *'Never know when these might be useful.'*

Jess looked greedily at Tom.

Harry picked up on her enthusiasm. While looking at Jess and in a more serious tone, he suggested, "don't over-indulge her."

"No way!" he said. "And, thanks, that makes life easier for a while. Perhaps this time, Albert might not be coming back. I know how to keep her level, and I'll be keeping a tight control over this stash."

Tom and Jess then explained what happened on the night Harry was attacked. When Albert got bored and tired from beating Harry, his men dragged him away.

Once they'd taken Harry away, Moses started shouting at Albert for lying to him about Harry dealing drugs. He berated him for the three of them being frightened by one man and was livid about being dragged out of bed, to fix Albert's hurt pride. This was not the turf war Albert said was happening, and not what Moses expected.

"You lied to me and I've dirtied my hands in your shit, again!" He nodded to his two minders in Albert's direction.

"No one lies to me."

Jeff and Eddie gave him a small taste of what Albert did to Harry.

After Moses left, Tom and Jess followed Albert's two men dragging Harry's limp body away. They'd taken him about a mile, which they thought was far enough. Albert's two men then threw him off the harbour wall into what they thought was the river.

"We were really scared," said Tom ashamedly. "When they dumped you over the wall, you splashed into the wet sand and stones on the riverbank; the river was low. They laughed, expecting that'd be the last time they'd see you. Either you'd die out there, and the tide would take you away, or you'd not dare come back. Job done."

"After they left, we jumped down to check you out. Your boots and coat were missing, but dunno what else," Tom continued.

Jess piped up, "we first thought you were dead, but I found a pulse. We couldn't leave you there, so we dragged you up to the road and then to the shelter just down the road. You're heavier than you look."

"We managed to get them to call an ambulance and waited outside in the shadows. When it arrived, we told them we were your friends and we saw you fall. Once you were safe with the ambulance people, we left fast, sorry."

"There'd be too many questions; we couldn't hang around the shelter in case anyone saw us with you. If word got back to Moses or Albert, we'd also end up where you were heading."

Harry patted Tom on the back and said, "so, maybe this time you can be the guv'nor here now? And no more payments," Harry projected for all to hear.

More quietly, he continued, "I'm not saying where I'm going, but I need to get away from here. Hopefully I'll be back soon. Look after each other."

Tom looked a little more confident than the last time, but Harry could still see his uncertainty.

The siblings took this all stoically. However, when he handed over some of the money he collected from Jeff and Eddie, their eyes lit up. "This is to keep you going while I'm away. This place'll soon be crawling with nasties. You both need to get away from there, at least for a while."

He apologised for having to leave them with all this mess and then left the building. Moses' car was where Jeff had said it would be. Harry exclaimed, "wow," but not too loudly, when he found a large bulging canvas bag in the boot. It contained packs of £50s, €500s, and $100s.

With all his planning for possible outcomes, he never thought he'd strike gold to this level.

He removed the bag, closed the boot, then laid it on the passenger seat. Sitting in the driver's seat, rifling through all this money, he estimated from a cursory glance that there was over £100,000. Running off did spring to mind. However, he knew he wasn't yet in any position to take himself up on his own offer.

This money was his way in, and he had a debt to pay.

Then even better! Underneath the money, he found ten 1kg packs of what looked like cocaine, plus several large bags of crystalline powder and tablets.

Harry suspected the contents were Bath Salts, Bloom, and Ecstasy. He was no expert but knew enough to realise this haul was over £200,000 in street value.

"What on earth was a low-level pusher like Moses doing with this amount of drugs?" he again said out loud as he sat in the car. "Just no way Moses was in that league!"

Further thoughts and reassessing plans would have to wait. He needed to be away from here fast, especially with what he carried in the car. He started up the BMW and calmly drove away.

10. STAKEOUT

The reasonable-looking hospital clothes enabled Harry to rent a cheap room in a seedy hotel. He was grateful for the cash Moses and his minders so generously donated. It would pay for his accommodation and other necessary expenses.

One of the first things he bought was a hoodie. Many people wore them to cover their heads from the cold. In this neighbourhood, it was useful to avoid standing out. So, he'd not be out of place wearing one with the hood up, covering his beaten face; he had to keep a low profile.

He parked the car a good distance from the hotel. If the car was found, it would be outside any search area, should there be anyone interested in finding him.

Harry was a dedicated shower-taker. However, for his first night in this room he took a hot and very long bath. "Ahhh," he exhaled as he slipped into the hot water. It felt wonderful to soak away the aches and pains, and he had many.

His dinner-cum-supper was a room delivery pizza and a couple of beers. He was then ready for a welcoming good night's sleep.

Over the next couple of weeks or so, this room would be his refuge and base of operations. There was nothing at all respectable about this establishment, and that meant it was perfect for his needs.

Even though he was trying to be incognito, human nature will have its way. Being a newcomer to the area, he was a potential customer. On his second night, he was offered various drugs inside the hotel and on the street and propositioned by a lady who came to his room. He declined. The following night, another lady of differing proportions offered her services. The subsequent night, a young man knocked on his door and smiled enticingly when Harry came to the door. Harry laughed as he shooed the man away, thinking about the enterprising pimp who was going through all the sexual flavours that Harry might be interested in.

Before the pimp could come up with yet another offer, Harry had a NOT-so-polite word with the manager. The offers stopped; he really couldn't afford to attract attention.

The hotel was far enough from Moses' turf and the influence of others like Dexter for him not to be noticed. On the other hand, it was also close enough to allow him to observe activities without excessive travel. To survive and complete what he had to do, he needed information on the various players he was likely to come up against. Most challenging of all, he had to find a way in.

Harry knew he had to rest and recover for a minimum two-week period as the doctors recommended. However, time was marching on, and he couldn't sit cooped up in his room while there was work he needed to do. After a couple of restful days, it was time to explore and prepare, even while in recovery.

Harry needed ears, as well as his eyes on those involved with Moses and his business. So, he placed an online order for some basic surveillance gear using Moses' credit cards; they still worked. The equipment one can buy as a consumer these days would be more than good enough for his needs. He hoped that Moses had good credit; fortunately, he did.

Setting up an email address linked to a burner phone was always a convoluted process. However, he'd done this before, and it was no more complex this time around.

It was the delivery address that would be the biggest challenge. He took a qualified and cheeky risk and addressed it to Moses' house as a priority order. It's always easier to match the address on the credit card to the delivery address.

Harry knew he'd have had to get into the property anyway to set up the listening devices, so getting the stuff delivered there, on balance, seemed a reasonable option. That was the worst-case scenario, and he'd a best-case plan.

Modern parcel tracking is wonderful. The online tools and the people in their call centres are most helpful when the customer has to change arrangements. Once ordered, all he had to do was have it redirected to a 'local' drop-off location. In this case, it was a corner off-licence shop far enough away from their house not to be frequented by Moses.

During the days the parcel was in transit, he watched the general comings and goings of Moses' house. The property was part of a terrace of houses that stretched down either side of the street. Almost all its houses had small badly-maintained, and overgrown front gardens. These small areas were supposed to offer the residents a modicum of privacy from passers-by. Nowadays, most had old appliances and household furniture rotting in them; as did Moses' house. If some had once tried to keep a tidy garden, they'd have given up a long time ago. He didn't blame them; it wasn't a nice area.

Moses' house was a typical three bedroom affair for this area. Downstairs comprised a living room in the front, dining room and kitchen to the rear, and a toilet added onto the back. Upstairs, it had three bedrooms and a bathroom. Some properties had extensions, as did this one. There was a back garden, or rather, a yard with a back wall and a gate. The rows of terraces backed onto each other, separated by an alley at the rear.

The occupants of each house could easily see the comings and goings of their adjacent neighbours. So, unseen access to the property was not going to be easy. He had to watch and see when there might be an opportunity to break in without being noticed.

Dressed for begging on the street and wrapped up in his newly acquired sleeping bag, he watched. He planned to sit, huddled by the pavement at the end of the road. However, a bus shelter was near where he'd initially planned to 'work'. The shelter gave him a good view of the occupants' and visitors' comings and goings. It became his base for watching the house. The good thing was it was dry, or at least dryish.

While with Tom and Jess, he learned how to engage and attract the attention of passers-by. He learned early on how to avoid the attention of possible dubious characters that might inflict grief. It was this latter skill that he played on over the forthcoming days.

One of the first things he found out while living on the street was that most people preferred to ignore street beggars. By employing added measures to dissuade them, he hoped he could watch undisturbed. So Harry chose to sit there, staring into space, occasionally rocking his body back and forth while humming inane tunes of sorts. When someone came by or was too close, he argued with himself.

People tend to take a wide berth around anyone showing signs of mental illness. It makes them feel uncomfortable. And many people with some form of mental illness live on the street; there's often nowhere else to go. Harry's actions could therefore be more extreme to eliminate any chance of unwanted interaction; hopefully, not too much to have the opposite effect and attract attention.

Saying that, there's always the exception.

A couple of elderly ladies seemed to take pity on him. They always dropped a few coins and made it their duty to try and engage Harry in conversation each time they passed, even though it was only, "young man, how are you today?" A couple of times, they even dropped him a meat-spread sandwich. Normally, people on the street would appreciate this attention. However, Harry needed to be inconspicuous, and their interest in him was not what he needed. So when they approached, he ramped up his humming, rocking, and arguing.

During one of his episodes talking to himself, he incoherently mouthed, "those lovely old biddies are going to get me killed!" He couldn't let them hear, in case it might upset them.

Despite all his deterrent behaviour, a few other braver and generous passers-by also dropped a few coins, albeit without even casting him a second glance. Otherwise, he was effectively ignored. He could watch invisibly.

None of the people entering or leaving Moses' house donated anything. "Mean-spirited blighters," Harry light-heartedly whispered to no one around after they walked by.

In reality, he was happy they kept away; and to themselves.

During these first days, he was able to build a general picture of the types of people visiting and going in and out of Moses' house. Or rather, it now seemed to be Jeff's and Eddie's house.

He was especially keen on those that looked to be the higher-up-the-ladder types. He needed to know the movers and shakers, the top people behind all the drug trade in the area.

When he picked out potential individuals or groups of interest, he followed them in the BMW to find out where they lived.

Sometimes he couldn't follow by car. That's where simple everyday technology took over. He used a burner mobile phone, linked via a maps application which he could track via his own burner phone. He had to be careful of interference from the strong magnets he attached to the phones. He placed the gaffer-taped packages under the arches or elsewhere under the cars when he could. After all that, they still sometimes dropped off. However, he was still able to identify most.

Over those days, he travelled a lot, building an outline picture of the main people involved, where they lived, their security arrangements, with whom they spoke, even down to their preferred sexual flavours and preferences. It's amazing how inconspicuous a beggar can be.

The parcel eventually arrived. A now smart and stubble-bearded Harry picked up the parcel from the off-licence. Moses' credit card and driving licence picture, which was so unclear it could have been anyone, were the only verification items required. Mind you, he still displayed a swollen face with numerous cuts and bruises. So, he really could have been anyone; and he played on that.

Back in his base of operations, i.e. his hotel room, he checked out the contents of the newly arrived box. Inside, were two battery-operated voice-activated radio mics and a battery-operated receiver/recorder. The system had a stated operating distance of up to 100m.

Allowing for walls, he expected he'd have a safe range of 50m. When he tested his equipment under real conditions, it had an even better range than expected. He'd already identified a location for the recording device; under an old shed roof, at the bottom of the opposite neighbour's back garden.

He planned to strategically place the two radio mics in the house to hear what was being said and going on inside. At last, he'd be able to fill the gaps in his knowledge and understanding of the people involved.

Being one house in a terrace, the only access could be through the front or the back. This was a highly populated and busy area and people seemed to be always around. Next-door houses were occupied, and their lights seemed to be on until the early hours, signifying activity. Rear windows looked down at others' yards and the alley. It seemed an impossible task to sneak into the house. No matter how much he checked out the area and house, it was all a negative.

People would notice someone acting suspiciously or making noises breaking into the property. Even worse, they might act upon it. After careful consideration, he rationalised the solution would be crazily, actually brazenly, simple; he hoped.

He'd Moses' key to the house. During the pocket-emptying escapade in the warehouse, he let Jeff and Eddie get their keys back. So, there was no need for them to get access by forced entry and in so doing, have to change the locks.

Harry never expected Jeff and Eddie to believe he'd evicted them. Even they knew it was all bluster for show. If Harry did try to move in there, it wouldn't be long before he was painfully, or most likely, terminally evicted.

While observing the property, he'd not seen any issues with them having access or anyone changing locks. He knew, or rather, he prayed that audaciously going through the front door would be the simple and obvious way to get in. He'd also seen others using keys to get in. That meant they wouldn't have wanted the hassle of updating everyone with new keys.

Having built a pattern of all those people using the property and their movements, he identified a few possible time windows of opportunity. It was a hard choice, but the best one seemed to be early-to-late evening. As well as the covering of the dark, his observations suggested this was the least risky time. This was their time to be out and about supplying drugs.

Since others had keys to the house, anyone could turn up unexpectedly. The upside was he'd not be out of place as one of those random visitors.

Similar to the vicinity of his hotel, younger people around here also wore hooded jackets, especially the visitors to this house. His hooded head would, therefore, not be out of the norm. While his beaten-up face was healing well, he was still unrecognisable.

So, all in all, he was pretty safe, at least as safe as one could be on the streets in that area.

11. CAUGHT OUT

The following morning, through early evening, he continued his simulated begging and watching in earnest, with only the shortest of natural breaks.

Evening came with Jeff and Eddie heading off for their rounds at the usual time. As far as he could see, no one was in the house. Assuming their pattern didn't change, the pair shouldn't return for at least two to three hours.

He extracted his dark and hooded branded clothes from a bin where he'd earlier placed them. He changed in a nearby alley and made his way to the house. In front of the door, he pretended to fumble with his key. This action gave him a few moments to listen for noises coming from within.

"Not a sausage," he mumbled to himself, hearing nothing. All seemed clear inside.

He put the key in the lock, and it unlocked the door. Success! He smiled to himself that all was going swimmingly well as he quietly entered, then closed the door behind him.

While staking out the place, he noticed that only a few short discussions took place on the porch, so that was a no-no for a mic. It made sense that people would go into the rooms for sensitive discussions, rather than in the hallway or elsewhere.

So, he decided to hide one microphone in the front room and the other in the back diner/kitchen. He could have added extra mics, but that would have meant more time going through the recordings. He was only one man after all.

Suddenly, he heard noises and stood still.

The upstairs hallway light came on, followed by clumping and stumbling on wooden floors. The stairway light then lit up. A female voice started shouting while descending the stairs, "Eddie, you cunt, you promised to leave me a line!

I need it! You promised!" She was screeching by the time she reached the foot of the stairs.

Standing at the bottom of the stairs, she looked around, trying to decide where Eddie was. She was sweating, obviously strung out, with a noticeable sway. The woman, not much more than a girl, was only wearing a semi-closed dressing gown which left nothing to the imagination. While very skinny, almost emaciated, she was obviously attractive to the likes of Eddie or Jeff.

She saw Harry standing in the living room doorway and shrieked, "you're not Eddie, where's Eddie?" Then after thinking for a few moments, "so, who the fuck are you? What're you doing here?"

Harry stood there gawping, mind racing for what to say or do next. He cursed under his breath for foolishly believing all was going so well.

"Like what you see?" said the girl sarcastically, thinking he was staring at what was under the dressing gown. "Eddie'll fuck you dead if you touch."

Recovering his composure, he delivered her a big smile. He remembered his contingency. "I'm Joe. Eddie asked me to pop in to get some stuff." He waved his keys. "And while I was here, he said I was to give this to you."

From his pocket, he extracted one of the bags of white powder that he'd kept back from Tom and Jess. He held it out to her.

"Hi, I'm Melanie," she suddenly beamed as she snatched it from his outstretched hand. Without a backward glance, she ran up the stairs. After some rustling sounds from above, it soon became quiet.

Harry hoped that after taking her fix, she'd forget the whole episode or at least put it down to a vague memory. But that was a consideration for later. Right now he'd a job to finish.

Once both mics were affixed and their operation tested, Harry exited the back door, then the gate into the alley behind, all using Moses' keys. He stashed the recording device in the place he'd earlier identified. It gave him quick access for retrieval, data extraction, and battery change. Most importantly, it was safe from prying eyes.

Unlike TV programmes, there were no experts and a big team to support him in a fancy van at the bottom of the road. It was all down to him. He'd have to watch the comings and goings by day. When back at the hotel, he'd scan the recordings. It would be a pain, but if he was going to get through this, it had to be done.

****

Over the next few days, Harry watched all the comings and goings. In the evenings, back in his room, he listened, trying to make sense of what was happening. Due to the mics being audio sensitive (voice-activated), he didn't have to listen through dead space, only when sounds were recorded.

For most of the telephone conversations Harry couldn't hear what was said on the other end. However, he got the gist of the exchanges.

The face-face conversations were different and clear. He soon learned the voices of Jeff, Eddie, and their most regular girls, so his only challenge was linking the voices spoken to that of the house's visitors.

The first really useful piece of information was hearing a call on Eddie's phone. Eddie said to Jeff in a panic, "it's Dexter, why's he callin' me, what d'I do? He wants the stuff, and you promised he'd have it all by today!"

"Put him on speakerphone," ordered Jeff.

"Where's my fuckin' stuff!" a voice said.

"We've been trying to find the dosser what nicked it. He's disappeared. Probably out of the country with all the money he stole from Moses," said Jeff. "We told Moses to sort your stuff out first before he dealt with the tramp in the warehouse. But he was livid 'n' not thinkin' right. Didn't want anyone else dealin' on his turf. He told us to "shut the fuck up" and said your gear'd be safe in the car while we fucked that dosser."

"Don't give me that 'it was Moses' fault', shit again," he sneered. "There's no Moses no more!" he screamed. "And I don't give a whore's fanny how he got my stuff. You were the minders. He's only one dosser. You should have dealt wif 'im."

"That wasn't just a dosser. He was some sort of Kung Fu expert," interrupted Eddie.

Jeff continued, "that guy played Moses, then done 'im. He's got Moses' gun an' we don't want to mess with him again; not alone. When we find him, you

91

need to be there."

"First, find the cunt. I'll be there to deal with him. If not, I'll be dealing with you both."

"Got it, boss."

"Find it all fast, or we're all fucked!"

"But, you're the man, what do you mean?" queried Eddie.

"Tell that nephew of yours to shut the fuck up. He's got shit for brains. Yes, the gear's mine. But right now, I've no gear, so no cuttin' and baggin', and nothin' to sell. That means no business, and we'll all probably be dead with someone else in my territory."

"Even worse, I still have to pay that fuckin' distributor with that stupid posh name, Bloodworth. The dosser's got the drugs and the money. The Bloodworths are the real deal!"

Harry could hear a whistle, assuming from Jeff.

"Now the serious shit!" he screamed. "The money in the envelope's for De Silva. He gave me some new gear on approval, wot I've already shifted. He's also the man! An' we don't mess wif 'im either."

"This shit's got two of the biggest bastards after me, and that means you as well!" Dexter was now screaming.

"So, educate your twat nephew on this fuckin' business, or he ain't lastin' long."

Hearing their exchange, Harry now knew what he'd earlier suspected. The money and drugs in the bags never belonged to Moses. Moses wasn't equipped to move in those higher-up-the-food-chain circles. It all made sense. And it gave Harry a great, albeit a risky, way in.

Over the next day or so, Jeff delivered further 'lack-of' progress reports to Dexter, who was not amused.

A couple of days later, an expensive 4x4 drove up. A large man, who Harry took to be muscle, exited the passenger seat. He opened the rear roadside door and, out stepped a mountain of a man. He dwarfed the other big man.

The large vehicle seemed to rock with relief as he exited. Even though man-mountain was so large, he was no fat sloth. He exited the car with surprising ease, strode up to the house, followed by the other man, and hammered on the door. Jeff appeared and was met with a large fist that struck him squarely in his face. He was sent reeling into the house and collapsed backward on the floor. The larger man picked him up by the scruff and effortlessly dragged him inside.

The other man followed them in, slamming the door shut behind.

The smaller man opened the house door after a few minutes and waved in the direction of the 4x4. He stood there waiting as the driver got out and opened the kerbside rear door.

Out stepped a man of medium build wearing a ghastly light blue suit epitomising what would have been worn in a prohibition speakeasy. On his head he placed a wide-brimmed hat which matched his suit. He then walked up to and through the open door. It was gently closed behind him.

"What a poncy poser!" exclaimed Harry under his breath.

A couple of minutes later, all exited the house, slammed the door shut behind them, and drove off.

Harry couldn't wait until evening came. He looked forward to hearing what just transpired.

No police came as a result of that incident. With so much noise and illegal action going on in this neighbourhood, who was really going to call the police and get involved?

Later that evening, back in his room, Harry eagerly listened to the day's recordings. He looked forward to the big-fella-and-poncy-bloke episode; he wasn't disappointed.

Harry could hear a lot of pleading from Jeff and Eddie and screaming from the girls. It was interspersed with shouts of agony, coinciding with several thumps and furniture being broken.

A deep voice said, "Mr Dexter sends his compliments."

"Ah, so that was the man-mountain," Harry quietly spoke in his room.

There were more thumping noises and grunts, interspersed by cries of agony. The girls continued to scream. He mostly heard Eddie pleading with the attackers.

Harry unsympathetically smirked.

Some moments later, he heard the door open and click shut. Shortly after, he heard another voice. "Do you need more encouragement from Marcus here? You've till the end of the week, or next time, Marcus'll finish you good. I ain't going down with you two cunts. Before the shit hits the fan, your fucked bodies will be on display for De Silva and the Bloodworths. They need to know I was serious about sorting your shit," explained who Harry took to be Dexter.

There was a slam that sounded like the front door closing. Then Harry could hear a lot of cursing and swearing about what they'd do when they found that dosser, i.e. Harry.

Over the next few days, there were regular calls to and from Dexter for updates. They often used speakerphones when on these calls, which made understanding those discussions straightforward. They continually promised Dexter they'd find Harry and the money, and pleaded when there were further threats of violence.

During those days of watching and learning, Harry's body made good progress recovering. The aches reduced, the swelling subsided, and the stitches, at last, had been taken out.

As well as investigating Aloysius Dexter and the circles in which he moved, Harry was particularly interested in the Bloodworth and De Silva references made during the conversations.

And, within those circles, Harry found his way in, his mark, and his target.

12. CLOCKED

Harry had been following Dexter regularly. A few days later, Dexter met a man in a rather loud and garish club, one who he'd met earlier. After all his observations, Harry knew this man to be Andrew Bloodworth since he'd built up a picture of him. Bloodworth was one of Harry's marks to get him in.

From the body language of Dexter and Bloodworth and the uncomfortable looks on their minders' expressions, this wasn't a friendly meeting. Their earlier meeting displayed a similar tension.

Harry guessed this was, at least in part, about the missing drugs and money. Bloodworth's body language, leaning forward and gesticulating, suggested he wasn't amused. The minders from both sides sat quietly, watching and waiting in case anything got out of hand.

One element of his mark's entourage set him apart from the rest. It wasn't the muscle guys who were there for show; as expected. It was the rather smart, yet understated-looking guy who was always quietly in the background. This man was highly observant, his face expressionless. His eyes roamed the establishment, watching everything but said and missed nothing. He could be a problem.

An imperceptible glance at Harry, after which the man no longer looked at him when he swept his gaze across the people in the club, suggested to Harry that the man had clocked him.

After the group parted ways, Harry carried on carefully (non-) drinking and chatted up a hostess. In reality, Julie, as she introduced herself, did the chatting up. She did her best to make a dent in Moses' and the duo's cash, attempting to order the most expensive of this and that. Once she realised her strategy was unsuccessful and he declined her offer of a place to stay for the night, she moved on to another potential punter.

Harry assumed the following hour or so, sipping his coke while negotiating with the young woman, was long enough to remove any suspicion of him watching the meeting. It was time to leave.

By the time he exited the club, it was late evening. It was during that lull when there were few people around. Most were still at home or indoors enjoying the pub or dinner out before the nightclubs properly kicked off. The buses were still running, so he decided to head towards the nearest bus stop, which he could see a short way down the road.

He heard soft and fast footsteps coming up behind. "So, what's wrong with Julie? Not your type?" a voice asked. "Or maybe a woman's not your preference?"

Harry turned around and faced the innocuous-looking guy from the club. "Julie's habits are a bit too expensive for me, not that it's any of your business."

He then visibly calmed down and said, "listen, my friend, if you're her pimp, I don't want any trouble; she moved on to another mark anyway."

"Nope, not her pimp," said the other man in a soft-accented northern voice. "But I am an associate of the man you were trying hard not to pay particular interest in this evening. I also saw you doing the same two days ago outside Luigi's."

"Dunno what you're talking about, you've got the wrong guy." Harry defended himself in a faltering tone, "I was just having a drink." He tried to hurry away.

However, Mr Innocuous was good at this. While not big, he was still very imposing and able to block Harry's path. He'd managed to manoeuvre Harry into a dark alley, and then confronted him. "So, you're not police, or wouldn't be trying to get away, or at least you'd be challenging me. You're not in the trade, or we'd have your mates around by now. You're not a journo or you'd be bleating human rights. Let's see. Is she checking up on her husband again?"

"Honest, I don't know Mrs Bloodworth," he blurted out a little too quickly for his pretend lie to be convincing.

"I never mentioned her name," responded the innocuous man so softly that Harry could barely hear. Harry automatically leaned forward, straining to listen, which was exactly what the other man wanted.

Wow! He was fast!

The stumpy club that Mr Innocuous swung towards Harry's head missed him by a hairs-breadth. Had Harry not expected such an attack, the blow would have struck him heavily in the temple with such force it could easily have been fatal.

There was no chance for the quietly spoken man to swing again. A bullet to the man's thigh from Moses' little gun at close range shattered his femur, and he collapsed. Harry fired another into the man's stomach and again into his chest. All were in brief succession and fully disabled him.

The man tried to reach for his gun, but it was futile; he was too weak from the three shots he'd taken. He lay there looking up at Harry, saying nothing, waiting for the inevitable.

Harry took the man's gun and shot him with it. The first clipped his head. For the second shot, he stood closer for a more accurate shot to the head; which finally killed him.

It was a rather messy, painful, and unprofessional-looking killing. Harry felt sorry for the guy since he was only doing his job, but not well enough. However, the kill had to be done that way. Harry stripped the dead man of everything valuable and made a fast exit.

He dumped the wiped weapons in a wheelie bin a couple of streets away.

The clothes Harry wore, plus some of the others he'd acquired over the past couple of weeks, were donated to a distant charity shop the next day. These shops are a great way to get rid of contaminated clothes, especially when bundled up with others. They'll be washed, ironed, and distributed without trace from where they'd come.

13. DEBRIEF

The next evening, Harry went for a drink in a busy bar he'd found. It must have been the only bar in the city with a public telephone located at the back, amongst the coat rack, near the toilets.

While people-watching from a table at the back, he remembered his dad telling him a story about the wife of one of his friends.

The wife called the public telephone in the pub her husband regularly frequented. That telephone was also beside the toilets. As the phone rang, a guy came out. He picked up the receiver, listened, then shouted out, "Oi, is Davy Taylor in!" He could see a man gesticulating, waving, and voicing the word, NO! The pub went quiet. The man holding the phone then replied to the wife, "he says he's not in darlin'," then hung up the phone.

Almost everyone in the pub burst out laughing and cheering. As the telephone man walked past his dad's friend, he said in a deadpan tone of voice, "tell 'er we're not yer messaging service mate."

Harry brought his thoughts back to the present. Seeing that all looked innocent and harmless around here, Harry discretely used the public telephone to make a call. It was picked up after four rings.

The female voice immediately said, "you're over two weeks late."

He privately called her 'Dragon-Lady' due to her caustic and often rude behaviour.

Without sympathy, she continued. "Heard you were in hospital. Officially, you had a fall, according to the police and medical reports, badly bruised, cut, and concussed. Had to stay in four nights."

Then more sternly, "word is, you'd a careless lapse of judgement and took a beating. Not what we expected of a man with your pedigree and training. Can I assure management that all's well and there will be no further repetitions?

And you're back on the job at last, albeit delayed?"

'Thanks for the kind words, m'dear.'

Harry's actual response was a sigh and a, "yes." There was nothing else he could say. Conversations with her were, at best, abrupt.

"Good, but before you start the debrief, the police found a body in the river a couple of weeks ago; broken neck, fractured wind-pipe, a Jeremiah Williams. Goes by the name of Moses. Mini-dealer-cum-pusher. Hallmarks of a professional kill. Know anything?"

"No idea. Pity though. He was initially going to be a way into the organisation. Things have moved on, however, and we're still on target," he responded.

He knew she'd enough dirt on him already without his admitting to anything on the telephone; or anywhere.

From what he had learned during their conversations, if not related to the mission's success, deniability was her preferred method of dealing with this sort of information.

And as if on cue, she responded matter-of-factly with, "looks like this will be a case closed as unsolved."

"Also, on the subject of dead people, a Mr Julius Mercier met with an untimely death yesterday. Ex-Foreign Legion, looks like a mugging, two assailants, had to be shot five times before finally killed. A rather unprofessional botched robbery and killing. He works, or rather worked, for a drug distribution business run by a couple who go by the name of Bloodworth. Could be linked? Know anything about this one?"

Harry feigned indignation. "No idea. I don't do botched and I don't mug."

"Of course not." While the controller was a lady of few words and expected the same brevity, clarity, and accuracy in return, she often delved into unnecessary sarcastic responses.

Harry had never met her or any of her associates, apart from the man in the local prison cell. He didn't even know who his employer was. It was, however, safe to say that his brief was sanctioned somewhere in the establishment's food chain.

It was uncomfortable not knowing who held so much power over him. That power could be used to have him killed, or at best, maimed for life. These people had connections reaching into many places within the authorities, and elsewhere.

On the plus side, the pay for this Op to an offshore account was good, assuming he could survive to spend it.

"Commence the debrief," she said.

While Harry had never met her, he often imagined her during these updates. He would see a taut stern face, hair pulled up in a bun, wearing a tweed dress, sitting in an aged oak-panelled room in an old musty building somewhere deep in the bowels of the city. Not a sexy image.

He gave her the salient points. When finished, he then requested information on his mark, Andrew Bloodworth.

"Now isn't that a coincidence? The second murdered guy, Mr Mercier, worked for this Mr Bloodworth," she said with more than a hint of sarcasm.

Harry said nothing, it was best this way with her.

So, she left it at that. "I'll have Mr Bloodworth's information for you in two days; same time. Don't be late and try and avoid getting beaten up again, it's most inconvenient. We have a lot invested in you and it would be such a waste having to start again."

After those kind words, Harry hung up and ordered another pint. Sitting at a small table by himself, he wondered who his employer was. Would he really, be allowed to walk away after all this finished?

Two days later, back in the same pub, his controller gave him the information he requested and it was even better than he expected. As well as his mark, Andrew Bloodworth, his wife was also included in the telephone briefing.

She opened with, "our Mr Andrew Bloodworth is a qualified pharmacist. For the first part of his career, he worked for a large pharmaceutical company. He then found work overseas for charity organisations. All locations were conveniently in those countries where drugs were either made or grown. Our assumption is that while there, he made contacts and built his overseas illicit drugs supply chain.

"While travelling overseas, he came proficient in weapons in the guise of self-defence. On his return, he was able to use his chemistry knowledge and his contacts to build a strong business. He is ruthless. Multiple kills have been attributed to him, but nothing proven. Like most egotists, he's been known to stray into other beds, much to the anger of his wife."

"Which brings me to his wife, Molly. A quite appropriate name for a drug dealer's wife eh?" she commented, referring to one of the street names for Ecstasy.

That bit of almost-humour from his controller was rare.

"Now, she's a most interesting lady and is the big advantage he has over many others in his business. She is ex-witness protection, highly trained in all matters security, and highly capable in combat."

"They met in Mexico, where she freelanced in close protection. She ran the team hired to protect him and some others as they moved through various villages throughout the countryside. It's believed that a number of the killings attributed to him, were done by her. She has zero scruples and is extremely dangerous."

"She knows her husband likes a 'bit-on-the-side' and in this business, there's not much she can do about it. She can't leave, that would be dangerous. She can't eliminate him since this is a man's world, at their level anyway."

"You never know, she might even be happy with him," his controller said, with an overt distaste that she didn't hide in her tone. She obviously had no time for the type of woman that would accept that behaviour from a man.

The controller then talked about the Bloodworth's business and financial dealings.

"They avoid cash whenever possible, preferring to use international offshore accounts, as do most of their suppliers."

"They are avid users of the dark web as a good medium for introductions. However, knowing that much of this is now monitored by governments, they engage with caution."

"They love crypto currencies. Being unregulated and difficult to track, these are a great medium to move money. However, their in-country customers still use cash, which is laundered through hotels, restaurants, gambling, sex workers, and anywhere cash is king. They're also involved with large commercial ventures, using the cash to bribe and coerce deals; for example, they'd buy a derelict property and use cash-in-hand workers to renovate."

That was as much he had ever heard her say in one go.

"Does that give you what you need?"

"Thanks, that was really useful."

She finished with, "you need to get this mission back on track. Make contact, ingratiate yourself, use your charm, whatever you need to do to move things forward; and try not to kill anyone; unnecessarily at least."

The line went dead.

14. RETURN

The next day, Harry checked out of the hotel.

Dressed again in his street-living wear, he went to find Tom and Jess so they could fill him in on what had happened this past couple of weeks or so. They weren't easy to find. It was late when he eventually tracked them down in one of the nearby streets. They were pleased to see him; but very frightened. They went into an alley to talk so no one could see them together.

Harry expected there would have been at least one visit to garner information on his whereabouts. However, he didn't expect the questioning would have been so physical. Bad bruising and cuts still showed on both their faces. When they walked and talked, he could see they were in pain. He knew the bruising was as bad or worse elsewhere.

"What happened?" Harry asked.

Both Jess and Tom explained that Jeff and Eddie had come around. Albert had taken great pleasure in telling the duo that Tom and Jess were best friends with Harry. He said the siblings were in touch with Harry and knew how to contact him.

Tom started, "Jeff told us he needed to know where you were, and urgently. He was terrified and said you had money and drugs that belonged to Moses' boss. That bastard Eddie, the younger one that wanted to mix it with you, really hurt Jess."

"And he also beat Tom badly," interjected Jess.

"We couldn't tell him anything. We knew nothing. Eddie took his time hurting Jess in front of me." Tom had tears in his eyes as he forced out, "he enjoyed himself hurting her! There was nothing I could do to stop it. I'd have told them if I knew!" Then apologetically, "sorry."

In Tom's eyes and face, Harry saw the resignation of people in his position who could do nothing when a victim of brutality.

As Harry listened, his anger towards Jeff, and in particular, Eddie, grew. While he was livid with them, he was equally angry with himself. However, he did tell Tom and Jess to keep out of harm's way. And he did give them money to help them do so.

Harry tried unsuccessfully to rationalise there was nothing more he could have done. But deep down, he knew his actions had harmed them; again.

Normally, he planned and executed all his missions in a controlled and measured way. However, after hearing and seeing what had happened to this pair of innocents, he was beside himself with anger. These two didn't have a cruel bone in their bodies. He felt awful being the instigator of what had happened to them.

And whether or not Tom and Jess knew anything, it was abundantly obvious that Eddie took great pleasure in extracting nothing. Bullies have a way of taking out their anger and fear on others, and Eddie was a nasty one.

There was nothing more he could do now. "Eddie will get his," he promised them through gritted teeth.

They told Harry that Jeff, the older one, could see that Tom and Jess were clueless, so he eventually intervened and got Eddie to stop.

Jeff had been around the block and knew the game. He used his newfound gratitude from Tom and Jess to get them to promise and contact him the minute Harry appeared or if they knew where he was. He gave them a phone with his number plumbed in and said, "call me as soon as you hear anything, or I won't be able to stop Eddie next time."

Tom said, "we're not going to tell them anything, but please, you must leave now and never come back."

"Listen, don't worry about me. Call Jeff after I leave," Harry said. "Let him know that I'll be visiting Moses' place tomorrow afternoon. I'm going to sort out this problem and no one will hurt you both again. This time I promise."

"By the way, what do you know about this guy Dexter that Moses was involved with?"

Tom and Jess, between them, told him what they knew.

His first name was Aloysius. Dexter's father was a failed boxer who wanted his son to follow in the same trade. He expected his son to be the champion that alcohol and drugs prevented him from becoming. And a champion needs a proper name to go along with his future boxing success. They had a distant German ancestry, and since Aloysius comes from the old German 'famous warrior', that seemed a good fit.

The father's string of beatings in the ring and then afterward in street brawls, plus a severe alcohol addiction, destroyed him. He never lived long enough to see his son blossom into a low-level, high-grade scumbag.

The father never considered the impact of anyone enjoying the name Aloysius in the schools and neighbourhood where he grew up. Fatherless, of less than average height, and with that name, he initially suffered a lot of teasing and bullying, but not for long.

While his father was alive, he taught his son how to box and street-fight. Dexter was vicious and uncontrollable in a fight and never gave in. Soon, the victim of bullying became the bully.

Later in life, Dexter showed that he was a cunning operator. He soon learned that the nastier he was, the more he was respected; or rather, feared. And he enjoyed the fear he engendered in people.

What made him even more dangerous was his sharp mind, easily out-thinking his competition. Mind you, most of his competition to date had drug-addled brains.

This was useful information for what was to come the next day, and he thanked them for being so candid.

It was night before they separated. Tom waited for almost half an hour before he called Jeff, passing on Harry's message.

****

That night Harry entered Moses' house for the penultimate time. He needed to clear out the equipment and prepare for tomorrow.

15. PAINFUL NEGOTIATION

It was early next morning that a now tidier and clean-shaven Harry made his way to what was now Jeff's and Eddie's house. He hadn't eaten yet, so on his way there, he stopped at a local Scottish-Turkish-run greasy-spoon cafe. It plagiarised a well-known international brand, with a play on the owner's name. It was called MacDougals.

Before the occupants rose, Harry planned to enjoy a comfortable breakfast in the house. So, he bought half a dozen breakfast MacDougal muffin meals with tea and coffee to take away.

"It would be rude to have breakfast in someone's house and not bring along an offering," he grinned inwardly at the humour of it all.

Harry found a space close to the house and parked Moses' car. Armed with his stash of food, he unlocked the front door and walked in.

No one was up yet; not a sound from downstairs or above. He went into the kitchen/diner in the back to enjoy his breakfast in advance of the arriving occupants. The sight disgusted him. Even from his time on the street, he'd never seen anything as foul as this.

His earlier forays into the house were in the dark. While he'd smelled bad odours, he never saw the mess in daylight, only in heavily diffused torchlight.

There were dirty plates and pots around the sink. Old takeaway cartons and pizza boxes littered the room containing food remnants. From the mould on the left-over food, a lot of this had been there for days, perhaps weeks. There were what looked to be rat or mouse droppings in the corners. He couldn't find a clean space anywhere to lay down his offering.

"What a bunch of dirty 'bastards'," Harry growled. "Street living is cleaner than this!"

He surveyed the open sewer around him. Harry didn't expect a pristine kitchen but never thought anyone could live like this.

"Ah well, here goes my peaceful breakfast," he said out loud to no one in particular. And in disgust, he swept everything off the table with a crash and a clatter. As well as making space for the banquet he'd brought for this bunch of slobs, he knew the noise would give them a rude awakening.

A stark-naked and startled Eddie was the first to appear, knife in hand. He uttered two words, "fuckin' bastard!" and then lunged at Harry.

Harry was now in better shape from the last time they'd met. He danced away from the lunging and swinging blade, picked up a breakfast barstool, and toyed with his attacker. Holding the stool by its legs, he used it to parry Eddie's ineffective knife swipes. Each time Eddie lashed out, Harry struck him in the face with the stool; hard, very hard.

"Fuck you," screamed Eddie while repeatedly striking out at Harry. Eddie also included variations of, "bastard and cunt," every time the barstool collided with his face.

Harry was enjoying getting some form of revenge for the unwarranted pain inflicted on Tom and Jess.

An increasingly bloody and battered Eddie was getting increasingly angry and frustrated, made worse by seeing Harry grinning back at him. The blood was streaming down his face. His earlier gun-butt wound had opened, and his crushed nose and lips dripped blood. He struggled to see as the cuts to his forehead and eyebrows seeped blood into his eyes.

Harry heard noises of other people coming, and was getting bored with Eddie's futile efforts. He parried what was to be his victim's final pathetic and petulant knife swipe and ended the playtime by striking Eddie over the head with the stool. Eddie crumpled into a heap on the floor.

While it would have given him immense pleasure to have punched and kicked this little toe-rag after what he did to Tom and Jess, he erred on the safe side. One thing he learned a long time ago in any brawl was to use whatever weapon was around.

Jeff appeared in the doorway. He saw Harry but said and did nothing. He then took in the scene. Eddie was on the floor, and Harry stood above him, still holding the bloody stool; it was obvious what had happened. His heavily bloodied bully of a nephew was slowly coming to his senses, but he still didn't move. He was too worldly-wise to react in haste.

"Hi Jeff, please come and join me for breakfast," smiled Harry, "I think we need a hearty meal before the boss arrives, don't we?"

"Oh, and please send down the two girls. It'd be nice to have some female company, and I'd like to know where everyone is." He hoped the girl he saw earlier wouldn't recognise his now-shaven, un-bruised face and smarter appearance from when they last met in the hallway.

Harry used the brown paper bags and the copious serviettes to cover a seat by the coffee table and proceeded to enjoy his breakfast.

Eddie had sufficiently recovered to get himself to a seated position against a cupboard door, not too close to Harry. He'd had enough.

"By the way Jeff, children shouldn't play with knives. So tell your nephew the next time he picks up a knife in my presence, will be the last time he picks up anything."

Harry hoped the demeaning way he referred to Eddie would encourage the lout to try again and take the consequences. He looked down at the bloodied, naked man. "If I'd have wanted you dead, I'd have done it at 2 am this morning while you were shagging upstairs. You sleep well afterward, don't you?" he smirked.

Both girls appeared in the doorway. Melanie was wearing clothes this time. As Harry had hoped, she didn't seem to recognise him. They stared around the kitchen, speechless.

"Eat," Harry open-handedly gestured to them all.

The girls recovered, grabbed some food, and ate hungrily, to the obvious indignation of Eddie. He expected them to come and offer him sympathy and a helping hand, but they completely ignored him.

Still seated, Eddie blurted out, "how'd you know how many of us are here? You said you'd be here this afternoon. And, who the fuck said you could come in here anyway?"

Harry held up his hand to stop the questions. "You'll remember I said you were homeless? So, you should thank me I've let you stay so long, at least so far. Now, when do you expect the boss?"

Jeff set his phone on a sideboard, went over to Eddie, and helped him to his feet while trying to calm him.

"Eddie, how's about you putting on something to cover your danglies?" smirked Harry. "You and they don't make a pretty sight." He then feigned shock and horror at the look of him. The young women giggled as they ate.

Seeing the bruises on Eddie's body that were not delivered by him just now, he gloated, "that big bugger Marcus does pack a helluva punch. I'll bet he enjoyed smacking you around, almost as much as I did."

To Jeff, Harry said, "now, I'm assuming you called the boss and told him I was here? When's he expected?"

"What are you going to do?" replied Jeff.

"Offer him a muffin, some fries, and a cuppa, what else do you think?"

He became serious. "I'm not here for trouble."

"I popped in to see Tom and Jess yesterday. They told me you'd both been over asking about me." He stared malevolently at Eddie. "You hurt my friends, and I hurt you. They knew nothing. You got off lightly; this time."

Eddie gave a shiver, whether from cold or fear was anyone's guess. But he said nothing. The look on his face was pure hatred.

"I was surprised to learn from them that a gentleman called Mr Dexter had been looking for some stuff that was in Moses' car. I didn't think to check. Why would I? I don't want trouble with him, so I checked and found a stash in a bag, in the boot. I've come to return it all; not touched anything. The envelope Moses carried is also with the rest."

And to twist the verbal blade into the two minders, "if only you lot had told me then, this wouldn't have been an issue for Mr Dexter. I want to clear any misunderstanding with him and be on my way, that's all."

Jeff picked up his phone and talked into it. Harry already knew by the way he'd laid the phone someone was on the line. And it was almost certainly Dexter who was listening.

Harry's explanation of his lack of knowledge of the car's illicit content and then pinning the blame on the two was for the benefit of Dexter. He had to make sure this was all a mistake caused by Jeff and Eddie. At least then, he might stand a chance of his plan succeeding.

Jeff said, "he said he'll be here in about 20 minutes."

"Then enjoy," said Harry again, gesturing to the food on the table.

Marcus appeared 15 minutes later. The others deferred and stayed clear of him. By their nervous looks, the big man inspired fear. And after what he did to Eddie and Jeff, it was clear why. This man was not to be messed with.

Marcus scrutinised Harry, then came over and said, "stand, slowly, arms up."

Harry complied, knowing to resist would not be a good move. Worse still, bringing any weapons would not have set the scene as he wanted.

Once satisfied that Harry was clean, man-mountain grunted into his phone. A minute later, Dexter entered with one of the men he'd seen earlier with Marcus.

Harry stood to one side and gestured to the seat he'd been using. Trying to make light of a potentially risky situation, he said to Dexter, "at least the paper's clean."

Dexter stood a little inside the doorway. He nodded to Marcus in Harry's direction.

The big man hit Harry hard. He then looked at Dexter, who nodded, so he hit Harry again. He looked over again at Dexter, who shook his head as a 'no'.

Harry was relieved. He expected there'd have to be some face-saving retribution since the loss of product would be hurting Dexter and others in the drug supply chain. Worse still, it was a blow to his ego and credibility. However, Harry didn't expect the two blows from this monster to be as bad as this. While he knew how to ride a punch, this man was big and powerful, and it hurt; badly. And Harry was still hurting from his earlier beating.

Eddie, now partially covered, beamed with delight at Harry receiving a 'slap'. He was keen to join in but was held back by Jeff. "Uncle Jeff," growled Eddie, "one of these days, you're going to get in my way once too often, then I'm going to have to kill you."

"Possibly, but I made a promise to your mother, my sister, before she died," whispered Jeff as he held onto Eddie's arm. "Like it or not, I'm looking after you."

Now satisfied that punishment had been delivered, Dexter sat down and looked at Harry. "You've caused me a loada shit. I want my money and all the stuff back. I've also lost a shit load of money while I was fixin' the distribution channel gap that poor old Moses left."

He took a handful of fries and slowly ate them. No one filled the silence until he spoke again. "Now, I've come to collect, and if I'm not happy, Marcus here," he nodded in the big man's direction, "will finish what he started."

Harry was still worried that Melanie might recognise him from before. He said to the other girl, "under Eddie's bed is a canvas bag. Please bring it down and give it to this gentleman here?" He already knew who Aloysius Dexter was but was naturally feigning ignorance.

"You can call me Mr. Dexter," he said, as he continued to graze on the fries.

The girl looked at a confused Eddie, who nodded in affirmation. A couple of minutes later, she reappeared and held out the bag to Dexter, who waved her away. Dexter gestured to the other man that came in with him, "Bob open it and tell me what's there."

"I don't do drugs, I don't sell drugs, and don't touch them in any way," Harry said in a quiet, apologetic tone of voice.

As Bob checked the contents, Harry added, "whatever you're into is no concern of mine. It's all there, I promise. Honest, I didn't even know it was there until I was told yesterday. Then I had to go to the car and bring it over as quickly as possible. I thought it'd be the afternoon before I could get here, but as you can see, I got here early." He lied ever so convincingly.

After a few moments of checking through the bag, Bob responded, "it's all here boss."

Eddie jumped forward and said, "honest Mr Dexter, he took it," pointing at Harry. "I didn't know it was here. If I'd 'ave known, I'd 'ave brung it over to you."

"Of course, you didn't know. You know nothin' about anythin', shit-for-brains. You're not stupid enough to cross me, and too stupid to see your mate here planting the bag," he gestured in Harry's direction.

"Mr Dexter," said Harry politely, "I wasn't in a good place after the beating I took from them and had to deal with the situation quickly and efficiently. And

I'm sorry what happened to Moses, but they left me no choice." Harry lied about the Moses reference; he was getting good at this lying lark.

He then tried to further reason with Dexter. "Everyone knows Moses and these two idiots were killing your rep, and even worse, your customers, with all the shit he cut into your product. So, maybe what happened was for the best in the long run. Also, your hands are clean, and now I owe you, whatever you need. I don't want to know anything further and want to leave and not look over my shoulder."

Harry finished with, "are we good?"

Dexter looked him over, thought for a moment, then said, "if I choose to deal with my people, I sort them, no one else. Get it!" This was said loudly for all to hear.

Harry nodded and looked down in acquiescence.

"Marcus here," gesturing to the giant, "has shown you, in the way he does best, my displeasure about one of my boys' death. And yep, what happened to Moses was coming to him anyway. You're right, I can now safely deny all knowledge of what happened to him, and it's you what's in the frame. And it's me what's got you by the balls."

Dexter then looked down at Eddie. "So, what happened to you?"

"He hit me, with that stool."

"Why didn't you hit him back?"

"He wouldn't let me," he whimpered. "He played with me; he enjoyed it, the bastard!"

"Shame I wasn't here," grinned Dexter.

Dexter was still smiling when he turned back to Harry. "I own you now, and you'd better remember that! So, this time we're good. Screw up again, and it'll be you in the river with a chain around your fuckin' neck. When I shout, you come, got it?"

"Yes, boss." Harry thought the 'boss' reference was a good touch.

"We'll talk again when I'm ready," he added.

Harry followed up. "I like living in the old warehouse and would like to continue staying there. That means I'll keep an eye on things for you and be there when you want to call in that IOU. No one will mess with that patch while I'm there."

Dexter thought, then nodded in agreement.

Harry turned to Eddie, "Tom and Jess are off-limits. Get it?"

Dexter also turned to Eddie, who was about to say something in response, but Jeff put a hand on his shoulder and nodded no. Eddie grunted in acquiescence but shot Harry a stare that could have soured milk.

Harry half-offered his hand to Dexter, but Marcus stepped forward surprisingly quickly, barring access. Harry deferred and pulled back.

He slowly went into his pockets, extracted, then lobbed Moses' car keys to Jeff, "I've no use for that old jalopy now."

He left the house to enjoy his new home, at least for a while.

16. HOME SWEET HOME

Later that morning, Harry arrived back at the derelict building. Tom and Jess were waiting with terrified anticipation.

Seeing him coming towards them unscathed, they shouted for joy. Jess ran over and hugged him tightly. He winced as she squeezed hard for such a frail-looking young woman; his stomach muscles still ached from Marcus' punches.

They both knew where he went and suspected who he was meeting, and what could have been the worst result.

"All good," Harry said smiling. Then there was joy when he explained that things would be OK for all of them, at least for the time being.

"You're now definitely in charge and have the mansion," he said to Tom while pointing at Albert's ramshackle concoction of boxes that was now their home.

"And even better, Eddie and I had a nice talk. He won't be coming around again, and confirmed by Dexter."

As a closing request, Harry asked, "Got any more of your delicious sandwiches? I'm starving, and I need to eat somewhere cleaner than I did for breakfast."

****

Jess and Tom were sitting by their new home when they saw Harry returning from wherever he'd been. He'd reported in.

She gave Tom a resigned look.

"You don't need to, he's not expecting that."

"Of course he is. With him, I know it'll be OK. I need to thank him."

Tom shrugged his shoulders and hoped for the best.

Jess walked over to where Harry was sitting, reading yesterday's evening newspaper. As she approached, she gave him a big smile, which he returned.

Harry had seen her walking over. He was expecting what was going to happen sooner or later. He knew she was in a dark place and felt valueless. His creating the situation earlier, then leaving them to face what Eddie gave out, made Harry feel awful. There was no way he could hurt her again. Jess wasn't much more than a child and had suffered so much in her few years.

From what Tom had explained, she believed her only value to others was through sex. Through her teenage years, this was the only value men, and sometimes women, saw in her. She grew up knowing that sex was the only currency she could offer. He was no counsellor but knew dismissing her offer would be yet another in a long line of rejections. And then she would feel further devalued.

Harry motioned her to sit next to him. When she sat down, he put his arm around her shoulders.

She expected this to be the forerunner of sex. She forced a smile.

He gently said, "Jess, before I came here, I'd no one, no friends, and no family. You and Tom are the only people I have. Please don't take that away from me. I can't lose the only two friends I have for the sake of a bit of rumpy-pumpy."

It was like a weight had lifted from her shoulders. The tension released in her, and Jess burst out laughing. She give him the biggest of hugs. After a few moments, she placed her head on his shoulder and just sat there next to him, chuckling.

"What's so funny?"

After some moments, Jess said with a smile, "that was the expression my father used to my mother with his usual nod and wink. He'd whisper to her, "rumpy-pumpy?" She'd giggle, and they'd disappear upstairs. Tom and I knew what they were up to, and we always laughed about it."

On the other side of the warehouse, Tom looked at them, nodded, and smiled. He left them alone to talk.

She reminisced about her father fondly for what seemed like hours, talking about the good times the four of them had. The tears rolled down her face as she sat with Harry, chatting about the enjoyable time of her life, now in the distant past.

There was little joy for her these days and until recently, little hope. She looked up at Harry and silently wondered if maybe things could change.

"My dad died when I was still in primary school. They weren't well off when he was alive, and with him gone, my mother lost all will."

She talked about her family's decline. With no income, slowly things deteriorated. Her mother, who'd always liked a drink, drank more, became depressed, then started drinking even more heavily. It was a vicious downward cycle. It wasn't long before her mother lost her friends and got into debt.

She no longer cared about anything, neither herself, nor her children. The spiral of despair continued as the mother started to bring home various 'uncles' to her children to help feed her alcohol addiction.

They enjoyed Jess and sometimes even Tom. Jess was eventually taken into care for her protection. Tom was too old by then to go into care. In any case, he wanted to stay with his mother to offer what little protection and help he could.

For Jess being a beauty wasn't the advantage it would have been in other circumstances. It was her curse. Even in care, she was abused everywhere she was placed. And with that abuse, she became angry. Her anger turned into emotionally disruptive displays that people in authority couldn't manage. So, she was regularly moved around when she became too much of a problem.

Harry, at last, fully understood. What she had with Albert was better than being passed around everywhere. Hopefully, all this was in the past. He vowed no one would mess with this young woman again!

Harry thought about how he could make provision for the two siblings after this was finished and all debts paid. All his money wasn't going be of any use to him when dead.

Tom eventually came over, and the three of them sat and talked.

Sitting there and quietly talking, Harry relaxed for the first time in what seemed ages. Now at more ease with his situation and surroundings, he could appreciate the little things. He watched the dimming light of the sunset creeping up the walls that he'd never noticed before. Harry stared as it streamed through the broken windows. Finally, the final shimmers of light painted a mosaic of colour on the opposite graffiti encrusted walls, before it suddenly switched off.

He hadn't felt tranquility like this in such a long time.

****

Word had gotten around that Albert was no longer there. More and more people started to hang around the warehouse for its peace, safety, and anonymity. For some, it was an escape from the watchful eye of the authorities; for whatever their real or perceived reasons.

Many were there because of drugs, having lost everything to feed their habit. All too often, they had to take dangerously cut drugs that were cheaper and more damaging to their health.

Others had a mental illness. Some, like Jess, had run away, and there were many more reasons. What they all had in common was their wish for a safe haven. And apart from the charitable and council-run refuges, this was as good as it got.

With more people coming, it had to happen that Albert's greed got the better of him, overcoming common sense. He and his two guys appeared a few days later, a little high and demanding money. No one came over, nor paid him attention, let alone money.

He shouted for Jess. She blanked him.

His anger rose as he stood there being ignored by the "snivelling fuckers" who, only a couple of weeks ago, kowtowed to his every word.

"Oi you," he again shouted at Jess as she and Tom talked some distance away.

Albert walked up to them. "I've not had a shag in ages," he tried to grab her hand.

Harry watched from a distance, thinking wistfully, *'so charming, how could she refuse that brown-gap-toothed smile?'*

Tom and the others needed to deal with the situation. He was there as moral support, but also, just in case.

Tom stepped in between them.

"You can fuck off," Albert shouted to Tom. "It's none of your business wot happens wiff a couple! Wanna taste a bit of Woody?" as he waved his baseball bat around threateningly.

Tom didn't budge, and people started to gather around him. Encouraged by the support, Tom challenged Albert, trying his best to hide his nervousness, "no one wants you, we don't need you, we're better without you, you're finished here, leave, now."

Albert was stunned at Tom's, albeit reticent stance. He thought about striking out at Tom but saw more people gathering around to support the small, brave man. Albert was not that high. He could see that taking action wouldn't end up well for him. Even worse, his two oppos realised the situation before him and were already heading away. They cajoled Albert to do the same and get out of there.

Albert said into Tom's face, "you think you're fuckin' safe, well you ain't. Tell that poncy talking tosser friend of yours 'e's goin' to get his, and then I'll be back. And then I'll fuck the arse off that bitch sister of yours."

Jess visibly shuddered.

Albert stomped away, and people slowly dispersed without a word.

Tom looked in Harry's direction with a sigh of relief. He got the thumbs-up sign in return, signifying well done and that he was proud of him.

Relieved that his presence was no longer required, Harry now knew he could safely leave at any time; although happy to hang around for the moment. He wanted to enjoy the peace while he could.

17. COLLECTING ON THE IOU

During his discussions with Tom and Jess, Harry had set the scene for his official military background. He knew Dexter would ask them and others about him, especially if sometime in the future, he'd call in Harry's IOU, which he expected, he hoped.

He needed to know how trustworthy Harry was. And from how he protected Tom and Jess, he looked after his own. If nothing else, these two were leverage, if needed.

Dexter saw the aftermath of how he toyed with Eddie, who he knew to be tasty in a scrap, and a nasty individual. He would find out, in detail, what happened with Moses and how Harry could overcome five men and then get away scot-free. He'd also be interested in how Harry could evade their searches, but that would be a challenge since no one could tell him. However, the fact that Harry lived without detection would be telling in itself.

And, knowing the siblings, Harry was sure they'd over-elaborate on all his exploits and abilities. Anything to make him look good was not going to harm his plan. He also knew and could see that Jeff rated him, always keeping well clear. Eddie, who hated him, was not rated by Dexter. So anything Eddie said against Harry would be a positive.

A few days later, Dexter made his move. Marcus and another arrived at the warehouse as Harry was tucking into another out-of-date sandwich.

He went over to Harry and stood over him. "Mr Dexter wants to see you."

Harry looked at his stale lunch, feigned indecision about leaving such a gourmet dish, then smiled. "A lunch appointment, how pleasant, what's the dress code?"

"We go now." His low voice boomed his monotone, emotionless statement.

Harry stood up to leave and said to Tom and Jess who looked on with

119

concern, "no problems, I'm only helping Dexter."

Marcus grunted, "arms up," and he frisked Harry without coming too close. Harry's clothes were overdue a wash, and he knew he stank something rotten. Harry did his ablutions as often as possible, but washing clothes was more problematic.

Harry inwardly smiled, '*this monster was not designed for nuance, but nonetheless bilingual; English and Grunt'ish.*'

Harry also pondered the look on Dexter's face when an over-ripe Harry would emerge from his fancy 4x4. With any luck, his dirty stinking clothes would leave a lasting impression on the interior. He had visions of Aloysius flaying Marcus while standing on a ladder to reach him.

He needn't have worried on Marcus' behalf. Moses' elderly 525 waited outside. Dexter's driver waited for them behind the wheel of the sacrificial transport. Harry was sat in the back, with Marcus keeping well away from his emanating odours.

On the way to wherever they were heading, Harry had to ask, "so what's happening, and where are we going?"

Marcus responded with, "shut up," which killed any further conversation.

The Dexter residence was an expensive secluded house, set back in a quiet street. Harry had been there before while he was in convalescence-cum-surveillance mode. So he knew the layout. He made sure that there was a visible look of surprise and awe on his face as he looked around and peered into windows, while directed around the outside of the house.

They entered the kitchen at the back of the house. There was some rather noisy music in the background; in the case of eavesdroppers, he presumed. The authorities can be such nosey blighters.

Harry wasn't offered a chair but left to stand inside the doorway. Dexter entered soon after and made himself comfortable in a large chair by the kitchen table. Marcus and Bob stood on each side of Harry, but not too close to the force field of odours that surrounded him.

Dexter had with him what looked to be a military file. He laid the file on the table and pushed it towards Harry, uttering the words, "you make interesting reading."

Harry picked up the file and glanced through it. It was a copy of his official military file. He wondered with obvious concern how this man could get his file. He knew there was no point in asking.

Dexter then said, "got a job for you."

"I'll do anything but sell drugs, sorry. I don't do drugs either, and know nothing about them," Harry said apologetically.

"I don't need no more drug-crazed runners, all fuckin' ten-a-penny. But if I did, you'd do what I fuckin' tell you to," was the angry response to put him back in his place.

Then with a show of being intimidated, Harry nervously rattled off, "but I'm good at security and a bit of driving. I know Marcus here's doing a great job for you, so you don't need a minder. So, how I can help you?"

The latter was said with as much deference and apology that he could gush out without being too obvious.

Dexter replied with annoyance. "It's security. OK?"

Harry said nothing but outwardly gave a show of relief. Inwardly, he hoped he knew what was coming.

"Obvious you can handle you'self, and you don' want to be visible. Dat's exactly what's needed. An associate of mine needs help with security since he lost one of his boys. And not stupid muscle like Marcus and Bob here, is what he needs."

The two big men stood there saying nothing about what was said about them and in front of them.

"I want someone that owes me to be that help."

Dexter paused, letting it sink in. He continued. "Pay's good." He then pushed over the police report on Harry's quickly dismissed assault charge outside the nightclub.

"I was exonerated by the police."

"Their uncle, the club owner, currently don't see it that way. If you take the job, the uncle will be told you're off limits."

"Word is you dun 'em two shites one-handed while holding up a girl with the other. Impressive. A proper Lancelot ain't ya? You've got a rep. with that lot

121

already. They was going to come mob-handed when they found ya."

Harry couldn't say anything. The story of him rescuing the girl had been stretched, which wouldn't hurt his plan at all.

Dexter leaned forward and stared at Harry. "And for me, I have you on the inside."

There was another sheet of paper that Dexter smugly pushed over toward Harry. It was an internal Albatross Tactical Security email. "You might know this lot as ATS."

In the email, Harry read that he was a person of interest linked to the deaths of three of their men in Afghanistan. No one was to approach, merely pass any information up the food chain.

Now, this did take Harry by surprise. With a smidgen of panic in his gut, he quietly wondered how on earth this thug had links into, or with ATS.

There had to be a drug link somewhere.

Dexter continued, "the good thing 'bout all this, and very lucky for ya, is my associate likes discrete security and you fit the bill."

Harry offered up his best poker-face, as he tried to hide his shock at the information this drug dealer had on him.

All he could think was, *'just when you think all the bases are covered and the plan is coming together, a mega curveball appears from nowhere.'*

"I don't know anything about what ATS wants, it's going to end up as nothing. Yes, I was in Afghanistan, but spent most of my time in logistics," he responded, trying to be as calm as possible. "I never had any dealings with ATS or their men. There was zero cross-over. They supplied all their own stuff."

"If that's true, you won't mind me calling my mate in ATS and tell 'im where you are then?" Dexter said threateningly.

Harry thought about Afghanistan, the failed mission, the ambush that killed his best friend, and the deaths of the three ATS mercs. He couldn't have ATS learn about his presence or his situation. That made him vulnerable, and the consequences could be terminal. It would also jeopardise everything he'd been working toward.

Harry pulled himself back from his wandering thoughts. "I could do with being clean, with some form of normality and money. I know I owe you and if working for your friend could maintain my invisibility, and repay you, then I'm up for it."

"Not that you had a choice. And don't forget, you's my man in there. I'll leave you with Marcus to sort the next steps," finished Dexter as he walked out of the room.

****

Marcus took Harry to Dexter's downstairs guest bedroom. On the bed, lay a dark suit, shirt, shoes, and underwear. "Clean yourself up," said the big man in disgust, pointing to the en-suite. "Then get dressed," pointing to the clothes. As he left, his parting comment was, "thirty minutes."

"Thank god it's not Dexter's pink and mauve hand-me-downs," he quietly laughed after Marcus had left. "Would bugger my street cred back at the old warehouse."

Harry was out in twenty-five minutes. It felt great to be clean and in fresh clothes. The new clothes, albeit from a cheap shop, fitted reasonably well.

Bob waited outside the room for him and when Harry appeared, took him back to the kitchen. Waiting with Marcus, were two large, well-muscled men. No one made introductions. There was an atmosphere of enmity and distrust. The tension between them could have been cut with a knife. Not a word passed any of their lips.

The two new guys gave Harry a security check, as thorough as he'd have done on someone. Marcus and Bob stared at them intently but said nothing. They glanced over in turn at Marcus as they went through the checks. They knew the big man was someone to be feared.

The dynamics of the men suggested this was less an associate relationship but more a competitive-cum-supplier one.

Once the two newcomers were satisfied, only two words were said and they came from one of the two new arrivals, "let's go."

18. INTERVIEW

Harry was seated in the back of a large 4x4, with the other two sitting in the front. They obviously had no security concerns about Harry sitting there, unguarded, as they drove away.

While these two were ill at ease in Dexter's house, once in the car, their mood relaxed and they made small talk between themselves, ignoring Harry.

As they drove north to the city outskirts, Harry interrupted, "do you know why I've been asked to come with you? All I know is it's about a job."

The front passenger curtly responded, "yes we know what's going on, and no, we're not going to explain."

"Bloody hell George, give him a break. He's going to be working with the two of us," the driver retorted. He half-turned around, saying, "I assume that answers your question."

Harry sat back, pleased with himself. With any luck, this was him going to be in.

Almost an hour later, they arrived at plush suburbia. After a drive down a long tree-lined avenue, their vehicle stopped at a large double gate. Cameras on both gate pillars looked at anyone who arrived. Both driver and front passenger leaned out to be visible. After a voice acknowledged them, and with the swipe of a card, the gates opened.

They drove up a long drive to a large, stone-built Victorian mansion. From Harry's observations, there were at least four reception rooms downstairs, and the upstairs had at least twelve bedrooms.

Harry had already recced the house and gardens during a couple of evenings and nights during his investigations. He knew the locations of the discrete CCTV cameras within the premises and how the security teams worked.

No cameras pointed outside to view the street. Harry assumed it was to avoid upsetting their neighbours' privacy and to stop questions being asked about why a high level of obvious security was needed in such a peaceful and tranquil area. It was also dubiously legal.

There was a discrete guard always on patrol, supported by another monitoring the cameras. There were two 'pet' Ridgebacks, which looked more like large labs to the untrained eye, overtly roaming and playing around the garden.

The average thug likes to go for the more outwardly aggressive mutt that has a 'bull' somewhere in its name. However, Rhodesian Ridgebacks are highly intelligent, fearless, and completely loyal; the ideal protection dog.

These dogs had given Harry some challenges during his second visit. However, a couple of carefully and lightly doped sirloin steaks were enough to quiet them for a couple of hours. It was important they quickly recovered with no ill effects since any visible drowsiness would raise suspicions. Also, he was a softie when it came to dogs.

Now, in the daylight, the manicured and open garden, while easier to monitor security-wise, was quite beautiful. It comprised a lawn of close-cut grass interspersed with small shrubs and bushes. Although early spring, the garden was already of different colours and hues, giving it an almost kaleidoscope effect.

The awe showing on his face as they drove up the driveway was, therefore, pretty much genuine.

A couple awaited them at the front door. One was a lithe, dark-haired, rather attractive woman in her 40s, who Harry's eyes took in first; naturally. She was decked out in mucky dungarees and muddy wellington boots and was the reason for the magnificent garden.

With her was a smart, fit-looking man, who looked a few years older. He'd the tidy, stiff appearance of a senior army officer. He could also have passed for a banker but didn't have the look of a chemical engineer that Dragon-Lady advised he was.

There again, what does a chemist look like? he asked himself.

It was his outwardly formal, polite appearance that Harry suspected would make people underestimate this man. From the further information he'd gathered, people easily dropped their guard, and that made him even more dangerous.

The minder in the passenger seat got out first and opened Harry's door. This was no courtesy but was done to emphasise his close presence. Harry was perfectly happy to wait until beckoned. The dogs were already in position, sitting between the couple and the car. To the uninitiated, they looked so cute. Harry knew dogs and those two sitting there, without tails wagging, staring at him with unblinking eyes made him wary.

The woman smiled a welcome and held out her hand. She saw Harry's hesitation regarding the dogs. So she walked forward, and Harry slowly took her outstretched hand, and they shook. The dogs went back to sit by the man.

She offered, "I'm Molly, and you, hopefully, might be our new, em, driver. Welcome."

"I'm assuming this is all your doing? Lovely," Harry commented, looking around and gesturing to the garden. He knew the compliment would warm her to him, or at least do no harm.

She beamed, "guilty as charged." While she assumed he only meant the appearance.

Clearly the security aspect was also her doing from what the controller explained about her. So, showing his observational skills, Harry followed up. "It's not only the garden's beauty, the whole place is unobtrusively secure, most discrete indeed." This was an interview after all.

The older man stepped forward a little to take over the conversation. "I'm Andrew Bloodworth, to you Mr, and this is my wife, Molly, Mrs Bloodworth," with an emphasis on the 'Mrs'. There were no first names for these two.

"Yes, you're correct, we operate in a dubious world, and we wouldn't want to upset our neighbours' delicate sensitivities with any in-their-face security measures. We are pillars of the community after all," he smirked at Molly.

Molly chuckled in return, "of course we are, darling, if only they knew."

"Jenny, take Mr Logan's things to his room," said Mr Bloodworth to an older lady standing behind them.

"Ah, this is all I have," Harry gestured to the clothes he was wearing.

"In that case, please arrange some clothes and accessories for Mr Logan and have them sent to his room. Some of Julius' things might fit in the short term."

And to Harry, he said, "follow me."

Harry offered a nod of courtesy to Mrs Bloodworth, and then followed her husband into a modern-looking drawing room that belied the outward appearance of the house.

"Sit," commanded Mr Bloodworth, gesturing to a comfortable armchair. He poured himself a drink from a decanter. There was no offer of whatever he was drinking to the lowly staff, even during the interview process.

He sat down opposite the interviewee. "Before we get into anything else, you need to know that this room is safe from eavesdropping and regularly scanned," he said. "So, any business-talk in this house is only done here, nowhere else, especially outside," he sternly emphasised. "One doesn't know who might be listening. We can talk openly here."

"You come highly recommended," he started.

Harry smiled, but said nothing, awaiting his next approach.

"Impressed how you dispensed with Moses, then managed the minders, and the other riff-raff; efficient and calculated," he said.

"From your medical files and from what the doctors said about your recent beating, oops, sorry fall, we're surprised you were even able to stand, let alone deal with that lot. It was a bold move!"

"And there was that earlier incident with Mr Bradley and his nephews; nasty little tykes those two. Quickly closed them down while encumbered, well-controlled, and efficiently dispatched. Very professional. Now, where did you get that level of training? Definitely not normal marines."

He opened what looked to be an MOD file, and read out loud, "Harry Logan, confidential."

He then proceeded to read extracts about his pre-injury front-line service. "No nickname, just 'Logan', unusual for your lot. Commanding officer and peer comments; confident, extremely capable, glad he's on our side, and top in classes, now what classes would they be?"

Here's a really interesting one, 'high personal morals'."

Harry said nothing since this was rhetoric to make a point.

"Some of your officers questioned your ability to follow the chain of command. Then, additions to those comments from more senior staff that lives were saved as a result; on more than one occasion. Also says you're highly intelligent, you love your planning and preparations. Now here's some more, 'reads situations, reacts fast'. I like all that. Lots of redactions; even more interesting."

"You're an unusual beast, Mr Logan, a planner who can adjust on the fly, who's also a killer with scruples."

"We're in a rough, often nasty industry that deals with the dregs of humanity. Everyone who works for me needs to be willing and capable of doing whatever needs to be done. Are your morals going to get in the way of your job?"

Harry now needed to respond. "I don't hurt innocents, and I look after my team. I don't think there are too many innocents in your line of work, so not a problem."

"Yep, good point," concurred Andrew Bloodworth.

"You've met George and Ray. They are two muscle-bound heavies who are highly capable of reacting, deterring, and fixing. You'll team up with them since your skills complement theirs. Molly deals in all matters security, so you lot and the other in-house lot, report to her. We don't have middle management, that's too dangerous. With the exception of the two dogs out there, I know everyone can be bought."

"We also use 'freelancers,' as I call them, for any real dirty work that needs to be kept away from my home, business, and permanent staff. As the pillars of our community, we can't afford to hire people with excessively bad records."

As Bloodworth spoke, Harry realised his new boss was a cautious and sharp operator; not forgetting a proficient businessman. Harry nodded but stayed quiet. He was keen that his potential employer got to the point.

Andrew continued. "My last driver is no longer with us, you're his replacement. I heard the story about how you managed Dexter, and he's a nasty shit. I expect you owe Dexter for not killing you on the spot, and he's told you that you're his man in my organisation?"

Harry nodded in acknowledgement but felt he needed to defend his position. "I'm loyal to my paymaster. What I owe Mr Dexter takes second place to my fiscal loyalties."

Andrew smiled, guardedly accepting Harry's response.

He also had to ask his new boss, "what happened to your driver?"

"All you need to know is that he's dead. I'm also aware that you prefer a low visible presence, especially since ATS has an interest in you." He showed the same document that Dexter had shared.

Harry hopefully showed no sign of the anger and shock to find yet another person knew about his link to ATS. Bloodworth was well connected, and Harry wondered if he and Dexter shared the same source; which would make sense. Whatever the case, it was uncomfortable knowing criminals like these were getting this information. And, from where was it coming?

"You're not here because Dexter vouched for you; which he did, by the way. I don't trust him as far as I can throw him, so his support for you means fuck all. One reason you're here is that you're capable. As well your army and police records suggest, the word on the street is you're highly dangerous."

"Now, if you prove less than useful to us, you're out. If you're not who you say you are, you're dead. And Dexter gets the same. Got it?"

"Got it, loud and clear."

"Now, the second reason you're interesting, is your post-operational time in the army. Because of your injuries, you were office-bound. Assume they no longer affect your abilities?"

"Yes, 100% sorted years ago, although the army had a different interpretation at that time. Once tarred with a desk job, and if you're good at it, it's impossible to get back into frontline duties." Harry replied.

"So, you spent quite some time in their logistics, before being discharged. That means you know distribution and I like that."

"Welcome to the team, albeit on probation."

Harry was now in.

19. MERELY A DISTRIBUTION BUSINESS

Andrew Bloodworth paused to collect his thoughts. "I'm going to tell you enough about my business, so you understand your role here and why."

Harry half-smiled and nodded in anticipation. This was going to be useful; he hoped.

Bloodworth started. "I'm nothing more than a product distributor. While our business is distribution, we naturally import and even export; also some localised manufacturing."

"The product I distribute could be anything. Forget what bollocks people tell you about drug distribution. It's no different to any other wholesale distributor that shifts," he paused, then added, "for example, pharmaceutical products. Even the operation of your army logistics lot is similar."

"We distribute products the authorities deem as illegal. As an illegal operation, we have to deal with criminals. Being criminals, they tend to be the scum of the earth, customers, as well as suppliers. But just because they're scum, it doesn't mean they are stupid. What they are is ruthless, and to survive, so must I be."

"However, we have the added overheads of high security and invisibility from the authorities and competitors. Everyone in the drugs food chain can and will fight for survival, even kill."

"No one ever crosses me and lives, remember that!" he emphasised.

"Some perceive my business as being dirty. Others perceive the military's products and services as being even dirtier. "And depending on the dynamics of the country where you live will impact your perception."

"So, it's all about perception. During the US prohibition in the early 1900s, the manufacture and distribution of alcohol suddenly became illegal. Respectable businessmen became criminals. Then there's a new government

130

mandate, and suddenly it's again legal. After the end of prohibition, the now legitimate businesses had to pay taxes for doing the same thing. Think of all the money the US government lost during those years and how much ours is losing today?"

Andrew Bloodworth said all this without any hint of justification. It was all matter-of-fact. This was the business he was in, and it was as straightforward as that.

"Let's get back to distribution itself now. All distributors, whether selling illegal or legal products, have to compete by being better on price, product availability, delivery, and quality customer service. Customers can buy elsewhere. They are only as loyal as it's in their business interest."

Then he became more upbeat, "business is booming, with new products coming online all the time, creating new markets and opportunities. To survive, we must innovate, think forward, and plan. This is where I've got a lot of respect for the military. I'm hoping my lot can benefit from a fresh perspective that perhaps you might bring."

"You don't need to know anything about the products to do your job. Knowing the dynamics of distribution is the bonus that got you this trial. But remember, you're not here as an advisor. Any opinions you might have get kept within these walls and only given when asked. Got that!" he emphasised the last two words.

"I don't want to lose another useful man because he can't keep his mouth shut in the wrong places."

Harry nodded again and inwardly relaxed. The finger of accusation for the killing of Andrew's man, paving the way for him to fill this job, was being pointed to external players that Julius upset, or who wanted him out of the way. Harry's plan and its brutal execution had worked.

"Shouldn't I know what happened to him, especially if this impacts security and my role?" It would be normal for anyone else in his position to raise the question again; so he did.

"All in good time, then only possibly," he responded. "You're here on a trial basis, and as I said earlier, I don't trust you. Until I do, if ever, you'll work with the team on a limited need-to-know basis."

"No more questions about your predecessor. Let's get back on track."

Harry had sufficiently made the point, so merely offered a shake of his head and a lip-twitch of acceptance.

Andrew Bloodworth continued. "We buy in bulk, split, then sell in smaller quantities to 10s of customers, such as your Mr Aloysius Dexter. And, we take an ever-so-tiny profit in the process," he smiled at his joke'ette.

"Dexter, and his like, then split and often cut the product further, into commodity packages to sell on the street. He has 10s or 100s of customers of his own. Those, in turn, sell to 10s or 100s of theirs, and so forth."

"So, the 10s of customers I sell to, via the likes of Dexter and his customer base, gives us a market reach of millions."

"We and distributors like ourselves have to add value to the likes of Dexter. Our suppliers will only sell in 100s of kilos, even tons. That's no use to the likes of Dexter, who can't pay for those quantities, store, manage, or shift them. Our Key value to them is our product stocking and supplying in manageable quantities, as and when they need them. Also, we are their only link to growers and manufacturers."

"We don't confuse our roles, or cross over into others' areas of expertise. Confusion of roles and responsibilities creates conflict. People get hurt and die, which happened so often in the past."

"Oh, and while I'm on the subject of people getting hurt, if you're on board, those jokers you smacked outside that nightclub will 'forget' the incident." He smiled as he emphasised 'forget'. "Their uncle, the nightclub owner, will be told you're out of bounds. And that will be the end of the matter. So, you'll also owe me."

That was the same promise that Dexter made earlier. Harry wondered which of these two would deliver on it.

Andrew then talked about Harry's pay. It was an interview after all. He verified that Harry had an offshore account. The alternative would have been in cash. Unfortunately, such a large amount of cash would be an issue for Harry to get through and launder. As far as the UK taxman was concerned, Harry was on the official books as a lowly paid driver.

Harry again nodded and enthusiastically grinned at the mention of the money he was earning. In this game, money brings loyalty; as long as no one else is paying higher. "I'm in."

"Good," Andrew said, and then with a smirk, "not that you had much choice."

Andrew then explained the product strategy of their business, but without referring to any of his products by name. Harry was still not yet to be trusted. "We don't sell all kinds of illicit drugs. We distribute products within our specialist knowledge, expertise, and infrastructure. Each product we distribute has different dynamics in terms of; weight per £, shelf-life, packaging, transportability, etc."

"We sell these products into specific markets and territories. We don't stray elsewhere, and neither do our competitors. Some distributors sell into the same market and territories as us, but only by agreement. Others stay clear."

"Any deviation by us, or our competitors, would upset that understanding with lethal consequences. It had been a painful process to achieve an understanding with our competitors to bring some semblance of stability. So, we all meet, discuss price ringing, quality control, bringing on new products, and overcoming potential conflict."

"We are in potential conflict with other distributors, and we manage that via agreements. It's a complex business. As I said, same as any other distribution business."

"Also, Dexter and his ilk are always trying to pit distributors against each other, with the promise of more business. This had been bad for us in the past. So, as well as avoiding bloodshed, we distributors work together to keep prices and profits as high as the market allows, and that's good for us distributors."

"Customers like Aloysius have tried to move into the wholesale drug distribution business. They're deterred, not only by me but all of us. We all like stability. And yes, we rig the market. We make loads of money, and so what! There are no Competition Authorities for an illegal business, and we all like that."

Bloodworth finished this session with, "this is as much as you need to know, at the moment. I have work to do, and you need to get yourself sorted. You start your probation tomorrow."

At that, he called George, the grumpy passenger, to show Harry to his room.

20. THE TARGET

Next morning, over breakfast, Harry learned that the driver who brought him the day before was called Ray. George, he remembered, was the less than-helpful passenger. They were two of the three live-in security team who went out with the Bloodworths. The addition of Harry brought that number back to three.

Another three permanent security personnel were mostly house-based; in addition to the two Ridge-Backs. All six resident security personnel occupied separate rooms at the opposite end of the house to the Bloodworths. Excluding the rooms that the Bloodworths used exclusively (unless by pre-approval, or emergency), he and the team were free to roam the house and gardens at will, as one would expect.

Molly planned the downtime of each team member to coincide with the Bloodworths' movements and needs. The '*grunts*', the nickname used by Harry for the other five members, spent most of their time in the in-house gym and over-indulging in protein supplements.

With that schedule, Harry could then plan time to train, run, and exercise, with the occasional break for relaxation.

The downside was that it was over a week until Harry could get uninterrupted (and un-followed) time to grab a beer in one of the nearby upmarket pubs, by the river. He could have lost any tail, but that would have been crazy, obviously raising suspicions.

Being late was going to unleash the wrath of Dragon-Lady, his controller.

The pub was noisy and busy, which was good. No one could easily overhear and see him talking. And he could see if anyone was overly interested. Using a wired headset, he called in via a burner phone to give his report. He'd be able to hear her perfectly but suspected that she'd struggle to hear him.

'And that would be such a shame,' he sardonically thought; a bit petty, but what the hell.

Her first words were an immediate challenge, "you're late again." No more than he expected.

He tried to explain the delay with, "it's been impossible to get private time to myself…"

Annoyingly, he was cut off after the word 'myself' with an unsympathetic grunt, followed by, "so, you're in then?" It could have been a rhetorical question, but he never knew with her.

Harry knew his controller to be, at best, derisive. Sometimes like now, she was just annoying!'

After a pregnant pause from the shock of her already knowing that he was now gainfully employed by his mark, he could only respond with, "yes."

"Details," came the instruction from over the telephone. "And what's all the noise going on around you? Are you at a party?"

"Phoning from a busy pub to avoid being overheard."

Then in response to the first part of the question, "I'm working for the Bs as a driver-cum-security."

And before he could continue, "The Bs?" she interrupted.

"Bs for 'Bloodworths'," he explained.

"Then say their name. Don't confuse your report. Carry on."

Harry took a deep breath to get his thoughts in line. He proceeded with the business and operational setup.

In return, she responded, "that ties up with what we know and about how things work."

Harry carried on by summarising Andrew's monologue. "Their business is import and wholesale distribution of drugs, with some small manufacturing of local drugs like Bath Salts and Meth. They also adjust other products for the local market. They sell on to their customers in smaller quantities and packaging, who then re-pack in yet smaller quantities for eventually selling on the street."

She added, "we've also been following the money, and from what we can see, wherever possible, their money is filtered overseas and transacted overseas. For cash, they have other legit businesses through which they filter it. They buy derelict properties and use the cash to upgrade. They also have interests in restaurants, shops, bookies, etc. The tax man needs to be satisfied, in particular, the VAT man. So they pay their dues like any honest businessman."

"If you know all this already, why have you bent my ear about being late?"

"We don't explain our actions to you, but your job is to explain your actions to us."

This woman had a way of winding him up. He fought the anger that always welled up during these conversations, then forced out a strained, "Ah hmmm."

"Good, I'm glad that's clear," retorted control. Then in a somewhat conciliatory tone, "and having your on-the-ground confirmation of what we know is basic multi-source validation."

Then came the instruction, "now you're in position, the name you have been awaiting is confirmed. It's Jeremy de Silva. He's half Indian, half Brit. His father was a beach boy in Goa who knocked up his mother while she was on a girls' trip there in the 80s. He loves his Indian food, hates his roots, and particularly his dad. His dad died in a rather gruesome and unexplained manner some years ago."

After letting that sink in, Harry asked, "was he responsible for his father's death?"

"We suspect that was the case, but nothing that could be traced back to him, via any of our sources," she added.

"Oh, and one last thing that I don't know is useful or not," said Harry. "They seem to have agreements with other distributors and territories that avoid conflict and keep up prices."

"Now that is important and useful confirmation," was the appreciative reply.

"And that leads us to the next topic of our discussion. Your mention of distribution agreements confirms the continued existence of an illicit drug distribution group. We understand they meet quarterly, face-face, and their next meeting is a little over one week away. Your presence there is expected, no excuses."

"We understand that De Silva is involved with the group in a senior way, possibly chairman. This meeting will give you a good opportunity to meet him. The De Silva task must be completed within one month. So you have plenty of time to prepare, and we do know how you like to plan."

"Any questions before we close?" she asked matter-of-factly, as termination of the call.

"Yes!" responded Harry, a little too angrily. Then knowing that to deal with Dragon-Lady, he had to keep his cool, he paused and collected himself.

He then calmly said, "Dexter and the Bloodworths, both separately, have shown me my official files. How on earth did these low-lives get access to MOD and police systems? Was it your lot that passed the information? They both also know about ATS' interest in me regarding Afghanistan. They've got an internal ATS email asking about my whereabouts. Again, was that also your lot?"

"So many questions," she said curtly.

"You surprise me, I thought you'd have more brains than to think we'd be sharing the very same material we're holding over your head. Your official file is open to people with the right seniority and authority. We are not the mind police and cannot control greed."

"Rest assured, there is nothing in it that can cause you a problem. We've even added useful information that encouraged them to employ you, should this become available to them."

"So you expected this would happen?"

"It was almost certain. We'd have been surprised if it didn't."

"And you didn't think to let me know?"

"All the better for your genuine surprise. You weren't employed for your acting skills."

Harry then interjected with, "how safe is my unofficial file?"

"That information about your time in the army's logistics division is dangerous to all of us, right up to the top. It's closed to only a named few. If that was leaked, rest assured, it would be promptly dealt with," she answered assertively.

"And now a gentle reminder for you, management doesn't like to be questioned, and remember, you are not indispensable. Without our support, your friends at Albatross will know where to find you, as will the nightclub owner."

Then, in a more mollifying tone, "are we now finished?"

"Yes," he responded, metaphorically biting his lip in anger and frustration.

"Call in one week maximum next time. Make sure you find a quieter place to talk. I struggled to hear you." The line went dead.

After finishing with Harry, the controller dialled an internal line, "he suspects we shared his official MOD file, the police report, and that email about ATS' interest in him. Did we?"

"Outside your pay grade." The line she was on went dead.

21. OPERATION PLANNING

Harry spent most of his first few days around the house and the grounds. He used that time to check out Ray and George and suss out their capabilities. Since he'll be spending most of his time in the field with them, he needed to know how far he could rely on them in a tight corner.

They were equally keen on learning the same about him. Ray and George were two different beasts. Both seemed completely loyal to the Bloodworths and would be useful but in different circumstances. Ray was ex-paras with a lot of experience, capable and trustworthy. George's background was solely from the ring and cage; extremely capable in a brawl, but not much more.

Harry also spent time with the other staff members to understand how they fitted into the picture, trying to build a rapport with them. In those early days, Molly was often around, explaining to him the rationale for their security setup and the background. She missed nothing, watching, monitoring, and advising on everything security; she knew her stuff.

It was a tight ship, a testament to Molly's direction and, in no small part, to the late Julius Mercier. Harry even learned from her aspects of security that his earlier training hadn't covered. Much of her knowledge wasn't written in any training manual or training course.

It saddened Harry to think he had to kill Julius, a key member of his new team. He had no gripe with him. Over the time he spent there, he'd learned enough about him to build certain respect for the dead man. Sadly on that deciding day, it was either him or Julius.

Yes, Harry did intentionally set up the situation for Julius to act. However, Julius had a choice. He could have walked away, which would not have been in character or his role. Julius could have approached the matter differently since he thought Harry was a private investigator. And then there was the third option, to try and kill Harry. Julius chose the latter; his killer instinct caused his demise.

Harry tried to internally rationalise that he was no longer a cold-blooded killer and was out of that game. It was Julius who tried to kill him, and he only acted in self-defence. However, he wasn't convincing even himself.

From what he could find out, as well as being highly regarded by all, Julius was useful in a scrap. The consensus was that he could only have been surprised from behind and then shot when turning and defending himself.

Harry was so glad he'd invested in research while in recovery, getting to know about him and others. It was a wise decision not to have mixed it with the man, or the story might have taken a different turn.

Several days after that last chat with his controller, he and George were summoned to the Bs in their secure drawing room.

"Tomorrow, both of you will accompany Mr Bloodworth and me to some meetings with our customers and our wider team. George, you've done this before, so this is business as usual for you," said Molly.

"I hope you don't mind my asking, but this is short notice for us to prepare," Harry interrupted as politely as possible.

George stared at him angrily, clearly because Harry interrupted his boss, and he didn't like the newbie interfering.

However, before George could say anything, Molly responded to this perfectly normal question from a new team member.

"While new to you, this is what we do most days of the week. It's how we run our day-to-day business, and about time you saw what we do. I'm tagging along on this one since I want to see you working."

She then reassured Harry. "I've already set up the teams and covered off the security around most of this stuff. Consider this meeting, the briefing you'd have received before one of your regular patrols while you were in the army. To us, this is nothing more, or less. So, today's chat is a run-through of tomorrow's meetings, schedule, and activity. OK?"

Harry nodded with an appreciative smile. It all made sense. From what he'd seen to date, he trusted her judgment.

From this and other discussions with the Bs and others, he knew that the house was off-limits to their drug customers and suppliers. So, these necessary face-to-face business meetings were held in the various premises where the Bs did business, or on neutral ground.

The Bs never carried any product nor handled money. These were negotiation and planning meetings. All the background work was handled by trusted lieutenants, through operational staff.

Tomorrow was going to be Harry's first outside job with the team. It was Ray's day off, which left Harry and George as the Bs in-car support. There were always 'freelance consultants' travelling with them. In this case, two of them were in one car.

During this briefing, there was no explanation of what was happening during the forthcoming business meetings. All Molly gave them was a short list of addresses and meeting timings. They reviewed the routes and discussed security measures. The internet and online mapping tools gave them everything they needed to plan and review locations.

Harry wondered what these global organisations would think about their tools being used for such nefarious purposes. He never did raise the point, but the Bs could have given them a 5* review for supporting their illegal business.

22. BUSINESS AS USUAL

At the crack of dawn next morning, the day's work started. It was a tight schedule of meetings and travel. Harry was building a picture of his new employers as a very industrious pair indeed.

Harry was the driver for the day, with George sitting in the front passenger seat. Only George accompanied the Bs into their meetings. There was no way that Harry was going to be allowed to overhear conversations so early in his role with them.

The Bs had planned seven visits that day. The first three were to premises controlled by the Bs, and Harry assumed it was related to storage or production. The last one of the morning was to what he assumed was a customer. They had time allocated for lunch. The post-lunch meetings were much the same.

At each location where they stopped for business, he stayed relatively close by the car but still looked and walked around, checking out the areas and the people he could see. The freelancers stayed by the building entrance, smoking and chatting without a care in the world. They really should have been more alert and Harry contemplated picking up this potential risk with Mrs B.

At their last official stop, the customer's rough-looking and heavily tattooed minders intently eyed him and the freelancers. Most had bulky objects in their pockets, suggesting knives or other weapons. All postured and posed to each other. Some were overtly smoking pot without any care of being caught.

Harry looked around. All in one place, he saw what he considered to be the dregs of humanity. The phrase, 'they'd slit your throat for a quid' came to mind. He also thought back to today's earlier visits, where some of the people in the Bs' factories and distribution centres didn't look much better.

The Bs exited the premises with a couple of rather dubious-looking characters, who blended in with those outside. The smiles and handshakes all around were a testament to all being satisfied with the results of their discussion.

From the way they talked, the Bs were happy with what they considered successful visits and lucrative meetings around this area of the city.

Next on the tight schedule was lunch. And another phrase came into his mind as he thought about how long it had been since breakfast.

'*My stomach was thinking my throat was slit'*.

****

Lunch was scheduled in an Afghan restaurant run by, "my close friend Sharif," said Andrew.

It was positioned in an upmarket part of the city, on a narrow road off the main thoroughfare, with many other expensive boutique shops and restaurants nearby. It was a small, yet smart restaurant, long and narrow, with a couple of small tables outside, for those wanting to drink and dine al Fresco.

Parking was easy. The owners had blocked the front of the restaurant in advance of them coming.

Once in the restaurant, Harry could see that it was expensively furnished, with traditional-looking tables and comfortable chairs. This was no greasy-spoon cafe.

It was just before noon and still quite early for lunch; only a few people were inside. A couple of Afghan men sat at one table situated towards the front. They were finishing off their late-morning coffee as the group arrived, so didn't stay long. A couple with a child sat at the front of the cafe. Otherwise, all was quiet.

The foursome was seated towards the back at a couple of tables on each side of the narrow restaurant. Three of them occupied one table; the other was for Harry. In Andrew's opinion, it was close enough for support in the unlikely event anything happened, but not too close to overhear anything.

Harry wasn't happy about the distance between him and them. Molly saw the sense in Harry's argument and tried to negotiate for Harry to be a little closer.

However, they were both overruled by Andrew. "George is perfectly able to take care of anything in this restaurant. And for the first time today, we are among friends here. Relax, both of you!"

George had his back to the wall facing Harry, who also had his back to the wall on the other side of the restaurant. Harry made sure he could easily get out and support if anything went awry. The Bs were in-between. Molly faced the entrance, and Andrew sat opposite her, facing the rear.

Assuming Harry could trust George, between them they had 360-degree visibility of the restaurant. With multiple entrances, this was as good as they could manage with the resources available.

The freelancers were tasked to monitor the entrance, passers-by, and nearby cars. They enjoyed a sandwich lunch in their car.

Harry was tense. This was an unknown and confined territory. He needed to ensure their safety since these two were his way in to complete his job. He'd been focussing all day and wasn't about to let his guard down now.

The owner, Sharif, came over to greet his guests, in particular Andrew, to whom he delivered a bear hug. He beckoned the waiter over to take their orders. Once the other table's food was ordered, Sharif came over to Harry's table and introduced himself.

When Harry ordered his favourite from his time in Afghanistan, Sharif showed extreme pleasure. "Excellent. A house speciality."

After the orders were taken, Sharif brought over their non-alcoholic drinks. The four of them would not be taking any meetings while their senses were compromised by alcohol.

When the food came, Harry settled a bit, but was still watchful as he picked at his food. The Bs chatted and ate as if they didn't have a care in the world. In their business, being able to take safe time out was probably a rare occurrence; and they took advantage of this opportunity.

George gorged on his food, making it difficult for Harry to catch his attention or maintain eye contact. He didn't like that. He and George needed to be in contact at all times, even when sitting so far apart.

Andrew looked over to an intense-looking Harry. "Stop stressing," he said to Harry impatiently. "I've known Sharif and his brothers for years. This is one place where we're safe. If it wasn't for Molly's insistence, you'd be enjoying a

144

sandwich outside with that lot." He nodded in the direction of the freelancers.

Harry realised he was being over-protective; it reflected in the atmosphere around them. They didn't need a stressed-out newbie placing a damper on proceedings.

He smiled an apology back to Andrew and Molly.

And the food was fantastic! He'd only once ever tasted better. The Kabuli Palaw with yogurt and naan he'd had today, brought back memories of the last meal he'd shared with Ratty, at Rafi's house.

After the group had finished their meal, Sharif came over to check on the Bs.

"How was the meal, did you enjoy? Best food in town, eh?" After some smiles, acknowledgements, and more pats on the back, two other well-muscled men sauntered out of the kitchen, dressed in whites.

Harry was about to intervene when Molly gave him a nod of 'no', so he relaxed. These were the chefs, both were Sharif's brothers. Andrew and Molly obviously knew them and eagerly returned their happy-go-lucky banter, back-patting, and shaking of hands. After chatting for some minutes, and once the team was satisfied the group had enjoyed their food, the happy chefs went back into the kitchen.

During the meal, Harry's suspicion was confirmed.

Sharif only allowed people he knew into the restaurant. He turned a couple of men away. Another couple arrived, again with pats and hugs all around. If Harry wasn't mistaken, Sharif had surreptitiously patted down the man, but not the woman as would be expected. He sat them a little further in the restaurant, but again not close to the Bs.

A middle-aged-looking man arrived for a coffee. Sharif gave him one of the outside tables; he was taking no chances. Other people arrived, expecting lunch, and were also turned away. Sharif took great care of the Bs' privacy and security. Harry, at last, realised why they liked this place.

Sharif lost a lot of business today. Harry suspected that Sharif was more than a restaurateur; probably a drug customer of the Bs as well.

The innocuous couple and the child sitting by the door were also considered safe. What Harry took to be the husband, was doing what he hated. He cut up all the food, then ate one-handedly, while occasionally gesticulating with the other.

As he looked at the family at the front, Harry wondered why people go out together when visibly unhappy. And it showed. The man was trying to be jovial enough and was doing his best to interact with the little girl who ignored him. Whatever had transpired between them, the girl was definitely on the mother's side. The woman's face was angry; she was quietly mumbling all the time and clearly not amused with her husband.

'Happy families eh!' thought Harry.

He missed his ex-fiancée, and what could have possibly been with her. That was in the past. His life had taken a new direction. His current line of work was not a place for a family man.

Harry declined the sweet course, knowing that a full stomach can divert blood from the brain and other parts of the body. He wanted to stay alert for the next round of meetings after lunch and was content to sip his iced water and try to relax.

All was quiet and well-controlled by Sharif, probably one reason why this was a preferred eating hole, and not forgetting the great food. He looked over to Andrew and Molly and smiled in acquiescence that they were right about this place; he was wrong to be over-cautious.

If there was one thing that Harry had learned from today's meetings and over lunch, the Bs knew their business and security. However, he was new, and if nothing else, he could learn as he watched.

There was one argument, however, and that was over the bill. Andrew insisted on paying, while Sharif refused. It was eventually settled amicably; no payment was taken.

Danger!

As they were getting up to leave, Harry picked up on subtle signs only a trained eye could notice!

Molly picked up on both his expression and barely perceptible sign language. He prayed she'd also caught the risk. There was a faint twitch in her lips that confirmed she understood.

'Thank god. Yep, she is good!' he thought.

With further smiles and shaking of hands, the four took their leave. George enthusiastically led the exit, ensuring the way was clear. Molly embarrassingly knocked her bag off the table, tipping the contents onto the floor. Andrew sighed and waited for her, motioning for Harry to follow behind George instead of taking up the rear. This change hadn't been agreed upon, but no one noticed or cared. Harry did as requested.

It was all quite relaxed as Sharif and his brothers followed behind Andrew and Molly down the length of the restaurant. Harry smiled and commented to George about the fantastic food as they walked towards the door.

Unfortunately, Harry had a sneezing fit. He stopped and let out a sneeze. In preparation for another, he searched for a handkerchief.

This action covered his right hand making a violent swing to the right, his stubby in hand. The leather-encased cosh noiselessly smashed into the back of the man sitting with the woman and child. Harry took hold of the now unconscious man, gently lowering him forward onto the table. It was as if he'd just fallen asleep.

The man sitting at the outside table casually walked away.

The other customers didn't seem to notice, or if they did, pretended not to.

Harry immediately turned around and with Molly directed Andrew out of the restaurant, and towards the car.

Andrew started to recover his senses at what had happened. He was livid with anger at the incident. He shouted at Harry, "you fucking idiot, pulling that stunt in full view of my friends!" He waved in the direction of a shocked Sharif standing in the doorway.

Sharif asked what happened but Harry ignored him. With Molly's help, they gently but firmly bundled Andrew into their car. Once in, they quickly drove off, leaving a bemused Sharif and team watching.

Andrew continued hurling abuse at Harry as they drove away. "What was that stunt all about, you fuckin' idiot! Why'd you hit that guy? Sharif and his family are my friends and customers. And, and, at their place of business!" He stuttered as he tried to find the right expletives to vent his anger.

Andrew recovered enough to deliver a tirade of abuse, beginning with, "Fs, Cs, and Bs," as well as a few less common ones.

"Everyone was vetted. There was no risk! What the fuck!" screamed Andrew. He was astounded and shocked. He didn't know what else to say.

After a few moments of silently seething in the back of the car, Andrew re-started. "Sharif and his family don't need that visibility. And you hit that man in front of this wife and his brat. Not that I care about them, but they were witnesses! We don't need this fucking heat! They don't need this fucking heat!"

"If it's OK with you, I'm taking us all back to the house," said Harry to the Bs. "Can we cancel the afternoon meetings?"

And that suggestion brought more expletives from Andrew, who then said to Molly and George, "what do you think of this fucking nutter?"

Molly was on the phone ignoring him. She held up her hand, then patted his thigh to try and calm him down.

George, who didn't see anything, was quick to support Andrew in his accusations.

"Boss, he's a fucking tosser. You should have asked me to properly check him out. All you had was Dexter's recommendation, and he's a lying, cheating shit. Want me to fuck him over when we get back?" He gave Harry what he thought was a sinister look.

Then to Harry, George continued, "you've screwed up the boss' rep and you've fucked the rest of the plans for today. That means fucked deals and lost money. You need to go back to begging on the street where you can't do any fuckin' harm."

George was about to continue his tirade, when Andrew said to him, "shut your fucking mouth you half-brain, and don't swear in front of my wife!"

Molly eventually finished the call and softly said to Andrew, "I've just spoken with Sharif. He's dealt with the matter. He's really impressed with our new boy here," referring to Harry.

Andrew gawped. A look of bewilderment descended on him. "What are you twatting about!"

"He saved our arses," she responded. "I felt something wasn't right with the family, but couldn't put a finger on it. Harry caught the reason why before me. He then dealt with the matter, quietly and efficiently."

"Thank you, Harry, great job. I don't think even Julius would've picked up on this one, and I didn't until you caught my eye." Molly was now looking at Andrew to see if there was a chance he'd apologise; which he didn't.

"Harry, in answer to your earlier question, yes, please take us home. We'll reschedule the afternoon's meetings."

"And by the way, that was not the husband with the woman and child," she addressed all. "The real husband's a druggie and owes money. He's been held to make sure the woman and child behaved. That guy was executing a hit on us.

Sharif is dealing with the aftermath, and we're all good. He's so apologetic about what happened. He thought he'd everything covered."

She then said to Harry with a smile, as he watched her in the rear-view mirror, "Sharif rates you, and he's not easily impressed."

She then followed up with, "Harry, for George's and Andrew's benefit, could you please explain?"

As he drove back to the house, Harry explained what he saw. "Initially all was good. You're right, Sharif was doing a great job controlling the customers. However, towards the end of our meal, it was pretty clear something was up. The man with the family had his back to us. However, from his body language, I could see that he was aware of what was happening behind him, reacting to our every move."

"The woman was mumbling on and on. It became obvious she wasn't moaning to he husband but was giving him a running commentary on us. The husband was eating one-handed with his fork. Then as we were leaving, he decided to eat with his fork and the rather vicious steak knife that Sharif gives customers."

"There was another man who came not long after they arrived. He sat outside, nursing a coffee for a long time. He had a thick folded newspaper, pretending to read it. The man outside stood up as George was exiting the door."

To Molly, "your idea of dropping your bag let me get in front to deal with the risk. If I was wrong, I was happy to take a bollocking."

"I'm sorry, but I couldn't make a fuss earlier, or it could have warned them off. Even worse, they could have had a contingency plan. My sole objective was to get you both out of there and into the car. And also, I wasn't certain. It was only when we got up to go, that things fell into place."

Then Harry finished with a smile, and looking in the rear-view mirror at the Bs said, "and anyway, I simply gave the blighter a gentle love-tap in case I was wrong."

The Bs sat back and said nothing.

George stared ahead, fuming, desperately trying to avoid making eye contact with Harry. George realised he'd made a fool of himself from his outburst and threats. However, in his defence, he rationalised to himself, he'd have seen the issue coming if he'd sat in that newcomer's place.

****

Dexter phoned a number. When the recipient answered, he launched into, "that was fucking amateur time! He clocked your guys and dealt with the issue stone-dead. Sharif and his brothers had no chance to deal with Logan. All he could do was clear up your fuckin' mess. And, that's cost me in gear and rep with them!"

The man on the other phone then shouted back, "Logan owes you! If you'd have told him to back off during the hit as I told you, we'd not be in this mess!"

Dexter, now even more livid at the accusation, shouted back, "the plan was agreed, and we didn't know if Logan would play along."

Taking a breath, Dexter then shouted, "don't come to me again with your fuckin' half-baked, shit ideas for making me rich. If I see you again, you're dead and I don't care what fuckin' connections you have, you're dead, you're fuckin' dead!"

By the time he'd finished, he was screaming into the phone. He then hung up.

The man on the other line spoke growled to the dead phone, "not if you're fucked first."

And to himself, '*well Mr Logan, there's more to you than meets the eye.*'

He removed the SIM, crushed the phone underfoot, and threw the pieces away.

****

Later that day, Harry collared Molly. He needed a private chat.

"Mrs Bloodworth, I don't think I can say this to Mr Bloodworth, but for that hit to have been successful, Sharif and his brothers must have been in on it. They were there to take me out as I brought up the rear."

"I know. Let me deal with Andrew. Then I'll sort out our Mr Sharif, in due course."

23. BRIEFING

George had been avoiding Harry after his outburst in the car. After thinking about what happened and talking with Ray, he realised he'd gone overboard with his criticism. Harry most likely saved his life. Unusually for George, he was embarrassed and didn't know how to reach out to Harry.

No nudging from Ray was going to get him to talk to Harry, let alone apologise.

Harry enjoyed letting George squirm for the rest of the day. The following morning, over breakfast, Harry decided it was time to let him off the hook.

"By the way, thanks for covering our exit and keeping our banter going. Otherwise things would have gone a different way."

The world lifted off George's shoulders. Chewing on a large mouthful of bacon sandwich, he mumbled something incoherent while trying to smile. He gave Harry the thumbs-up sign.

Ray smiled and nodded in appreciation at Harry. All was good.

****

The Bs summoned Harry into the study after breakfast. He was offered a seat in a comfortable chair, a most unusual occurrence. Andrew and Molly were seated on the settee opposite.

"First, the word on the street is that someone wanted us out of the way," said Andrew formally.

Harry didn't say out loud the first and obvious thing that came into his mind, *'yeh, anyone with half a brain would realised that.'* So, he kept quiet, waiting for what was to come.

He continued. "The key thing is this. We now believe Julius' death was a hit, to get him out of the way and expose us. George and Ray wouldn't have been enough to prevent the attempt on us."

It was the closest thing Harry would ever get as an apology from Andrew.

Molly also commented. "With you being new and considered inexperienced and untested in the trade, whoever was responsible assumed we'd be at our most vulnerable. Your decisive action spun that perception on its head."

Andrew leaned forward, "I now know you can take care of yourself; and us. But watch yourself when you go out for your run or your pint."

Harry smiled in understanding. "Thanks, but don't worry, I always do."

Their serious warning to look after himself, was both unexpected and appreciated. It was, in truth, less a show of their caring side but more a professional statement of fact and their own security.

He knew the Bs had been keeping an eye on him during his solo excursions outside the house, which made perfect sense. He'd clocked the 'amateur freelancers' who were intently not watching him. They were a dead giveaway to someone with his experience and training.

"Whoever took out Julius might well be after you now, since you screwed up their plans. So, you'll have an even bigger incentive to do your job." Andrew said the last words with a forced smile. In a way, he was trying to say thank you, but not very successfully. Harry knew the words were well-meant.

"And the bloke I coshed?"

"His name was Fahim Jackson, a mixed-race freelancer from out of town," replied Andrew. "He was questioned by Sharif but knew nothing; or at least wasn't saying anything. He was found burned in a car. So, there is insufficient forensics to concern ourselves about."

"The kidnapped druggie guy, who that freelancer tried to impersonate, sadly died of an overdose," sneered Molly. "And his wife's disappeared. So, she's no longer around to talk about us, or anything else, for that matter."

The poor woman was an innocent victim. Harry didn't bother asking what happened to her, since that would have been a futile question. In any case, Andrew did warn him right at the beginning that for the Bs to survive in this business, they had to be ruthless; and they were that, Molly in particular.

"Her fucking husband didn't deserve her help. And she deserved all she got from staying with such a useless twat."

That was the first time Harry had heard her swear.

"And, in case you're worried about the kid, she's with family. She's too young to know what happened." The way she talked about the child could have had a possible smidgen of maternal instinct, but Harry doubted it.

"Also dead kids attract heat," she added. And that was the more likely reason the child survived.

"From what you said, he wasn't alone, and the other guy's vanished. We're sure he'd local help, but there's nothing on the street." Molly gave no hint of their earlier conversation about Sharif.

"One way or another, he'll turn up."

Harry appreciated the heads-up on what happened after the incident and their appreciation of his actions being justified.

"So, you're up to speed with what you need to know regarding that incident."

"Now that's over, we can now cover the real reason we asked you here now. There's a meeting in five days with my distribution buddies," said Andrew with overt sarcasm about the word 'buddies'. "You and Ray will be with me there."

"We meet in different locations once a quarter, and, we're hosting and organising the next one in this city. These are big events, and people will be arriving from around the country."

"It's important that you're clear on what this is all about. As I mentioned earlier, one way or another, we compete with everyone coming to this meeting. And there's a lot of bad blood. We also collaborate on specific deals. It's a complex arrangement. We call our group the 'Arbitration'. It was set up to keep distributors' blood off the streets. So we talk, negotiate, and agree who's selling what, to whom, and where."

Molly interjected. "We avoid conflict by ensuring clarity of each of our businesses. Previously, they were all man-bitching, spreading rumours, then fighting about who's doing what to each other. It was like being in a school playground with grown men tittle-tattling about each other."

Andrew looked over at her, sighed with resignation at her outburst, and continued.

"We use the meeting to define and reinforce agreements and boundaries. As a result, we've minimised the rivalry, bloodshed, and the unnecessary competition we've had for as long as I can remember."

"At this meeting, we all decide who distributes what product, to whom, and in what territory. In our worst times, the whole industry was getting too visible to the authorities. We needed to keep our side of the business as clean as possible. Not all drug distributors in the country are a part of this Arbitration. But, because we have muscle and coverage, we pretty much set the business agenda across the country."

"Saying all that, we have no control over our customers and what shit they cut into our products. So the nosey-parkers and press target their activities. The politicians and lobbyists spout about them, and as a result, they get the attention of the police. So, nowadays, we're less visible, and that's perfect for us," said Andrew smugly. "Dealing at our level is too complex for all their tiny piggy brains."

Molly took over the explanation. "Now for the security aspect. Each member can be accompanied by two of their own. Neither of us trusts you. However, you're sharp and observant, and that's important for me. What's also in your favour is that you know how distribution works. That's what's important for Andrew, and why you and Ray will accompany Andrew during the meeting."

"I don't attend the meeting itself because I don't have a penis!" she said, with visible indignation. "And that's where all that lot, keep their brains!"

She knowingly looked at Andrew, who smiled back but wasn't taking the bait.

"There'll be a lot of tension at this meeting. One of the people attending organised that attempted hit on us and most likely took out Julius as a precursor. Word's gotten out, and they all know it was one of them. They're most likely wondering who we're gunning for. People will be more nervous than usual, especially as it's taking place in our manor. I suspect they're also possibly worrying that one of them could be next."

"You need to listen, watch, and learn."

Then disdainfully, she followed up with, "we have a chairman that was voted in because he's got the biggest business and most influence. Also, the

Arbitration was his idea, so it made sense for him to lead, at that time. His name is Jeremy De Silva."

"I've already been planning the location logistics and security arrangements with him and his team. Since I know more than these self-important over-testosteroned thugs, they listen. I've slapped down many of their stupid ideas already, and they don't like it from a feeble wench like me, but they're learning."

Harry could see she didn't suffer fools gladly. He fleetingly almost felt sorry for De Silva's people having to deal with her.

"So, I'll be around on the day, but only in the background," she summed up.

Andrew carried on. "De Silva's a nasty, conniving piece of work. De Silva's the most likely person responsible for ordering Julius' hit and the attempt on us. We don't trust or like him, and vice versa, but business is business."

"His number two, Jock, is as bad. He's a seriously capable thug. Watch him. If anyone could have organised the kill on Julius, it was Jock."

Molly waited impatiently for her husband to finish the interruption. "Your job is plain and simple; watch Andrew's back and keep your nose clean. You don't talk to anyone but Andrew and Ray. No weapons are allowed, and no communications. There are no distractions since the meeting can be a highly tense affair, with lots of arguments."

"What's agreed at the meeting is sacrosanct and will be supported by all. De Silva gives the impression of playing fair, but those of us who'd prefer a new chairman are often out-voted. So, with all those male ego-fuelled emotions in one place, things can get fraught. But they cannot be allowed to get out of hand!" she stressed.

Andrew took over again. "And, with your experience in Distribution and Logistics, it would be interesting to get your feedback on the business. Not there, but when we get back. Remember, while there, no talking to anyone but Ray and I!" Andrew again emphasised the last point.

"Any questions on this, talk with Molly."

The conversation was over, and Harry knew he was dismissed.

24. ARBITRATION

The meeting was taking place in the five-star St Anthony's Court Hotel, kicking off at 7 am sharp. Previously, Molly told Harry these meetings tended to go on and on. There was a lot of procrastination and point-scoring from those in conflict with each other. So, an early start was important to get all the ground covered.

Over the next few days leading up to the Arbitration, Molly took every opportunity to highlight that any room full of "testosterone-driven" discussions would be full of time-wasting "bovine faeces" (her preferred phrase instead of bullshit).

She made no effort to hide her disdain for the male-only attendees. "These cavemen think they're better than me, and I get so damned infuriated. Most are nothing more than over-blown street thugs."

Harry always smiled but said nothing.

The hotel was located on the city outskirts, near the airport and just off the motorway. So, access was easy for anyone coming on the day, although most members arrived the previous day.

The Bs had been out with a couple of like-minded groups in preparation for the following day's proceedings. Ray and George accompanied them, being trusted and known by the people and minders they met; as trusted as could be expected in this industry.

The Bs, Ray, and Harry arrived early. Molly and De Silva's no.2 (Jock) worked with specialist freelancers to ensure the room was clean and secure. The authorities would have loved to know what would be discussed here, assuming they knew what was happening, which they certainly did. Harry's earlier discussion with his controller confirmed that.

In one of the Bs internal planning sessions leading up to the meeting, Molly imparted a story that she was proud of. "Each meeting we had, was observed by the authorities. They were interfering too much, undercover police as waiters and the like. Some groups were worried about being seen together; fully understandable. So, the filth needed a lesson to back off."

"Someone tipped off the local police, Special Branch, and the press about an Arbitration meeting last year. The bizzies were all scrambling over each other to get a piece of the action. They arranged a warrant and heavy-handedly raided the place, all armed and with dogs. They expected drugs, weapons, and evidence of criminal activity."

"The press were there en masse. Unusually, their presence didn't upset our law enforcement teams in any way. A highly publicised successful raid would have given the authorities tremendous kudos."

"The fuzz were eager to show off the results of their inter-departmental and inter-regional collaboration and intelligence gathering; and other bollocks. And let's not forget, a fruitful drugs raid of known drug gangs would have gone a long way in boosting the careers of some senior police plods."

"They found nothing! There were no drugs or weapons since all the attendees had to be clean for these meetings anyway. There was nothing at all incriminating."

"What that lot did find was a meeting, discussions, and supporting documents about best practices around industrial and commercial property renovation; most of our members dabbled in property anyway."

"The press had a field day. They accused the police of brutality, invasion of privacy and loads more. We even filed lawsuits. We dropped them later, after negotiations and their open apologies. It was a publicity mess for them. Careers were compromised. Questions were even raised in parliament, challenging the actions of the various authorities involved."

"Those authorities previously snooping around our meetings learned their lesson. Since then, they've backed off. Result!"

"I wonder who was bright enough to have set that up?" she asked in such a way to impart that it was her idea.

****

On the day of the meeting, there was no overt police or security services presence. Not exactly true. The street contained several unmarked cars with half-open windows, sporting large camera lenses.

They didn't see much of the people coming to the meeting since they couldn't see inside blacked-out cars. At the entrance to the venue, the attendees exited their vehicles behind well-placed advertising banners.

Although most participants knew each other, they had to negotiate a biometric scanner, then a radio-wave scanner before finally going through the security screening machine at the entrance. A couple of sniffer dogs walked up and down the waiting queue. No chances were taken that someone would sneak in a weapon, eavesdropping technology, or even a fix.

Once through the entrance, the attendees found themselves in a large ballroom. A pre-prepared buffet was at one end, and washrooms were at the other. There was no reason to leave the ballroom before the day's event concluded. No hotel employees were in attendance.

Of course, the organisers couldn't stop anyone from leaving; businesses had to be run, and people needed to communicate. Some even had to leave for that all-important fix.

For urgent matters, notes were passed into the meeting. When attendees returned from whatever they had to do, they were subject to a repeat of the entry security measures. If nothing else, that was discouragement enough.

The proceedings commenced with a welcome from the chairman, Jeremy De Silva. He reiterated the purpose of the day's activities and reminded all of how they should conduct themselves.

The chairman emphasised the importance of referring to products by name, only during individual grievance negotiations. Open discussions of product specifics with the wider group were deemed unsafe. No matter what security precautions were taken, there was always the risk of the meeting being monitored.

"We've collated all the complaints made by you lot about each other since the last meeting. You've each got a list of meetings in your pack. You must attend them to address your grievances and others against you. Conflict is bad for business."

"We've provided round-tables for your discussions. Use them. I'll adjudicate any impasse. If you still can't reach an agreement, it then gets put to the wider audience within your region."

Neither of these options was the preferred route for anyone to air their dirty washing, so to speak. So these small discussions were invariably successful.

"Good luck everyone."

The group discussions started.

Andrew's first meeting was with a middle-aged Chechen called Vladislav Mayrbekov. Both had accused each other of poaching customers, cutting in dangerous Chems, and creating a price war on the best revenue earners for them in that territory, i.e. 'Oxy', 'Spice', and 'Meth'.

The bad feeling was spilling into deals with other customers, and they were on the verge of a full-blown war.

After a heated discussion, it became clear where the blame lay. It was actually, and coincidentally, Moses, supported by Dexter, who'd started to pit each against the other.

Andrew smiled, to the annoyance of Mayrbekov.

"This wasn't the first time Moses caused trouble between us," to which the other nodded in agreement.

"So, I hope you didn't mind, but we took steps to stop his activities and close his business."

Andrew then looked in Harry's direction, who emotionlessly nodded in agreement.

"It was a clear warning for Dexter as well," added Andrew.

Mayrbekov looked at Harry and laughed, saying, "ah, so it was you, you killed eem."

Harry kept a blank expression as he rocked his head as a, possible, yes.

Andrew joined in the laughing since that had cleared the air. He added, "no, no, my friend, we are simple businessmen. We don't kill people, we merely," he hesitated and pretended to think for a minute, then said, "we terminate their contract with us." He heavily emphasised the word 'terminate'.

"I like that, eet is a good phrase." Mayrbekov laughed again, digging the minder on his left-hand side in the ribs with his elbow.

The discussion relaxed. Both parties were then able to agree on pricing for their main products. They even came to a what-where-who arrangement on some newer products.

This face-to-face meeting ended in handshakes and back-slapping between the two. Harry, Ray, and the other minders stood up, straight-faced.

There were other conflicts that Andrew had to negotiate, some caused by him and his people, others by those sitting opposite. There were even three- and four-way territory-based meetings. The biggest issues of the day, and apparently at every meeting, were caused by pricing and under-cutting. There were also issues around pitching to customers who'd earlier been agreed as being out of bounds for that product.

Everyone wanted to maximise the price they could charge to their common customers. Under-cutting was bad business for all here.

During one of the lulls in the meeting, while people took refreshments, De Silva's number two came over to Harry. Speaking loudly in a jovial Scots accent, "I've not seen you before at these meetings. Everyone calls me Jock."

Then quietly and softly, he leaned in and followed up in an overtly, sinister manner, "you're familiar. I know you from somewhere. Now, where would that be? Perhaps something I've read?"

Harry said nothing, keeping his best poker face in play.

Still leaning in, Jock tried again to needle Harry. "I know you, and I'm going to find out more."

Pulling back, and in a louder, jovial voice he added, "don't see Julius here today. Caught a bad cold?" he smirked.

Harry still said nothing.

Jock tried again to solicit a response. "And you're the newbie apprentice, Harry Logan, I hear."

Harry looked over to Andrew and caught his attention. Andrew saw who Harry was with and started to walk over. Once into earshot, Harry, at last, responded in a loud voice for all to hear, "do those chat-up lines really work for you with the boys?"

The guy's face reddened with embarrassment and anger. Before he could respond, Andrew bellowed for all to hear, "the hired help don't talk unless asked." His outburst, while outwardly aimed at both Harry and Jock, was directed at the Scotsman.

Without further word, his face now blazing with anger, Jock stomped over to talk with De Silva. From the stares in his direction, Harry could see they were talking about him. He wondered what they were saying.

"What was that all about?" asked Andrew.

"That guy says he knows me and was going to find out who I was. He was particularly interested in Julius and made some sarcastic comments about why Julius wasn't here," said Harry.

"I think he wanted to see if we knew what had happened to Julius. What he said sorta plays into what you suspected about De Silva's involvement with Julius' death." Harry used this opportunity to further turn the screw on De Silva and Jock in Andrew's mind.

In an apologetic tone, Harry added, "I didn't want to say anything back until you were in earshot, as you made clear. I couldn't resist the temptation to put him in his place after he was overly inquisitive, and trying to rile me. I'm assuming he's the guy you warned me about? Hope I haven't stepped on any wrong toes and created problems for you?"

For the first time since he'd known him, Andrew laughed. "No problem at all! Listening to you tongue-slapping that twat down was a joy to hear. He and Julius were always in conflict, same as De Silva and I."

Andrew explained more about De Silva's no.2. "The guy's Steven Carmichael. And yes, people call him Jock. It was the nickname given to him by his old SBS buddies. He's no ordinary minder. As I said, he's number two in De Silva's operation. My reference to him being the hired help would have grated on the little shit. He swans around as if he was the boss."

"He needed taken down a peg or two, and I also enjoyed doing that."

"Oh, I expect he already knows everything about you. All that was to put the wind up you. Glad you didn't succumb; too much anyway."

Andrew further explained to Harry that under all of this organised pleasantness is a deep simmering internal friction, not only about street dealings but how the Arbitration works. Many in the room weren't happy with De Silva's approach and high-handedness. The Bs and those others who supported them believed that De Silva and his cronies manipulated the meetings and the business outcomes to their advantage.

On the other hand, De Silva sees Andrew as a disruptive influence on others. During this Arbitration, Andrew had taken every opportunity to imply De Silva's people killed Julius and were behind the attempt on the B's lives.

"I suspect that was their first foray. Now they've sussed you out, and since you work for me and are most capable, you're a threat to them. As I said before, watch your back. Don't forget, it's also in your interests to keep us safe." Andrew gave a rare smile. This was a second humorous display, and on the same day.

"That Scots shit there," said Andrew nodding in Jock's direction, "is also ex-ATS and still has connections there. Influential people are behind that organisation. Don't forget they'd love to have a chat with you, whatever their reasons. Working for me keeps you under their radar and out of their grasp," said Andrew.

Harry wasn't sure.

Toward the end of the meeting, Andrew and De Silva had a private, heated, and highly gesticulated one-to-one in the corner of the room. De Silva came away fuming.

In the car on the way back, Andrew told Harry about their conversation. "I mentioned the attacks to De Silva. He got defensive, obviously guilty. He denied it and said he'd check it out and let me know."

He lightened up. He was looking forward to updating Molly on today's proceedings. His meetings had solved costly conflicts and also identified opportunities for him to sub-distribute other distributors' specialist products.

Once back home, Harry could hear Andrew extolling his meeting prowess and successes on the day. He was trying to wind up Molly. "It amazes me how a group of mere men could have such a successful meeting without any women present?"

Harry heard a thump, immediately followed by a squeal from Andrew. He then heard their laughter.

25. TESTING THE WATERS

Two days after the Arbitration, Harry had another free evening. It was hard to find a place where he could have a private conversation with his controller without being obvious. Calling from a mobile phone in a busy pub a second time was a bad idea, although he was tempted. It would have given him great pleasure to wind up Dragon-Lady.

Harry decided it was best to use the old pub with the payphone again. He sat down with his pint, sipping, reading his book, and watching the comings and goings around him. There was no rush to make his report. He first needed to watch and wait, making sure of the lay of the land before making his call.

To anyone here, using the public phone wouldn't raise any eyebrows. However, if anyone he knew saw him making calls from there, the consequences would, at best, have been unhealthy.

Since the incident at the restaurant and the Arbitration, the tailing of Harry had effectively stopped as far as he could tell. That is unless they were using proper professionals now; which he doubted.

As Harry was coming to the end of his pint, he saw Steven 'Jock' Carmichael watching him through the pub window. Jock walked in with another man, looked over at Harry without any acknowledgement, then sat at a table near the door.

Harry didn't believe in coincidences. His immediate interpretation was trouble afoot, and wondered if Jock was looking for payback. He raised his glass in the direction of the two men and mouthed the words, "still in a huff?"

There were too many people here for anything to kick off, so Harry sat and waited to see what might transpire. He was about to order another pint when De Silva walked in. De Silva ignored Jock and Co and sauntered over towards Harry. He sat down opposite and said, "good evening Mr Logan. What a coincidence. Can I call you Harry?"

Harry said nothing. He studied the man opposite and waited for his next move.

"Can we buy you another pint?" he nodded towards the other two, emphasising he had muscle with him, in case Harry hadn't noticed. If it was an effort at intimidation, it didn't work.

Harry lifted his pint glass as a yes, still deploying his best poker face.

De Silva turned around and motioned to Jock to replenish Harry's beer. The look on Jock's face, being sent to buy a drink for Harry, was not one of amusement. Jock said something to the other man, both smiled. The other man went up to the bar, ordered a pint and a large whisky, and brought them over to their table.

He gave the double to De Silva. As he handed over Harry's pint, he accidentally, on purpose, banged it on the table, splashing some of the beer onto Harry's crotch. It was enough to be an issue but insufficient to create a fuss. As the beer delivery man walked away, it was Jock's turn to lift his glass as he mouthed some words to Harry.

"That was a bit petulant," Harry said to De Silva, referencing the departing man.

"Your friend Jock can be a bit tetchy when someone accuses him of being an Arse-Banger," defended De Silva.

Harry grinned at Jock, picked up his glass in appreciation, "if the cap fits, wear it, my mother always said." He distinctly mouthed the words as he spoke. If Jock couldn't lip read, he knew De Silva would relay those words.

Then to De Silva, he said "I don't like people nosing into my business."

"Then you're not going to like this," said De Silva as he passed a file over the table, Harry's file.

"My Mr Carmichael over there hasn't seen this but would be very interested in knowing what's in it. He'd be particularly interested in your last Nangarhar Province mission, at the same time and area that some of his friends disappeared."

After letting that sink in, he came out with the explosive, "that mission where you were attacked en route and almost lost your leg, was compromised by certain elements within ATS. They informed the rebels who ambushed you.

Unbeknown to your masters, your team was interfering with ATS' drugs sources."

Harry tried to keep a straight face. He wasn't surprised De Silva had the file, considering who else had shown it to him. However, he was astonished that De Silva knew even more detail than Dexter and the Bs. Most of the Ruperts and his mates thought it was a local in their compound who somehow leaked information. He never mentioned the evidence he'd picked up from the dead men.

Hearing what De Silva told him was confirmation that ATS was directly involved, not just rogue elements. Someone in the know had passed them information on their mission details. He had his suspicions, but kept them to himself.

Harry changed the topic. "Where are you getting all this?" And since this man had no military background, it begged the follow-up question, "you're not military, so how are you putting this all together and in context, albeit bollocks?"

"Sometimes having friends with the right connections is useful. Now here's another bit of gossip for you. Jock is still run by ATS." De Silva contemplated Harry's expression as he sipped and savoured his expensive malt. "His links with ATS have proven very valuable to my business."

"Why are you taking the time to tell me all of this? I'm a nothing, a few weeks ago, I was living on the street and enjoying people not shitting all over me." Harry realised he was slowly getting in deeper and deeper over his head in completely different shit.

"A nothing? Mmm, if you say so," said De Silva with a knowing smile.

At that, De Silva stood up. "I enjoyed our chat, we should do this again. Enjoy your pint."

He walked out, followed by Jock plus one.

Harry finished that second pint, taking his time, thinking about the implications of what he'd heard.

He couldn't risk calling in today and would have to bear Dragon-Lady's sharp rebuke when he next had an opportunity.

He took a taxi from the pub straight back to the Bs' house. Walking home

166

would be ill-advised that evening since he didn't know what, or who, might be waiting for him outside. However, deep down, he knew that in the immediate term he was safe. Otherwise why would De Silva have come and talked to him?

Harry decided not to tell the Bs about this meeting since their reaction might screw up his plans. First and foremost, he needed to advise his controller. De Silva had sounded Harry out. Not knowing why, and what he'd heard, worried him.

'What was this man's game?'

Harry was beginning to feel exposed. His controller and her bosses needed to find out who was sharing his file, especially the latest ATS involvement and perspective that De Silva shared.

****

After the meeting with Harry Logan, De Silva and Jock privately talked over a couple of large malts.

"OK dump, what'd he say," demanded Jock impatiently.

"Firstly, remember that I run this operation, and you're only an employee, so back off."

"And you remember, it was me, what brought you the ATS deal that turned your dead drugs distribution network into the largest in the country. Without me, you're nothin'."

De Silva took his time to respond. "You are replaceable, I'm not," he jibed.

Jock thought better about continuing this argument. He'd bide his time. "As you say, boss," came his attempt at appeasement. "We've both done well out of the deal, let's not screw this up now by falling out."

De Silva smiled in concurrence but could see the signs. One way or another, they were heading for a parting of the ways.

"Don't worry, he still has no idea you were involved in the failure of his last Nangarhar op, and that much was obvious. However, he was already suspicious about ATS' involvement."

Jock raised his glass in acknowledgement, took a large final swig, and then left

De Silva to contemplate their discussion.

****

Now he'd gotten his thoughts together, Harry was ready to call his controller during his next day off. Unfortunately, pubs and other exposed places were now out, so he conceived a new and safer method of contacting her.

Fortunately, he'd stashed his street gear in a 24x7 storage facility. Moses' credit card was still paying for this service, which was at least positive. The storage location was quite a distance from the Bs. So, that evening, he took a bus, then a taxi there. It wasn't to avoid and lose prying eyes, but more to identify if there were any on him. There weren't.

After retrieving a large bag, and out of sight in a local park, he donned his street gear and hid his good clothes out of view, up a tree.

With his hood pulled up over his head, he bought a cheap disposable phone and two cans of strong beer from a local supermarket close to where he changed. He paid cash in small denominations.

The assistant didn't give him a second glance. It was not unusual for dodgy-looking people to come in and buy cheap phones. What they used them for was none of her business, and it was safest to keep it that way.

Harry called his controller from a park bench while going through the motions of drinking from the can of beer wrapped in the carrier bag he was given. The other was opened, emptied, and lay at his feet.

She started, "this is not acceptable, you're again…" The controller tried to admonish him, but before she could get to the word 'late', Harry' aggressively interrupted. "I'll start! De Silva and his boys found me just before I was about to call you on Tuesday. Ten minutes later, they'd have found me on the phone to you."

While talking with her, he was giving the outward appearance of talking to himself, not that there was anyone around at this time, early evening when it was dark.

"And what the hell have your lot gotten me into!" he whispered an exclamation into the phone.

Harry summarised the conversation with De Silva and his obvious suspicions. He finished off with, "and did you know about ATS' involvement with De Silva before you got me up to my neck in this shit?"

After a pregnant pause, "apology accepted," his controller sarcastically and curtly responded. "Now, stop and wait."

There was a muffled conversation and the rattle of high-speed keystrokes. "I've passed this up the line. While we wait for a response, you can now give your report on what happened during the Arbitration, which was supposed to be the real purpose of this very tardy call."

Harry, barely stifling his anger, went through the Arbitration meeting process and interactions, including the De Silva and Andrew Bloodworth discussion.

By the time he'd finished his de-brief, the controller said, "I've had feedback from above about your De Silva pub meeting. There are more dynamics at play than we first considered. He's reaching out to you, and that's unexpected."

"Unexpected? Well isn't that a surprise?" he said with as much sarcasm as he could muster. "Coz it was unexpected to me as well!"

"We also suspect he will instigate a follow-up. We believe that conversation with you was staged to check you out and your reactions to the information he supplied."

"Nah, I'd never have thought that!"

With no response from the controller to his sarcasm, he then continued in the same way, "I thought you lot knew everything in advance?"

Still no response.

Dropping the sarcasm and calming himself down, he followed up with, "it's so good to see that you lot are also blind-sided, as I've been all along with this."

Harry knew his comments were not a wise choice of words. He was only human after all and needed to get that outburst off his chest.

It was almost like his words were ignored; perhaps they were. She continued as if he'd said nothing. "We need more information and more time, so the action on De Silva is now on hold. Understood?"

Harry was too angry to immediately respond.

"You need to confirm," she said earnestly.

"I confirm that the hit on De Silva is now on hold, "he said drolly. "Until I hear from you, boss."

She then finished the call with, "When are you able to call in again?"

Harry reinforced to the controller that the contact process was becoming difficult. He could only suggest several options when he might be free and able to again make contact.

She had little choice but to agree.

After the call finished, he crushed the phone under his heel and picked up the pieces. During the two-mile walk to the storage facility, he deposited the destroyed SIM and phone parts in various locations and changed back.

After re-storing the bag, he again took a taxi to the Bs' house.

26. SIMMERING CONFLICT

Over the next few days, the Bs and De Silva had several heated telephone discussions. De Silva felt Andrew implied he was responsible for the attack on the Bs and the killing of Julius. It didn't help their discussions when Andrew corrected him. "I wasn't implying anything. I was telling anyone who'd listen, it was your lot who killed Julius, then tried to kill us."

During their last call, De Silva was more conciliatory. "Andrew, we've gotten off on the wrong foot at the last Arbitration. We need to clear the air. We know that since the last Arbitration, sides were being taken. It's making everyone nervous."

They both knew that tension was not good for business. Competitors and customers alike would capitalise on their friction, at their expense. They agreed on a face-to-face meeting the following day, over lunch in a loud, public restaurant. They preferred meetings like these to be planned at short notice; it reduced the risk of other parties interfering, perhaps a setup.

On these calls, Molly was always included, as was Jock on De Silva's side. On the final call to agree on the meeting logistics, Harry, Ray, and George were included, but in a listening-only role.

De Silva told the Bs that Harry wasn't welcome to the following day's meeting. "When my man was making polite conversation at the last Arbitration, your Mr Logan insulted him, for no reason, and in public. This is not appropriate behaviour at my meeting. I'm expecting your other guys to attend tomorrow."

That suggestion, or rather instruction, was like a red rag to a bull.

Andrew bellowed like a bull sniffing a heifer in heat, "you're meeting, my arse!"

Molly placed a hand over the phone and whispered, "the shit's winding you up, dear. Don't let him get to you."

Mr B composed himself. "We are all equal in the Arbitration, there are no bosses. That meeting was hosted by me, in my manor, it was my meeting," he emphasised the 'my'.

"You were invited as a member. As a courtesy to you being chairman, we permitted your involvement in preparations." Andrew quickly followed up with, "don't overstep your lack of authority."

He allowed some moments for his reply to settle into De Silva and those listening in on the other side. He followed up, "do you remember the membership unanimously agreeing on a rule that all support staff keep their gobs zipped?"

"Of course. It was my idea."

"That rule applies to all, including your staff. Your subordinate, Mr Carmichael, came over to my man and started the conversation, which my man repeatedly tried to ignore. If your people can't follow your instructions and the rules of the Arbitration, I shall request they be excluded in the future."

Andrew was on a roll now. "I shouldn't have to remind you of the physical fights in the early days. It was these that brought about your request for this rule. Harry attracted my attention. Only, when I was within earshot, did he politely put Jock back in his box. It was your man who wasn't following orders. Or are you calling me a liar?"

De Silva didn't know how to respond to that challenge without taking the discussion into a place where there'd be no coming back.

So he settled on, "of course not, but your man insulted Jock."

"What he did was close down their discussion, which he did; most effectively, I might add."

It was all a bit of pre-meeting posturing.

Andrew then finished with, "perhaps it's best Jock not attend this meeting since he's too sensitive to be in this game."

"Jock will be there."

"In that case, Harry will also be present. One doesn't know what might

172

happen, and as you very well know, he's most useful," the implication of De Silva's involvement in the attack was clear.

"OK, OK, both Jock and Mr Logan will be at the meeting tomorrow," conceded De Silva.

Harry realised that De Silva played Andrew to ensure Harry would be present. But the question was why?

****

For the meeting the following day, Harry was again driving, accompanied by George in the passenger seat with Andrew in the rear. Molly stayed at home working on their business. As usual, she wasn't amused when excluded from these meetings.

"Side-lined again! That twat knows that we run this business together. I'm going to get a couple of balls sown on and my tits removed," she grumped with expletives that were unusual for her to use, then said goodbye.

As was the norm, they were accompanied by another car with a couple of the Bs' freelancers.

When they arrived at the planned meeting location, another two of their freelancers were already there. They, plus two of De Silva's men, had earlier tested the surroundings for bugs and eavesdroppers. While Harry had some experience in this field, these were professionals. Harry could add no value by getting involved, let alone questioning them.

"Nice to meet you again," De Silva said to Harry with the not-too-subtle implication of the meeting they'd had in the pub. Harry's worried look before he could compose himself, was long enough to give De Silva the confirmation he needed.

De Silva now knew Harry hadn't mentioned their pub meeting to the Bloodworths. Having chosen not to say anything, it was highly likely that Harry had an alternative agenda, or was at least interested in knowing what would be De Silva's follow-up. And it was now obvious to both, that each of them was interested in that follow-up.

Almost immediately, De Silva supplemented his comment with, "I seem to remember you at the Arbitration having a pleasant chat with my man Jock here." He smirked, as Jock gave more than a hint of pique at being called 'my man'.

Harry didn't respond but had to admire the cunning way he handled the introduction.

Harry and Jock hugged all the opposing security personnel like long-lost friends. As agreed, they found neither weapons nor eavesdropping equipment. It was obvious to all others around that they disliked each other. Their own pretend hug was a highly awkward affair for both.

Neither De Silva nor Andrew could hide their amusement at Harry's and Jock's discomfort with the procedure.

The two leaders were saved from the embarrassment of a search by the opposing parties.

The restaurant was large, busy, and noisy. However, they had a large, comfortable, private table at the back, separated from the general public. There were six at their table.

Andrew and De Silva sat at the same side of the table, with their backs to the wall. Harry sat at one end close to Andrew. Jock was at the other end, close to De Silva.

George and the third person from the De Silva group (the same minder with them at the Arbitration) sat opposite the other bosses. They were the sacrificial lambs in the unlikely event of any violence. George was next to Jock, and the other man was next to Harry.

While no danger was expected, this arrangement gave their bosses maximum protection and them the clearest visibility of the restaurant. And not trusting each other, they wanted the best visibility of any risk.

Even with all the checking for external surveillance, the discussion between both parties was going to be generic. They avoided reference to the specifics of anything illicit. De Silva and Andrew danced around the preliminaries as usual in these meetings. Then they got into the details.

Listening to their differing positions, Harry soon understood the significant divide between their approaches to elements of their business. Harry saw that there was no love lost between these two.

De Silva wanted to exercise more control over their customers to maintain the

174

quality of their supply to the users. He believed sick or dead customers from badly cut products were bad for business. Even worse, he didn't like the resultant attention of the authorities that could lead back to them; no matter what steps they put in place to isolate themselves.

In addition, a bad rep. creates opportunities for others to enter the market, even worse for business. He used the example of Dexter being about to deal with Moses and the dangerous product he was putting into the market that was killing his customers. "That's before your boy here solved our problem," said De Silva nodding in the direction of Harry.

"That was Dexter's motivation not mine. Mr Logan wasn't a member of my team then. He just happened to be there to shoulder responsibility away from Dexter. Let's not forget, he acted in self-defence."

Andrew re-emphasised his position. "We cannot control everything. If we get involved in others' businesses, it will backfire. I believe in the principle of laissez-faire, as promoted by the 'Froggies' in the 1700s." He forced a smile, trying to break a bit of the ice that always built up at these meetings.

It wasn't reciprocated.

Undeterred, Andrew continued. "Many others in our business also share this view. Our approach is simple; leave our customers to operate their market, without interference. We stay outside and above it all."

He wanted De Silva to see that his argument had a solid business foundation. "Trying to ensure our customers sell clean product into their market wastes time and resources. Don't forget, it can create dangerous conflict with them. They don't like interference. If we try, they'd see us as entrenching into their business."

"What you're proposing is bad for business and we don't want bad feelings out there. It can cause a shit-storm. And that WILL attract the attention of the authorities."

Andrew then used an analogy. "How would you like it if our Asian and South American suppliers told us how to manage our business?"

"In summary, our position of staying out of our customers' businesses is the more profitable, healthy, and prison-free approach. And as you said, Dexter was going to deal with Moses in any case, so no reason for us to get involved."

Andrew then threw a curveball into the discussion, "isn't it strange that some of our more dubious customers have been picked up by the authorities in recent times? And it's not only mine. Other distributors have also said the same."

De Silva's curt response was, "coincidence."

"Coincidence my arse! We've raised this issue loads of times during the Arbitration. Business and products were lost. Fingers were pointed but all we get is you and your cronies ignoring us."

De Silva wasn't about to rise to the bait but defended with, "or it could be that the authorities are targeting you and your friends because you're more visible. After all, your customers are putting their heads over the proverbial parapet."

De Silva's reference to Andrew's 'friends' was to the supporters of the Bs agenda at the recent Arbitration meetings. Their diametrically opposed views were divided across the Arbitration membership. The Bs were seen to be the most vociferous in their pushback against the drive by De Silva and his side to tidy up their customers' activities.

Their meeting was tense since both were fixed on their rationale. They continually cited instances that supported each of their positions.

Like many business meetings of this ilk, it ended without a resolution. However, they did agree to continue talking, to try and resolve the gaps in their positions. At least that did bring a reduction in tensions.

Neither wanted the situation they had before the Arbitration when blood from all sides stained the streets. They did agree on one thing. This conflict was giving their customers and outside competitors a wedge to crack open their hold on the distribution market.

They knew they had to resolve this gap between them and work on finding common ground. The upshot was that they agreed to meet again in two weeks but in a different place. As usual, they'd agree on details closer to the time; to ensure security.

As a goodwill offer, De Silva suggested offering access to his Spice supply route. His product was considered the best in the market, and even better, it was cheaper than other sources. If Andrew was interested, there was the carrot of discussing this suggestion in more detail during their next meeting.

176

That brought a smile to Andrew's face. He looked forward to sharing the potential offer with Molly.

Back at the house, Harry and George were with Andrew as he told Molly he'd secured a sub-distribution agreement with De Silva for his brand of Spice. It wasn't exactly what was stated, but close enough as far as Andrew was concerned.

While she was pleased about the offer, her response was not as supportive as he expected. "Listen, Andrew, I know it's a good offer. I'd have loved to have been there to see the whites of his eyes, but we can NOT trust that man," she told her husband, splitting out the word for emphasis.

"He's never offered anything free without wanting some concession in return. Please tell me you haven't promised him anything?"

"Absolutely not," was his definitive reply. "I know he's trying to soften us up, and I'm not daft."

She mulled over what she'd been told. "I don't think the next meeting will happen. He made the mistake of offering access to his lucrative Spice business. There's no way he'd let you in."

"He's up to something. I don't like it. We need to be cautious. I'll warn our people to keep on their guard." Harry could hear the concern in her voice.

'She's a smart lady.'

Harry's, albeit limited, experience with De Silva to date was the man was a smart and ruthless operator. Fortunately for the Bs, Molly also knew it.

27. CHANGE OF HEART

Harry and the others in the household security team were asked to join Andrew and Molly in the drawing room later that evening.

Andrew opened the meeting. "Listen, everyone. We need to be frank with you. The De Silva discussions are going nowhere, and he's up to something. Whatever it is, it's not going to be good for us. We have to be vigilant in case there's another attempt on our lives, which could even be targeted at this household."

Molly came in next with, "any questions, now or any time, let me know. I'm taking point on this issue."

The team raised numerous questions, which Molly dealt with, trying to ease some of their concerns. The team was less worried about themselves, and more about their bosses. Harry knew it was as much about financial loss as it was loyalty. If anything happened to their employers, their lucrative offshore payments would cease.

Once she'd answered all their concerns and all was clear, as much as it could be, they started to leave.

"Harry, stay behind for a mo." Once the three of them were alone, Molly asked, "you've not said anything, and looking at you, I know you've thoughts around this."

"I agree with what you've done and said. You are right to put us on alert. However, if De Silva's lot does try anything, it won't be here, too messy."

"If they had any brains, it's most likely to be done when you're out, especially if they could link the hit to your drug operations. The police and others will be too busy patting their backs, as a result of their anti-drug efforts, to investigate the detail."

Then apologetically Harry finished with, "sorry, but you did ask."

Molly said, "you're right."

She then came out with, "but we've got an ace in the hole, an inside man in De Silva's organisation who I've been cultivating. Our mole confirmed the hit on us was sanctioned by De Silva."

"Our source agreed to set up the situation for us to deal with De Silva once and for all. We're awaiting further information from him. We want you to be involved since we've decided we can trust you, on the hit side anyway. And, there'll be a handsome bonus."

"And as you suggest about De Silva hitting us outside, I like the idea of having this hit done on him as an internal feud, at one of their locations."

"Are you in?" she asked.

Saying no at this point would be foolhardy, so Harry's only response could only be, "yes, of course."

"Who is your inside man?"

"His number 2, Jock," she replied.

****

A few days later, it was Harry's day off. The Bs were out with George and Ray. This was the perfect opportunity for Harry to report back to his controller. He again went through the same call setup process as before; a new disposable phone, from a different shop, and two cans of strong, disgusting lager.

He needed to urgently debrief his controller on the recent meeting between Andrew and De Silva. He wanted to particularly highlight De Silva's game-playing during the introduction, the offer to the Bs, and Molly's cautious approach to dealing with this man.

He also needed to mention Jock seemingly working for the Bs as their inside man.

When Harry finished his update, his controller responded, "that reinforces our revised thoughts and how we need to proceed."

"Your attention is no longer on De Silva. Previously, how you dealt with the security team around De Silva during the execution of our agreement, and particularly Mr Steven Carmichael, was not of any concern to us. However, things have changed. Your target is now Mr Steven Carmichael. And I'm sure you'll be fine with that since he was always your focus."

"Why the change?" asked Harry.

"The less you know, the longer you'll be able to enjoy the spoils of your efforts," came the reply. "You have two weeks to complete the job."

She hung up, leaving Harry to rethink his strategy. It was all up in the air again.

He reversed the disguise process. Now back in his job attire, he decided the need for a pint in his local was too hard to refuse himself. Not that he was a copious drinker, he just needed uninterrupted thinking to better review and plan for his revised target. And of course, beer would be excellent lubrication for his thought process.

If he was really honest with himself, he just fancied a pint.

****

Nursing his beer and looking into space, Harry was nonetheless ever vigilant. A heavy-set, squat man watched him. He'd the look of a failed ex-boxer; cauliflower ears, multiple nose breaks, and facial scarring. Harry did his best to pretend not to see him, but this man was so obvious, it was hard to avoid him.

Halfway through his beer, Jock strode into the bar, made his way over, and sat opposite Harry. He leaned in close and stared at Harry, doing his best to intimidate him.

"Down that pint. We're leaving," was the brusque command. "De Silva wants to see you."

Standing by the bar near the door, Harry could see Jock's shadow from before, plus the squat man who'd been initially watching him. They sat nearby.

Harry didn't fancy his chances with them all, especially with Jock in the mix. However, the bar was busy, and he was by now quite well known here. Well, he was at least on nodding terms with some of the worthies who propped up the bar. He knew there was no chance that Jock 'n' Co would try anything now and here.

Harry previously took great pleasure in winding up Jock and saw no reason to change. He flippantly said to the Scotsman, "let me check with Mr and Mrs Bloodworth and let's set something up that works for them. I'll get back to you."

"Now," ordered Jock.

"Fuck off," said Harry. "No way am I leaving here with you. I'll be dead if my bosses find out."

"If you don't come now, you'll be deader."

Harry chuckled, wondering how one could be deader than dead.

"What're you laughing at?"

"Private joke mate, between me and myself." Harry grinned. It could also have been partly his release of inner tension.

Harry became serious. "How do I know that it's De Silva who wants me? You might still be holding a bitch grudge from our last chat."

Jock called a number, briefly spoke into the phone out of Harry's earshot, then handed his mobile to Harry.

"So, you don't trust Jock," said De Silva.

Then flippantly, "well, you're a good judge of character. In case you're wondering, strangely, he doesn't like you. It seems that your whole attitude towards him is upsetting; Jock's got such a delicate nature."

Harry wanted to educate De Silva that attitude is more a state of mind and what he should mean is 'behaviour', or even 'demeanour'. However, he kept those thoughts to himself.

"Anyway, rest assured, it was me, who sent him over to get you. I know the Bs are out. So you're obviously at a loose end and could do with some pleasant company. And you're not going to be missed. Oh, and I promise that Jock and friends will be on their leashes; for today anyway."

Harry grunted, "OK," and handed the phone back to Jock. He took his time finishing the pint. Close to the end, he gulped the last large mouthful, quickly stood up, and said, "what are you waiting for, don't sit there all day, I believe he wanted me now."

He stormed out of the pub and waited for his entourage to catch up. That action allowed him a few moments to surreptitiously place his now silenced work phone in a plant pot outside, so he'd not be tracked. It also meant winding up Jock, which was definitely not a bad thing.

"I'm going to take great pleasure slicing open that smart-ass gob of yours before I properly fuck you over," said Jock to Harry as they walked over to the car.

Harry smirked. "Not today. Remember, your boss says you have to play nice."

28. DAMNED EVERY WAY

They drove up a long driveway to an extravagantly gaudy mansion, the sort of house that De Silva would have. The location was no surprise to Harry. From earlier recces, he knew where they were.

They entered the house via a side entrance that opened into a large utility room and walked through a short hallway to a large panelled door. The squat man opened the door, and Harry followed Jock inside. The second man, Jock's shadow, brought up the rear. The door closed; the third man waited outside.

De Silva stood up. Jock and Co walked over and took their positions behind their boss, one on each side. He greeted Harry with an outstretched hand, who ignored the gesture.

After looking at Harry for a few moments, he eventually said, "I've got a job for you." There was no point in him responding since there was more coming. "You're going to top the Bloodworths, and we're blaming that twat, Dexter."

Harry laughed out loud. On the way there, he knew there had to be something serious afoot, and he suspected it had to be about the Bs. This idea was one of the options he thought would be suggested, but he assumed it would have been only Andrew.

Molly didn't have sufficient credibility with the wider membership, so couldn't be considered a danger to his business. De Silva wanted to leave no stone unturned; she was, after all, a very capable killer.

Of course, Andrew and Molly were not nice people. In truth, they're unscrupulously bad. However, that didn't put them on his list. If so, they'd be in the queue behind many others, equally bad or worse, such as this lot standing in front of him.

Quickly recovering, Harry retorted, "you dragged me from my pint, to talk rubbish! No chance. Ain't gonna happen! Even if I wanted to, Molly's sharp. I'd never get away with it."

Jock and the other minder moved towards Harry. "I told you he'd tell us to piss off. We've wasted our time bringing him here."

That move forward prompted a sinister response from Harry, who'd planned his response to this request.

Harry glared at De Silva, outwardly ignoring the others but still keeping them in his wider field of vision. "Do you really want us to mix it in your home? And, I'm assuming you've family around as witnesses, or worse, to be frightened? Because, I can assure you, I don't go down easy. I'm sure you'd not allow those two imbeciles to use noisy guns in your house."

In acceptance of Harry's comment, De Silva ordered, "he's right, cool it you two." When they wouldn't move back, he hissed at them, "back!" Jock and Co still didn't move. The other man didn't respond to his boss but, instead, took his lead from Jock, who wasn't giving way.

De Silva walked in front of Jock and waited, not saying a word until they both moved away from Harry as requested. Once they'd backed off, he looked at Harry again.

Harry tested them. "I knew it. So it was you lot behind that botched hit on the Bloodworths! You were incapable of doing it yourself, so you're asking me."

De Silva glowered at Jock; it was the confirmation Harry needed.

Half laughing, half sneering, he said to Jock, "I might have guessed that balls-up was down to you. It was always obvious a hit was going down. George would be eliminated by the man outside and Andrew by the family man. Sharif and his brothers were the backup muscle to take me 'n' Molly out."

Jock said nothing. There was nothing he could say. Harry was right, it was their botched attempt.

"Molly and I knew Sharif and his crew were involved. Andrew, for all his faults, would never believe that Sharif would, or could turn. Unfortunately, money and power are wonderful pivots. So it was pointless suggesting it to him, even by Molly."

"We all assumed your organisation was behind it. Because it was such a botch-up, we all suspected that it was Jock himself who organised it. Who else could

184

conjure up such a shit plan!" sneered Harry, baiting Jock with his comments.

Jock stepped forward and said, "you bastard," but before he could say anything else, De Silva screamed, "stop, no one shits on my doorstep!"

Harry continued his goading. He needed to take control of the situation from these people and get them to act rashly. It was his only chance of getting out of there alive.

"It was never going to work. Even if your people got the plan right, it was always going to be messy. But to make matters worse, they screwed up. A 360-degree screw-up."

Turning round to face Jock and Co, De Silva said, "you two out. I need to talk with Logan, and you're not helping the discussion, being in here." Out of Harry's view, he conspiratorially winked at Jock.

A seething Jock relaxed a little and gave in. "Don't worry, I'll be right outside."

De Silva nodded in agreement.

The two men walked past Harry, petulantly bumping shoulders into him. Once they'd left, Harry couldn't help commenting, "your boys are a bit tetchy."

De Silva ignored the quip and gave him a genuine smile, "please sit down." He pointed to a comfortable armchair next to the fire.

"I've some cheapo whisky," said De Silva pulling out a 30-year-old well-known quality blend. It was an attempt to lighten the strained mood and a gesture of appeasement, which had succeeded. The dynamics of the situation had now changed.

Harry, now a little more relaxed, nodded in appreciation. De Silva poured a healthy measure of the 'cheapo' whisky into each of their glasses; each measure was worth as much as a bottle of decent wine.

De Silva, clicked a switch and some loud background classical music kicked in. "Now, no eavesdroppers." He added, "let's clear the air with a once-in-a-lifetime warning, no one refuses me, especially when I have some real shit on them."

Harry toyed with the response, "*a first time for everything.*"

His choice was taken away when De Silva continued, "and for your information, the hit on the Bloodworths then and now, was and is, not my idea."

Harry was expecting De Silva to try and reason with him after removing the tension he and Jock were creating together. That statement surprised him. A sip of the amber nectar, savouring its warmth in his mouth, and, as it gently slid down, it gave him time to re-order his thoughts.

From the discussions with his controller, it started to click into place. However, he couldn't show understanding, so he looked at De Silva blankly.

"I don't normally explain myself to the likes of you, but you need to understand what's going on here," opened De Silva. "And, I have a proper business proposal for you. There's more to you than meets the eye, and you're sharp. Now, that makes you potentially valuable, as well as dangerous. So here goes."

"I was doing well with my business until a few years ago. I started to get a lot of bother from the filth. My supply channel was being shat-on everywhere I looked, and started having difficulty getting product. What product I could get was being tracked to where it was stored. I was regularly raided. My people were being lifted and banged up. I owed money for product shipped to me, which was sitting, impounded."

He took another sip.

"The upshot of all this was my distribution channels were crying for product, which I could NOT supply. Competitors were getting wind of my problems and trying to muscle in. I was losing money, then people. My business was unravelling. If you're targeted, suppliers give you a wide berth. Customers avoid you because they're losing trust."

"It all smelled of bacon, fucking Pigs! I either had a leak or worse still, there was an undercover pig in my organisation. It was all slowly going tits up."

"Then Jock and his mate, Fred, the one in the room just now, approached me with an offer. They have new supply connections of quality gear, a line of credit, and new people to help me get back on track. Jock could even tell me when police raids were about to happen. A deal with them would ensure the integrity of both my supply and distribution channels."

"The downside was that they wanted 80% of my profits. It took me a while to decide, but since I had no profits, the 20% seemed a great offer, at the time. And it was, over the last four years, business boomed."

"It was their idea to bring the various factions together to control the distribution market; our Arbitration meetings. There was one proviso from their side. I had to keep my product and distribution channel clean. If any of my customers screwed with quality, we deal with them; whatever it takes. Why this needed to be the case, I still don't know. But that was the deal. As it transpired, it made sense."

De Silva warned Harry, "by the way, Jock was special services and well able to take care of himself and deal with others. I don't know why you've so much of a beef with each other, but you don't want to mess with him, unless on your terms."

De Silva continued when Harry merely shrugged his shoulders.

"By the way, and in case you're interested, Fred's real name is Frank West, also ex-forces. As usual, your military types do love their nicknames. Usually, they're hard, macho ones. But the link to the murderer, Fred West, was too close, hence his nickname 'Fred'."

"Jock is the real deal, and Fred is also no mug in a scrap, but short on the brains front. I expect you know this already."

Harry nodded yes and took another £5 sip of whisky.

De Silva paused, also taking a drink. With his thoughts re-ordered, he continued. "I've recently found out that behind Jock and Fred is an outfit called Albatross Tactical Security. This Albatross lot is into all sorts of people-and-hardware security shit, mercs, prisoner security, off-books overseas stuff, weapons, and more. They're also rumoured to be into 'dodgy dealings' the authorities can deny. They're well connected with the military, the fuzz, and some say, the spooks."

Harry said nothing, merely listened, with the occasional sip. There was nothing De Silva was saying that he didn't know, or at least suspected.

Then, with a combination of frustration and anger, De Silva said, "their 80% cut of my money is their off-books fund. It's making them, someone, or some people very rich!"

"Now, this is what you need to know," said De Silva. "The file I showed you was given to me by Jock, who got it from his mates at ATS. So, whoever is involved there, knows everything about you. I'm not supposed to let you know that they know about you. So, I'm also taking a risk here."

"Now, the big warning for you. Once your hit on the Bloodworths is completed, you're next. But first, they want to have a detailed discussion with you about what you know. And, as you're fully aware, Jock doesn't like you, so he's gonna enjoy that discussion."

De Silva continued. "I now know the shit I went through four years ago was set up by ATS to fuck my business. It was all too suspicious about my losing business and them coming in with an offer. You can guess, they have people working for them in the pigs."

"They're stealing my 80% and I want it back. I've built up my team. My customer base is run by me, and only me. Now with my own people and connections, I've become a risk to them."

"And by the way, the Bloodworths' accusations are correct. Information on other distributors' dealings is being given to the filth but not by me. Saying that, their lost business is coming my way, at least that's OK."

"However, Jock and his mates in ATS are playing a dangerous game with elements in the authorities, pretending to be the nice guys while double-dealing. At the moment, I'm outside those activities and very much locked in and with no control. Or so they think."

"The upshot is that those two shites, Jock and Fred, outside that door, need to disappear. Only then can I take back control of my business and all my money."

Then De Silva came up with the hot one. "I want you to do this, and I'm prepared to pay and pay big." De Silva paused and savoured his whisky, giving Harry time to mull this over.

Both De Silva and his controller were now making the same request. With De Silva being on board, Harry could count on his support in the process; that would make the job easier. Even better, De Silva was prepared to offer a lot of money, over and above what his controller was paying, for the same hit.

He wondered if his controller had wind of the changing dynamics, hence the new target.

Then came the next bit of good-health news. As well as the offer of money, De Silva offered him Jock's job as a further incentive.

Harry wondered how that job offer would go down with this controller. Assuming it happened. He was in no rush to tell her.

First, he needed to get all the different dynamics at play, aligned in his head. So, he mulled them over, one by one.

Kill one. He had to overtly show to De Silva and Jock that he agreed to the hit on the Bloodworths. He'd need to build a credible plan that he'd need to share, to ensure he was actually on board. The downside was that if he did that job, then he was next. While the Bs were alive and the plan was developing, he assumed he was safe.

Then there was the second kill demand. The Bloodworths want his help with a hit on De Silva. Jock was behind organising that one. He also suspected that Jock had done a deal with the Bloodworths to hand Harry over to Jock's ministrations. He now realised why they included him in those discussions; otherwise, why would they trust the only new person on the team?

Kill three. His controller and whatever organisation she represented, plus De Silva, now wanted Jock eliminated. After this kill, there was no way his controller's organisation would let him walk away. He'd already walked away from another part of their organisation, and they knew he'd again do the same. This time, he knew too much; he'd either have to be in, or dead.

With all these kill demands, and on different people, it felt like being in a musical game of pass the parcel, and he was the parcel. Parcels often get discarded after the music stops. That is, unless they're valuable to the players, particularly, the winner.

On top of all that, he'd have to face the promise he made himself. When he left the service, he vowed he'd only focus on what he was good at and what kept his conscious clear. He wasn't good for much else apart from security for hire. This time he was adamant, it would only be that. Killings on request had now ended.

He'd promised himself he was no longer in the game of quasi-officially dispensing his employer's justice. People were again dragging him back into their dark, devious world, using him to eliminate people; without scruples.

Eliminating Jock and Fred was the no-brainer. There were no scruples for these two. Whether he set up the circumstances for them to try and eliminate him, or kill them outright for what they did to Ratty, was worth the exception.

Then it would, at last, be truly over.

After all the internal pontificating, he enthusiastically accepted the hit on Jock and Fred, to De Silva's delight. It was a simple decision. No matter what happened to him, they were getting theirs; he vowed and hoped.

De Silva, now quite pleased with himself, said to Harry, "now, when those two are invited back in, you are going to accept the Bloodworths' hit on the understanding that I've coerced you. As far as they're concerned, I've got something on you that can't be discussed in front of them. Got it?"

"Basically, they don't know, that you know, they know about the file," said De Silva, smiling at his little tongue twister; as did Harry.

Jock and Fred were called and smugly walked back into the room.

"He's in," said De Silva, meaning Harry accepted the hit. De Silva's parting comment to Harry was, "you've two weeks and I want this to be clean, with the blame pointed at Dexter. Got it!"

Harry acknowledged with a reluctant nod.

Jock wasn't satisfied. "I want to hear it from your lips, Logan. We don't want any misunderstandings."

"I'll kill Mr and Mrs Bloodworth within the next two weeks. Happy?"

"Very happy indeed," smirked Jock. He was enjoying this a little too much.

As an afterthought, Harry asked, "why Dexter? You're tying my hands."

Jock interrupted, "because I owe that bastard, and I want it done that way."

Harry left with Fred and the squat minder in the car. "Back to the pub?" said Fred looking into the rear-view mirror at Harry.

"Yep, I need a drink," was his response.

Nothing more was said until they got to the pub. Fred's parting words were, "two weeks, you're not such a cocky shite now, are you?"

****

While Harry was en route back to the pub, Jock said to De Silva, "the twat took the hit on the Bloodworths. I'm impressed with your powers of persuasion. And then afterward, I'm going to enjoy doin' him over, bit by bit."

De Silva grinned but said nothing. What Jock didn't know was that he and Fred were the cheese in his mousetrap.

Then, a worrying thought came to De Silva. This all assumed Logan could deliver. He'd seen Jock and Fred in action. Theirs would be no easy hit.

****

Andrew Bloodworth's mobile pinged, advising a new Secure App message had arrived. Attached, was a recording. As he listened, a rage overcame him.

He screamed out, "Molly!"

When she appeared, she was about to admonish him with, "don't bellow like that to me in the house, what'll they all think about me?"

However, she only got the "don't bellow" out before he growled, "listen to this, now!"

After hearing the recording of Harry saying he was going to kill them, Molly checked the tracker App on his phone to find his current location. He was still in the pub.

Her response was immediate. "The bastard! He's meat! I'll get some extra boys. We'll have a party when he's back from his drink."

The recording was from Jock, their 'friend' in the other camp.

29. WHEN THE MUSIC STOPS

Harry stood outside the pub blank-mindedly watching Fred and Co drive away. He took a deep breath, entered the pub, ordered a pint, and sat at a small quiet table. While nursing his beer, Harry mulled over his internal conflicts.

Yes, he'd killed, but in action and while wearing the uniform but he was out now. He tried to justify to himself that he had changed and moved on from those angry times.

While he'd set up the situations for Julius and Moses to want to kill him, he rationalised they had a choice. They didn't need to come after him. What he did to them was purely in self-defence. In his mind, that didn't make him a cold-blooded killer; he kept trying to tell himself.

He was happy to make the kill on Jock; that was unfinished business. No one but his controller knew that. From everyone's perspective, he was a killer-for-hire to commit cold-blooded murder. Even though everyone on each others' targets was lower than pond life, he was out of that game.

So his conscience should be clear. However, no matter how often he said that to himself, it didn't feel that way. He knew that if he survived this one, there will be other demands, and he'd be back in that murderous cycle.

Then came the real issue to be addressed. No matter what course of action he took, he'd end up dead. He needed protection. That meant being too valuable to the organisation controlling him, perhaps also De Silva, even the Bloodworths.

However, now was not the time to mull over the rights and wrongs of what he'd done or may have to do.

He first needed to sort out his immediate issue. The solution was simple, in principle, as all best plans should be.

He'd level with the Bloodworths that he'd been pulled to De Silva's house and tell them what he knew. They'd have the muscle and resources to help him deal with Jock and whatever people in ATS were involved. He had to move quickly. He could use De Silva to set up Jock.

****

Molly had taken control of the situation. Checking her location App, she saw his mobile pinging his location at his new local pub. She dispatched Ray and others to pick him up, and no excuses.

While a car with four men made its way to the pub, he was inside, wrapped up in his thoughts and his conscience, unaware of the danger.

When the car pulled up, Ray said to the others, "stay here, but stop him if he leaves alone. I don't want to spook him, so I'm going in there, natural-like."

Ray entered the pub with a relaxed, smiling demeanour. He played it cool. However, no matter what, Harry was coming with him.

He wasn't there!

Ray asked the barman, "seen Harry, supposed to be meeting up for a pint."

"Yeh, been in twice, you've just missed him, left 10 minutes ago. He'd a headache and was heading home. You staying for one?"

"Nah, I'm good, 'night."

Ray called Molly, "he's not here."

"Damn." She checked the location app. It showed him as still being there. He'd left the phone somewhere in the pub. She was now certain he was in cahoots with De Silva.

"He's ditched his phone, get back! Keep an eye out for him. If you see him, call me first."

They had a welcoming party waiting for him. Two men were in a car across the road, and two extra were secretly waiting at the front gate. The dogs were let loose but calmly sat alongside Molly, plus two extra men, in the garden. Another two were with Andrew in his room. All were armed.

They'd have to wait for him to return, hoping he was unaware of their plans.

****

Harry didn't stay long in the pub. He left his barely-touched beer and made for the exit.

The barman looked over and asked, "beer OK?" Since working for the Bloodworths, Harry had been coming in every few days. He was now considered an up-and-coming regular. The barman was just checking; it's good to keep new customers sweet.

"Pint perfect as always. Had a tiring day and have a headache. Seeya," he said as he walked out into the fresh night air.

Harry didn't head straight back but instead chose the long way. This would give him time to weigh the options. How was he going to explain that their man inside De Silva's organisation was actually planning to kill them?

He also had to flesh out the execution of his kill plan. He needed to set up Jock and Fred and go through what he needed to complete the job.

Delivering a complete, well-thought-out plan to the Bs would be key to selling them the story. Sauntering towards the house, his mind explored the various options and the endgame of each. It was like running through the various strategies and outcomes in a game of chess.

He'd only been away for a few minutes when he realised his work phone was still in the plant pot. "It'll have to wait," he mumbled to himself. He didn't need interruptions, he needed to focus.

Back into his planning thoughts, it wouldn't be any surprise to the Bs that De Silva wanted a hit on them. He was struggling with the toughest sell, and that would be accusing Jock, their new inside man. So, he needed to get this right in his head and keep it simple.

Jock and Fred had been playing everyone. He orchestrated the attempted kill, and he'd been grassing to the authorities about the Bs and others' customers. De Silva, although not innocent, was effectively their front man.

He smiled as the plan started to gel in his mind, giving him a little more spring to his step. Eventually, the plan was in place.

However, he still didn't trust Jock not to pull a fast one. So he kept to his

194

indirect route, keeping in the shadows as much as he could, all the while maintaining a watchful eye in case Jock and Co waited for him somewhere in the shadows.

****

It was very late by the time Harry reached the avenue that led to the B's house. After replaying his plan and the various outcomes and push-backs with the Bs, he'd a good picture in his mind of how this would work. He prayed Andrew and Molly were still up and prepared to listen.

Although engrossed in his thoughts during his walk back, he was still aware of what was happening around him. He'd clocked a fast-driven car, full of large bodies, heading towards the Bs. Were they bringing in additional freelance muscle?

Not long after, another car with what looked like Ray and three other large bodies inside, drove down the road, much slower than the speed limit. Few do that unless on the lookout for someone.

If there was an emergency, he wondered why they didn't call him in. Then he remembered, he'd left his work phone in the plant pot. Dammit! He was in the dark.

Maybe he was wrong and people attacked the house? Perhaps De Silva's discussion with him had been a ruse to get him away from the Bs? Had he left them exposed?

He was only surmising, and he had to be sure.

Harry stayed in the shadows as he walked up the tree-lined avenue. He found a dark spot some distance away from the house and watched. He could see all the house and security lights were on. Almost certainly something was afoot.

A car parked opposite the entrance to the Bs looked like it contained a couple of large people. Who were they working for? Were they waiting for someone, perhaps him?

He needed more information, but it'd be crazy to scale the wall as before, assuming there was added security. Harry used a new burner phone and called the in-house Bloodworth security.

He excitedly told them that he'd scored and reassured them he'd be back in time for the start of his shift in the morning. This was a normal reporting process, so the Bs' security could keep track of staff out of hours. Normally, this would have been logged with, "lucky bugger," or a similar comment.

Without any response or comment, he was immediately passed through to Molly.

"Where are you?" she immediately asked.

"Hello Mrs Bloodworth, met a friend. Sorry, lost my phone and phoning in to confirm all's good. I'll be back in the morning for the start of my shift. It's unusual to hear from you at this time of night. Is everything OK?"

"No, no problem. Just working on plans after the earlier discussion." He could hear the tension in her voice even though she was trying to keep her speech calm.

"I'm worried. I want to ensure that all the in-house people are in, for everyone's safety."

"No problem, there's a taxi rank nearby. I can be back in 15-20 minutes," Harry replied.

"No taxi," she responded. "We'll send a car to pick you up."

"Are you sure? I don't want to put anyone out. I can get to you quicker in a taxi."

"I gave an instruction!" she said sternly. "I need your arse safely back here now! I'm sending a car to you. Are you still at your local?" Unusually, she sworn and that meant she was stressed. Mentioning his local, he knew she'd also been tracking his phone. It could be out of concern, but on the other hand, she could be looking for him.

With all the discussions he'd been having, it didn't take a genius to work out that the probability of him being the subject of the activity was high. Her response confirmed that.

Harry gave an address for a shop about a fifteen-minute drive away from the Bs' house. He waited and watched.

Within a minute, a car screeched out of the gate heading in the direction he'd given. If there was a problem at the house, they'd only have sent a driver, perhaps another. He could see four large bodies in the car as it passed him.

He was right. They were coming for him. He felt sorry for the people at the address, but they'll get through it.

His plan of going in and explaining to the Bs was scuppered.

Damn. His initial suspicion was now confirmed. Could this last meeting with De Silva have been leaked? If so, it was back to square one. Somehow they'd had tabs on him. Could it have been their pet inside man, Jock? And if so, what game was he playing?

Perhaps getting Harry to De Silva's house was a ruse to implicate Harry. Maybe Jock had evidence of his visit? He remembered that final verbal confirmation of the hit on the Bs.

If Harry was right, he'd underestimated the man, and Jock's priority was to get rid of him.

Where was De Silva in all this?

He slowly walked down the long road, away from the house, speeding up as he got further away. In so doing, a new plan started to build in his mind. This one would give him the satisfaction of dealing with Jock and Fred himself, but it was more dangerous.

Once out of the vicinity and undercover, he phoned Molly back. In a put-on stressed voice, he said, "OK, the truth, I'm in hiding. I don't know what to do! So, I'm out of here," he said in a panicked and rushed voice.

She tried to interject. Feigning panic, Harry babbled, not letting her get a word in. "I was picked up by Jock and his boys. He used the same information you have on me, forcing me to agree to kill you both. No way was I going to do that after what you'd done for me."

She tried to but in with a, "don't worry..." but Harry talked over her. "Jock is trying to take over your business, then De Silva's. He admitted to setting up the hit on you, not De Silva. I had to agree to kill you both to get out of there alive. You're both in danger. I'm gone. Look after yourselves." Before she could reply, he hung up.

Harry made another call, this time to De Silva. "Is Jock with you?" he asked.

"No. You can speak. You sound a bit wired, are you OK?" asked De Silva.

"The Bloodworths found out I was with you this evening and are now after me. Jock is playing a double game with them, so watch your back. The upshot is that the deal we discussed alone is now game-on. So bear with me with what happens next. OK?"

"OK…" came a hesitant response from De Silva, then, "what are you going to do?"

"Best you don't know. Call Jock and when he comes, put it on speakerphone. I need him to hear what I'm about to say."

He also needed to know if De Silva was also involved.

He could hear De Silva shouting to Jock that he had to urgently come. There was silence for a couple of minutes. There was an opening, then a shutting of a door. Harry could hear Jock approaching, a little out of breath. "What do you want?"

"Not me, him," Harry could imagine De Silva gesturing to the phone that had Harry on the other end.

"Good to hear from you," said Harry. "I'm assuming you're both listening. I've thought about your request that I make a hit on the Bloodworths. I'm declining. Firstly, I don't kill for hire. If you want the hit done, use Jock. He gets paid enough to do your dirty work; isn't that what he's hired for? Mind you, perhaps he's only full of shit and bluster. When push comes to shove, his sort hasn't got what it takes."

Harry could hear Jock breathing hard as he leaned in toward the phone. "Logan, you're dead, you're fuckin' dead," he shrieked. Harry could hear him ranting and uttering expletives in the background as he paced up and down the room.

Harry had hoped his insults to Jock would anger him to rush in and act rashly. He needed even the smallest advantage.

Harry, continued, "don't come looking for me; I'm going to ground. If you do, I know too much about your game. I'll blow it open. In the meantime, I've told the Bs that Jock was behind the attempted hit on them. I told them that Jock demanded I do the proper job this time, threatening me with some information De Silva has on me."

Harry then said, "basically, I told them Jock admitted he and his people were too incompetent and he needed a professional. And that's why they dragged me to your house."

Harry stopped his monologue. He waited, grinning from ear to ear in satisfaction as the tirade of expletives continued at him. Once they'd sufficiently died down, Harry followed up, "Listen, Jockie, my boy. The Bs were after me, but now you're in the frame. They're coming for you and your bum-chum Fred. Now, it's you in the shit. I'd get away quickly before our Molly gets to you."

Harry felt a release of tension and spontaneously laughed after his outburst to Jock.

"And, Mr De Silva, stay clear of me. Keep your other dogs on their leashes, and I'll stay quiet about your business."

There was a pause and Harry could discern muffled voices. Someone was holding his hand over the speaker while deep in conversation.

"Deal?" Harry asked again.

"Deal," said De Silva.

Harry destroyed the phone.

Listening to the dynamics on the other end of the phone, Harry was certain that the De Silva offer was genuine; he hoped.

30. FINAL STAND

Sometime later, a street-dweller-attired Harry arrived back at the old warehouse. It was after midnight, and everything was quiet, apart from the ambient noises of the nearby docks. All the residents were asleep in their various locations around the old place. There was no sign that anyone of any risk to him was already there, not that he expected them to be. However, he wasn't going to repeat the same over-confident mistake that landed him in hospital.

He found Tom and shook him awake, then Jess. Speaking softly and with urgency, "get your gear, both of you. Get out of here now, no questions! People will be coming for me here, and I can't put you at risk again, or worry about you."

Before Tom could respond, Harry held the palm of his hand gently to Tom's mouth. "You're both in danger. You can't be around when they get here. They'll try and pull out whatever information they can get about me, and they'll not be as nice as Eddie."

A bleary-eyed Tom asked, "what's going on?"

Harry ignored the question, he'd no time for explanations. "Stay in a public place whenever you can, and use proper shelters. I'll be in touch if I can sort this out. If you don't hear from me, don't come looking. I'll be dead."

He pulled out some £20s. "This should keep you going till the heat dies down. Look after each other." He forced a smile at them both.

"And Jess, it would help you both to stay safe if you kicked your habits. Otherwise, you WILL get Tom killed. You need to know that he's in constant danger protecting you. He'll never leave you. And I'm not going to be around."

Harry hoped his parting shot and the last words she'd hear from him might encourage her to get proper help. They were good people, his closest friends, and he cared for them. It'd been a long time since he'd been as close to anyone.

Jess said nothing and quietly started to sob on hearing that this would be the last time she'd see Harry. She tried to reach out to him, but he left. Apart from Tom, he was the only person who cared for her, without any agenda; he actually liked her.

There wasn't much to pack, so they were quickly on their way. From the shadows outside, Harry watched them leave, ensuring they left without issue. He was relieved they'd be away from the action about to descend on this area.

He knew trouble was on its way. Everyone knew that here would be one of the obvious places he'd lie low. And he was not going to disappoint them.

He didn't expect Jock to run away; that wasn't his style. He'd riled the man, and that was useful. Angry people want revenge and make mistakes.

If someone did come for him, or rather, when Jock came for him, the warehouse would be the first place he'd look. They'd know Harry would lie low in a location where he might have the upper hand. This was Harry's turf after all. So, it made sense to find a vantage spot in or around these promises to view the comings and goings, but safe and secluded enough to be invisible.

The actual warehouse was out. It was too open and without vantage points. Even if it was a possibility, poor and innocent people lived there. He couldn't have them involved with what was about to happen.

He needed to be close by, and he had the solution. He planned to hide in the loft area of the large office building outside the entrance to the warehouse. It was a reasonably large open space, two flights of stairs up. From there, he could prepare his defence against whatever might come his way.

The access road leading up to the old fencing and walls surrounding the warehouse and the various derelict outbuildings was broken over the last one hundred metres or so. His visitors would come by car, and only someone who knew the road would try to use it, but only in the dry, and in a proper 4x4. It had been raining recently, so they'd be coming on foot, and he'd have early warning of their arrival.

There were other entry points for anyone on foot. However, in this weather, the paths were muddy and uneven. He expected they'd choose the least muddy of those entries to avoid ruining their expensive clothes; sad but true.

The graffiti-covered walls were cracked, and broken plaster littered the floor. The ground floor was covered with faeces, making unsoiled walking difficult. As a result, no one used the office block apart from as a toilet; and no one else would be at risk.

A wide stairway gave access to the first floor. The guard rail was broken and much of the concrete stair was loose and cracked. Access to the roof area from the first floor was even more dangerous. The heavily rusted narrow spiral steel staircase suffered missing treads, and those still in situ had sharp edges. All was in danger of collapsing from even the lightest of weight.

And because of all those issues, it was the perfect location for Harry's purposes. There were several areas of rotten flooring in the roof space. Knowing their locations gave him further advantage.

This roof space would have been a storage area at one time. There was a wide opening to the outside and the courtyard below. Decades ago, it would have been closed by double doors, but now only rusty remnants of hinges remained.

A massive beam protruded above and out of the doorway by about 1 metre. Harry assumed a pulley would have been affixed at one time, enabling items to be hoisted and stored in this space.

The courtyard below would have been the main access to the warehouse. It would have been via this courtyard that all the people who once worked there would have clocked in and out.

Sitting back in the shadows, this doorway allowed him to see far down the only access road; while remaining unseen. He could watch all comings and goings, giving him plenty of time to see any challenge facing him, who and how many.

He dumped his gear in a dark corner, then watched and listened. It was unlikely there'd be any visitors during the remaining night. This would be new territory for them, and they knew Harry would have the upper hand. Any attackers would wait until there was light to see. However, he'd learned his painful lesson, so he cat-napped during the last of the remaining darkness.

31. WHO PAYS THE PIPER

Morning came and went without issue. He watched the people who lived in the warehouse come and go as normal without noticing him. This reassured him. If the people who lived there didn't notice him up there, others definitely wouldn't.

He hadn't eaten for almost a day and felt hungry and thirsty. He needed to keep hydrated and sufficiently fed, so surreptitiously left for something to eat and drink, hoping to avoid prying eyes. After a hearty meal, he returned with a bag of food and drink. He didn't know how long the wait might be.

He approached the warehouse carefully, checking for tyre tracks, any puddles of cloudy water, or quality-shoed footprints in the mud. All good. No one had followed him. He'd made it back without incident. He now had to watch and wait.

Gingerly climbing the spiral staircase, something didn't feel right with the light, noises, and smell. Entering the loft room, he was shocked to see a large man silhouetted in the open doorway above the courtyard. He was standing, facing him, with his arms folded.

As Harry's eyes acclimatised, he saw a self-satisfied-looking Albert facing him. Wrapped in all his winter finery, over his fat, flabby body, he initially gave the impression of a formidable opponent. Harry relaxed. There was no immediate danger there, but there was the niggling worry that if he knew Harry was there, others also might.

"Got you this time cunt," Albert sneered through his brown teeth. As he talked, he was doing that dance of joy which was his usual expression of excitement when anticipating someone about to get hurt.

"Do you really want to mix it?" said Harry incredulously. His surprise, then niggling doubt at Albert's composure, quickly changed to a worry. Albert was a coward. If he was over-confident, there was a good reason; and that soon became clear.

"Nope, but they do," as he pointed to Jock cautiously making his way up the stairs to the first floor. He was followed by Fred daintily entering the building, trying to avoid the human excrement getting on his fancy shoes.

"They was asking about you, and who better than me t' tell 'em? I knows this place and knows where you'd be. He even gives me a ton to find ya, but I'd 'ave done it for nothin'."

Albert was dancing back and forth even more excitedly now as Jock started up the spiral stairs. "Told ya, I told ya I'd 'ave ya."

The vantage point Harry chose was only as good as the early view and warning it gave him of those coming for him. The downside was that if caught in that place, which he now was, there was no way out. He'd have to go through the two minders that he knew were more than capable of taking him. Then there was Albert as well. While not a threat alone, with these two, he was an added problem.

The only other way out was through that large double overhead loading door to the concrete ground two stories below. A jump would kill, or at least cripple him.

In any case, Albert was between him and the loading door, blocking that exit. By the time he could deal with Albert, the other two, or at least Jock, would be on him.

Jock took his time coming up the spiral staircase. He wanted Fred with him.

Jock shouted up to Harry, "was going to come mob-handed to rip this place apart to find you, but your mate Albert here told me where you were. Now you're away from the poncy Bloodworths, you're mine. I'm going to enjoy personally taking you apart."

Harry knew this was the end game. They say that in the final moments, your life flashes back in front of you. Into Harry's head, from nowhere, came a quote that Colonel 'Parkie' often used. It went something like this, "all problems are created with solutions. Relax, take stock, think it through, and you'll find it"."

Albert was the problem. Then the flabby, overly clothed, and ever so comfortably squidgy Albert became his solution. Seizing his opportunity,

Harry sprinted toward and lunged at a surprised Albert, who stood there like a rabbit in headlights.

Harry was a little over average height, lean, and well-muscled. His 90 plus kilogramme bulk, with the momentum gained from a few fast launching strides, hit Albert square in the chest. Harry grasped Albert's lapels, as his American football-style attack drove them both through the opening. Harry ensured he landed fully on top of fat Albert, who cushioned his fall.

On impact, the air rasped from Albert's body. There was the crack of breaking bones. Harry lay there, catching his breath. He didn't move. He first checked he was OK, and that none of the broken bones were his, which they were not, thankfully.

There was no sign of life from Albert.

'One down.'

Having been about to follow Jock up the stairs, Now it was Fred who was closest and first able to engage Harry. Fred could see their target wasn't moving. It was obvious to him his victim was at least winded from the fall, hopefully with some broken bones to boot. And that would make him easy prey.

"Wait, for me," Jock shouted.

Harry barely moved, which encouraged Fred to ignore Jock's shouts. He'd take advantage of Harry's weakened situation after that heavy fall and finish him off himself. He didn't need Jock for this easy kill.

As he ran over, he took out a nasty Fairbairn–Sykes fighting knife. Jock continued to shout at him to wait for him to arrive, "fuckin' wait you arse-hole!"

Fred was going to have the satisfaction of dealing with Harry himself. He'd show Jock. Fred's knife thrust downwards at Harry, who he could now see was slowly recovering and trying to get up.

The strike would normally have connected, but Harry was not as out of it as he appeared. Harry knew Fred had a reputation when mixing it hand-to-hand, so he let him be over-confident. His well-wrapped left arm parried the attack. He then grabbed Fred's knife-hand wrist to prevent the knife from striking him.

Fred was leaning forward and down, with his weight on Harry. He had the advantage. He felt a punch to his chest, then another to his stomach, but there was no strength behind Harry's strikes. Realising Harry was still recovering. He was in no position to defend himself, so Fred gloated, "is that all you've got?"

With his free right hand, Fred punched Harry hard in the face. "That's how it's done!" He punched Harry again, harder.

Harry rode the first punch to his face. There was nowhere to go for the second one which dazed him. He couldn't survive much more of these, if any. He continued striking Fred again and again, now in rapid succession.

Fred scowled at Harry's feeble blows as they repeatedly struck him in his chest and stomach. They were pathetic. He was going to take his time finishing him with more of his own before he sliced Logan open.

Fred's vision started to blur, his body started to feel weak. He couldn't understand what was happening? Then it dawned on him. Those weren't punches. Looking down, he could see blood pouring and spurting out of the many wounds to his torso.

To a now weak Fred, Harry uttered, "if you're going to mix it with me using our boys' preferred stick, you should've first learned how to use it."

The last thing Fred saw before he collapsed into a dead heap was Harry's red fist holding a long thin stiletto blade; the one he took off Moses.

Harry pushed him away, quickly got up onto his feet, and took a few steps towards where Jock would come. He wanted the advantage of a dry area. The mud and water between him and his attacker gave Harry the advantage. Jock, wielding a large knife, was now almost on him.

Jock stopped and stared at Fred's still body, lying in a pool of red; too late to see his friend expire.

"Stupid twat," he cursed at Fred for being so gullible to let himself be drawn in. He then turned and faced Harry, who now held a knife in each hand.

"You killed my best mucka, you bastard."

"And not forgetting the other three in the Afghanistan farmstead," taunted Harry, trying to rile Jock into a careless lunge as they danced around testing each other.

Jock had just seen Harry cunningly disable Albert before efficiently dispatching Fred. He was now only one and no longer as confident as earlier. Jock had worried about the noise of gunshots bringing the authorities. He wanted to deal with Harry personally but inwardly cursed that he should have brought a gun! And more men!

Jock was now more cautious.

Harry could see a wave of barely restrained anger rising in his opponent. He pushed harder to burst that bubble, "and you drove away, scared. You left them to rot in the desert as fodder for the wild animals."

Jock wasn't going to be further pushed into rash decisions. "The man that got away was Fred, not me."

Now he realised why Fred had been so keen to deal with Harry himself. It was Fred's mates who Harry had killed that day in Nangarhar.

"So, you hid while your mates did your dirty work." He pushed again.

"Nope. I was management, running the show there. I didn't get involved with low-level operational shit. I did, however, plan that ambush that killed your lot and your best mucka," replied Jock. "It was a great plan, so simple, and the Taliban took all the blame."

"But you fucked up in the house," replied Harry. "You sent nasty little amateurs, like him there, to do a man's job." Harry pointed a knife at Fred behind him, without even looking.

Jock wasn't taking the bait and ignored Harry's jibes, and in return, he was trying his best to wind Harry up.

"My Taliban mates then got to see it our way, and the politician was immediately topped. Topping your mates forced their hand. It was back to business as usual for our export trade."

Harry always expected another ATS man was behind it all, but never assumed it would have been Jock. He didn't think Jock had the brains to coordinate the attack and collaborate with the Taliban. Whatever the case, Jock was always his target; Fred was a bonus.

They continued dancing around each other, carefully probing each other's defences. They talked and stalked. Each tried to out-psych the other, waiting and testing for an opening.

"I'd been after your lot for the past 4 years. I thought you were the fourth man at the farmhouse and the person responsible for my mates' deaths. I got that wrong, but it's still you, even more now. All these years were about you, and you're not walking away from this."

If Jock experienced fear, he hid it well.

Jock continued to test his opponent, pushing back him back a little, and a little more. His confidence seemed to be rising.

"Let me introduce you to Mabel," waving what looked to be a ten-inch-long diver's knife with a serrated tip.

"I named it after my Auntie Mabel. She had the most vicious and sharpest tongue in my street. And this is just as nasty." He laughed, as he waved it in Harry's face.

Harry could see this man was a cunning operator. Any fear Jock earlier exhibited was now completely hidden, replaced with a big, beaming grin. His opponent's courage seemed to be building up. It was now Harry who was feeling a bit out-psyched. Jock was exhibiting a surprisingly growing confidence; he play-acted well.

Jock continued to smile and started to make more testing lunges at Harry, pushing him further back, inch by inch. Jock was trying to get to firmer ground. Harry was happy to play with him, waiting for him to make a mistake with his increasingly bold swings and lunges.

Jock seemed to have a change of heart. He stood erect, making more space between them, and put his hands up.

"Look," said Jock in a conciliatory tone, "you 'n' me got off to a bad start. De Silva sent me here to do you. But you're ex-forces like me and we needs t' stick together like. We're even now, and I don't hold what you did to Fred against ya."

Jock now stood still. He was relaxed and smiling even more now, yet still watching Harry for any opportunity. "De Silva's done, finished. The Bloodworths are next. You and me, we could take over. Wha d'ya say?"

"I'm gonna leave now with Fred."

Harry said nothing. He relaxed a little, stood more erect, waiting and watching. He knew Jock wasn't having a change of heart. But what was his game?

Suddenly, Harry felt arms around the bottom of his legs gripping him tightly, and the shrill voice came from behind and below, "I've got the bastard! Do 'im, do 'im now!"

"The shit's got a harder head than I thought," mumbled Harry, as he desperately tried to keep his balance. He couldn't deal with Albert, since that meant taking his attention from Jock. He could see Jock grinning from ear to ear, knowing he'd won.

Harry cursed himself for believing that the fat lump of lard was completely out after that fall, or better still, dead.

Albert wasn't able to stand due to a broken leg and other injuries. However, face-down, he was able to drag himself forward toward the fighting pair. Harry had psychologically mirrored Jock's upright position. His change of stance from a crouching to a more erect one, with his legs closer together, allowed Albert to reach out and wrap his arms around them.

Jock's seemingly over-optimism as Harry was backing away from Jock and towards Albert should have been a clue that something was up.

With Harry's legs now immobilised, he could only topple backward onto Albert, who grunted at the impact. Albert was no longer having the good day with Harry that he'd thought, as he cushioned his fall for a second time.

Albert screamed in pain as Harry fell on him, exacerbating his injuries.

Jock wasted no time and lunged forward to finish his powerless opponent.

Suddenly he stopped and stood there, swaying with a shocked look. A torrent of blood started pouring down the side of his head. He then collapsed under a hail of bricks coming from above.

Albert wasn't letting go, and Harry, now sitting on his back, needed to dispatch him fast in case Jock recovered. Leaning forward, he placed Fred's knife on the back of Albert's neck. With the heel of his other fist, he smashed down hard driving the knife deep, severing Albert's spine, and right through his windpipe.

Harry extricated himself from the dead man's grasp and immediately turned his attention to Jock who was seemingly unconscious and wounded. There was a bad gash and some other smaller injuries to Jock's head.

Harry looked up to see the smiling faces of Tom and Jess. These two had saved his life; again. He waved thanks.

The scene had to be sufficiently prepared for the authorities to close the case. Harry aimed to avoid the close inspection by the authorities. He knew that gang fights between the likes of this lot weren't overly scrutinised if the deaths were obvious. He also expected the controller's influence would encourage a quick closure.

Jock lay on his front. Harry stood on Jock's knife hand and removed Mabel. He turned Jock onto his back. Jock was still out of it when Harry finished him off with Fred's knife, which he placed back in Fred's hand after cleaning his prints. Harry also cleaned his prints from Moses' knife and then wrapped it in Jock's fingers. He'd remove Jock's knife from the scene.

Tom and Jess soon joined him at the scene of the fight. Together they removed any chance of finding fingerprints on the bricks they lobbed down. Harry cleaned himself, retrieved, and put on his other clothes. He burned the blood-stained clothes he wore.

With yet another burner phone, Harry sent a picture of the scene and requested payment with the message, "job done, once you make the transfer, I'll report."

To another number, he sent the same picture. He then called the number and said, "is that job offer still on the table?"

"Yes," De Silva enthusiastically replied.

"I'll be over in about an hour."

It was time to leave.

****

The taxi dropped him off at the entrance to De Silva's house. Walking up to the side gate, the security man on duty offered a half-hearted, yet warm wave as Harry walked through without question. They were expecting him. They knew what he looked like since he was now one of the team.

De Silva met him at the front door. This time, Harry took De Silva's proffered hand, and they shook.

To the man standing behind, De Silva said, "Graeme, this is Harry Logan. Show him his room, then around the place. He's on our team. Answer every question he has."

Graeme smiled a welcome.

To Harry, De Silva followed up with, "settle in, meet the team, and familiarise yourself with everything around here. I'll see you at 9 am tomorrow. Join me for breakfast."

At that, De Silva walked back into the house.

Graeme commented, "you are honoured indeed. None of us even had a cuppa' with the boss."

There was no sarcasm, purely a statement.

32. FACE TO FACE

At 9 am prompt the following morning, Harry joined De Silva for breakfast, as instructed. He found De Silva sitting at the head of the dining table with two other people. To his left was a stern-faced woman of indeterminable age, and to his right sat the same man who came to his police cell with the offer of a get-of-jail-free card.

The woman was slim, clearly worked out, and dressed in a formal dark trouser suit. Her hair was in the style of the 80s, which was a possible clue to her age, but that didn't help Harry, not that it mattered.

It all clicked into place.

So, this was Dragon-Lady.

"My controller?" he asked her.

She gave a quick confirmation nod.

Then directing a question at the other man, he asked, "does my controller have a name?"

"Yes."

Harry could have asked the question, "how do I address you?" but he knew he'd not get a definitive answer. They like their word games or lack thereof.

"OK then. Let's say Ms Smith, and you must be," Harry paused for dramatic effect as if thinking of a name. "So, let's say Mr Jones." Harry was overtly sarcastic to the other man, and in so doing, to her.

"You are permitted to address me directly," she piped up. With a wry smile, she continued, "since you have done a reasonably proficient job out there, you're allowed this one, but don't over-step the mark. And yes, Ms Smith and Mr Jones will do for this meeting."

"And for any future discussion," joined Mr Jones.

212

Harry started. "So, Mr De Silva was your man all the time. You got ATS to set up this drugs distribution business, with Mr De Silva as the front man, knowing that if it went belly up, they would all take the fall. ATS already has a bad reputation, and Mr De Silva's is as bad in your eyes."

He used the term 'Mr' in front of De Silva. He was now his boss, after all.

"Not exactly," she replied. "Mr Jeremy De Silva is a recent convert, and we've agreed to let bygones be bygones."

"As I understand, you're now in Mr De Silva's employ, yet you've not handed in your notice? No matter, you have our permission to treat this job as a secondment from us." Ms Smith needed to remind Harry that she owned him and his position within her scheme of things.

There was nothing Harry could say in response.

She changed tack. "I'm going to give you a bit of background perspective, so you can understand how to do your job."

De Silva and Harry leaned in. After all that had happened, this would be interesting.

"Here's the problem the country faces that we were engaged to help fix. People are hooked and dying from drugs; we all know that. However, many of the worst deaths and ongoing illnesses result from the even more dangerous substances cut into them.

They've hooked children into this industry, locally and by cross-county gangs. Addict-related prostitution is growing, as are crimes to feed drug addiction. Then there are drug-gang-related stabbings, worst of all including children. The list is extensive."

She let that sink in for a moment. "There was no way out of this spiral of decline. The Powers-That-Be, our masters, have their hands tied. Whatever strategy is employed to make a change will upset some very influential people here and overseas."

"And, to make matters worse, the public's getting tetchy. They all want something done but don't know what that is. Whatever our masters do is going to be wrong for someone. They passed this political hot potato to us, as they often do in these circumstances."

"With looming elections, they needed a workable solution without further delay. That solution would have to appease all those disproportionately influential lobbyists with minority agendas. A win here would see a second term. So, a fix had to be quickly made, hence the timeline you were given."

She drew a breath. "The US failed with alcohol prohibition, then back-tracked. The gangs that arose from prohibition didn't go away. They just changed their product focus. The US wasn't back to square one. They now had to deal with the added gangs who wanted to continue their lucrative life of crime. The authorities there had to learn about and then deal with a worse situation of their making."

"There's no way this country is ready for the legalisation of illicit drugs. That's a political no-no and would be the death of any political party."

"The definition of insanity is doing the same thing over and over again to achieve the same results. So, we've been insanely into drug prohibition, repeating behaviour that had previously failed. Even if we opened up the market, the organised gangs would then turn their attention to other crime as they did after prohibition."

"So far so good?" she asked.

Harry nodded yes.

"So, the solution was to exercise some control of the product on the street, without our masters getting their pretty little hands dirty."

"A deal was set up four years ago with ATS. Mr Carmichael was the go-between. We found an existing drug distribution organisation and took it over. We kept the face of the business in place, i.e. our Mr De Silva here. He had to be encouraged to agree to the ATS partnership offer, but eventually, he saw the light. At that time, Mr De Silva thought his partnership was a commercial venture with ATS."

"ATS was supposed to use their cut of the profits to invest back in cleaning up and controlling the channel. Their job was to remove those worst offenders, who were not playing by our new rules, either themselves or via police and customs raids and seizures."

She then showed a bit of annoyance as she explained, "It worked well, initially. However, the newly deceased Mr Carmichael, aka Jock, and elements in the ATS hierarchy got out of control. They stopped playing ball, all that money disappeared, and they played lip service to the agreement."

"Only snippets of information on those who were the worst of the worst were coming to the authorities; and then only to satisfy their own greed and agendas."

"Our masters were getting frustrated. Their highly publicised strategy of what they called, 'targeted attention', one of their most public promises, had failed."

"Mr Carmichael and Co. had become too big for their proverbial boots, both here and overseas where a lot of the product is grown and made. They thought they were invincible since they were well-connected and could look after themselves. They threatened to spill the beans if we stopped them; controlling both supply and distribution was a lucrative business."

"So, you used me. I was a perceived outsider coerced into sorting out your shit," Harry interjected. "So, this was a setup to get me on board. So, don't bleat to me about Luke and Co, you're no better than them."

"It was a lucky circumstance for us that you left one boss to join another, but all under the same master. So yes, we got you. And while we have you, Luke and Co will no longer expect you back. They led you a merry dance for four years. Compared to them, we ARE the nice guys."

"Don't forget, you had an agenda to find and deal with those behind the killings of your comrades. Only with our help, were you able to take out the real people responsible for your friend's death, Jock, and his colleague, Mr Frank West, aka Fred. So, while there was a little influence on you to get you to listen to the deal in the police station, you were a willing party," she said defending her position.

"We cannot control a multi-billion pound market from the outside," she replied. "Yes it's a dirty business, but you're no angel." Then came her verbal slap-down. "Don't play the indignant card with me!".

Harry said nothing, she was right. After what he'd done over the last four years, he couldn't challenge anyone. So, Ms Smith and Mr Jones were a different branch of the same diseased tree.

He now knew that during his time when officially in the Army's logistics department and performing 'precision surgery' as Luke would call it, he wasn't hunting the perpetrators of his friends' deaths. He only worked toward their agenda. They lied to him, time after time.

"It's good that you are filling the gap in De Silva's business and you're perfectly qualified for the job. The other lot trained you exceptionally well and I've thanked them profusely," she smiled, but only with her mouth. "So, consider the last couple of months as an extended interview."

"The important thing is this; our masters need to be seen to be managing the drug problem. They need information on the worst of the recidivists out there, so they could visibly deal with them. They need everyone to see that they can, "be tough on crime and the causes of crime"," she quoted a well know PM.

"Additionally, if fewer people die from drugs and we have fewer long-term ill, we save billions from the NHS budget. It's simple, effective, and efficient. And the right people get re-elected; even better, I get to keep my job. In return, you continue with your disgracefully high income to your offshore account," she finished.

It was Harry's turn to smile. "And yes, I received both balances to my account, thank you," he said to De Silva and the other two.

"More than one?" queried an indignant Ms Smith.

"Yes, it was a double-bubble payment. As well as your less than generous payment, Mr De Silva also funded the job and filled the gap, I call it my bonus."

"I never heard that!" she said firmly, knowing there was nothing she could do about it; now at least.

Harry then said, "Does that mean we're all good?"

"That's down to you, so we'll see, won't we?"

At that, Ms Smith finished her tea and stood up. Jones followed suit.

"I'll leave you both to discuss your HR policy," she said to De Silva.

As Ms Smith walked out, she delivered a parting shot to De Silva, "keep it clean, keep the information flowing, and we'll all live happily ever after."

33. STRATEGY ENACTMENT

Two days later the government announced the implementation of their long-awaited illicit drugs policy, which they'd been promising since the election four years ago. It was all over the papers. Various pundits delivered opinions about whether this was workable or more whitewashing over irreparable cracks.

This new strategy, after decades of failures, would simply focus their stretched resources where they could do the most good. Instead of targeting all parts of the illicit drug trade, they would focus on those sections and organisations of the drug trade that did the most harm to the youth, the nation's health, and domestic crime.

The local papers led with the story, quoting from the following government briefing document.

'The three elements of this Ternary Strategy:

1. We will half the drug-related hospital admissions and deaths during the government's next term. Our drug enforcement agencies will operate in conjunction with the local and specialist police bodies to identify those groups supplying the most dangerous drugs and substances.

2. We will reduce drug-related crime by 60%. It is common knowledge that comparatively few individuals commit the bulk of these crimes, to feed their habits. We will target them.

3. We must protect the young. We will target the removal of children from any illicit drug involvement. There have been too many innocent young deaths, early drug dependency, and a life of crime. We will commit to a reduction of 50% within two years and 75% by the end of our next term.'

Harry was hooked to the TV, watching the news about this policy. Most people in the country fervently wished for it to be a success. However, political parties had made promises before and prevaricated on lack of delivery.

There were the typical dissenters of any government policy, whichever party was in power. They felt they had to be visibly complaining. There was nothing any government could say or do about those who just liked to be heard, or wanted publicity for their own ends.

Some parties had real and credible vested interests, such as the police, prisons, judiciary, social services, and NHS. With repeated promises from many different governments over decades, they had jaded opinions about how this might affect them and their operational activities.

Against a backdrop of a worldwide illicit drugs pandemic, the big question raised by the press and all, was, could the government deliver on the drugs election promise they made four years earlier?

They would again wait and see.

****

The following day at PM questions, Harry watched the leader of the opposition challenge the government on repeated broken election promises.

"You promised the electorate that you would clean up the escalating illicit drugs problem. But...," she paused, allowing the baaing and braying in the chamber to subside. "...you have miserably, yes miserably failed..."

She paused again for dramatic effect, and in response to the further bleating of the dark-suited sheep. She then shouted above the noise "...and in every measure you had stated."

She looked to the speaker for support. After copious banging of the official gabble and requests for silence, the opposition leader carried on with her accusation.

"All we've seen is a growing burden on the already overwhelmed NHS. There are fewer drug seizures. More people are locked up for drug-related offences, more children are being used to run drugs and dying as a result. Your policies have resulted in increased drug-related prostitution. Do I go on?" She was now shouting over the noises.

"My learned colleague does not need my permission to go on," responded the Prime Minister, "she does an excellent job without any help from this side of the chamber."

Those on the benches behind him bellowed to the angry boos from across the other side.

The Prime Minister continued. "We inherited a mess from the previous government, your government." He pointed at the previous speaker, who was now seated.

"And it was only once we had a full picture of the depth of the problems your policies created...," he had his finger pointed at the opposition leader and used the noise of the opposition's bleating and cries for great dramatic effect.

Once the noises had sufficiently reduced, he carried on. "...only then, could we work with all the bodies involved to build our new strategy, the one we promised the country."

He then finished by saying, "over the rest of this term of government and into our next...," he was now almost shouting to be heard over the opposition's boos, "...we will be measured on our successes, against the targets we have set in reducing drug-related crime, costs, and deaths!"

He pointed to those sitting opposite. "Something you never did or even tried!"

The Prime Minister was screaming at the top of his voice by the time he'd finished.

He, at last, sat down, with a beaming smile, to a chamber filled with politicians standing from both sides waving papers and shouting across at each other.

He fervently hoped that the promises of better intelligence needed to support his commitments would be forthcoming. If not, he and his party would be out of a job next year and for at least another five years.

Harry switched off Prime Minister's questions, sat back, and beamed. He knew this time around, the government might, at last, achieve success in this policy; because he and De Silva were conspiring in the wings, driving its enactment.

EPILOGUE

At the onset of the following winter, Harry, Tom, and Jess were finally at their destination in Scotland.

Harry stood with his arms around the shoulders of the siblings, watching the cold-looking loch, surrounded by high misty hills and white-topped mountains. The long months of planning their exit, at last, showed fruit.

They hoped they were all at last free from their chains.

With a lot of counselling, Jess successfully completed her time in rehab and had been clean for over five months. In a way, she was fortunate not having a naturally dependant makeup. Her addiction was her need to withdraw from the daily abuse she'd faced. With nothing from which to withdraw, the self-harming stopped, and she was through the dreadful detox process.

During that time, Tom maintained a pretty much off-grid activity. He quietly did the legwork setting up their final location, IDs, and a quiet B&B in the west of Scotland. The lease was cheap. Being somewhat off the beaten track, it had little passing trade. That suited them perfectly. The fewer customers who used their B&B services meant a lower chance of being spotted. This was not a final place, but somewhere to take stock while the heat died.

Over the preceding six months, Harry supported the security around De Silva and was ever the reminder for him to stay honest with the deal he had. They further built the Arbitration structure. Whatever part of the establishment was his partner in crime, together they managed the worst of the drug trade's excesses in the country.

Those distributors and customers not playing ball experienced increasing raids on their supply chain, from overseas manufacturing, via imports, to their drug-running operations.

De Silva and the Bloodworths eventually managed to find a workable mutual ground with Harry as an intermediary. However, they, and others with the same opinions, continued to challenge when they felt the occasion merited.

The real explanation was never given to the Bloodworths. However, they started to see the benefits of controlling and investing in a clean distribution channel. In the main, they pretty much toed the line. And the Powers-That-Be, via Harry and De Silva, left them alone. As a result, their business also grew at the expense of others.

During those six months, the government proved its strategy had worked with numbers and statistics. The police and customs received more and better information on the worst of the drug-related activities, showing increased arrests and drug hauls. They were outwardly positive about the strategy's success. Crime also declined. The principal perpetrators were identified from within and given over to the authorities for prison and/or rehab.

Outwardly, the police were viewed as being more professional and focused. They were happy to take full credit.

The NHS saw reduced figures resulting from drug-related poisonings and abuse of the most dangerous of drugs.

Drug-related prostitution declined, as did abuse and children's involvement in drugs and crime. Social services were extolling the government's strategy.

And Harry continued to make even more money during those months until he'd a substantial nest egg put away to retire with the siblings; the earlier payments also helped.

****

They called it D-day, aka Departure Day.

On that day, Harry cashed out his local accounts. He transferred his offshore accounts to ones even further offshore that were better hidden from the scrutiny of his masters. Swiss accounts were fine while he worked for that 'lot', as he called them. However, these days, they're not so private, and his funds were at risk of seizure or blocking. He wanted his money outside of their visibility by D-day.

He posted his resignation to De Silva from the local post office, knowing it would arrive the next morning.

Harry took a train to Dover, paying cash. He then paid cash for train tickets to Southampton, Portsmouth, Harwich, Newcastle, and ferry tickets to Calais and Dieppe. He'd practised disguising himself, not only his facial and body features but his overall gait. His training in disguises during those four years while officially in the military's logistics served him well.

What disembarked from the busy rush-hour train in a dark, rainy Southampton was not the smart, fit, dark-haired man who gingerly boarded. Instead, was a grey-haired, grey-featured, sickly man with a pot-belly and slight stoop.

Tom and Jess met him in what looked to be a beaten-up old estate car, paid for with cash some months earlier.

They drove away to the next chapter of their lives.

****

The following day, De Silva forwarded Harry's resignation to Ms Smith, who notified Mr Jones and his team. Their expert opinion was that he could be anywhere in Europe, after having taken a ferry to France from one of those exit ports; or even further. They then offered the contradicting suspicion that was too obvious. He could have gone to any of the many locations for which he'd bought tickets.

There were other numerous cash transactions elsewhere in the country and abroad, some of which could be Harry or someone who looked like him. In truth, they couldn't even be sure that he bought all those tickets; or, that he could have bought additional ones.

"So let me summarise what you're telling me. All our over-paid and highly-trained experts have different opinions, and those are at best vague. They're all as useful as a glass hammer!"

"He's gone rogue," said an annoyed Mr Jones.

"So, you don't know where he is?" said Ms Smith straight-faced.

"Yes, ma'am."

"Good. Our other lot trained him well; very well indeed. So let's pat ourselves on the back for that, at least."

She recognised Mr Jones' look, wondering why she took this disastrous news so calmly. Ms Smith let him off the hook. "Now, let's not get too wound up about his departure. He thinks he's finished with us. What he doesn't realise is this is NOT his resignation. It's merely a sabbatical, that's all," she said, glancing through the data Mr Jones gave her. "He doesn't yet know it, though. And let's not tell him, eh."

"I don't understand?"

"This was to be expected from what we know of him. And before you ask, I'm not wasting resources trying to find him. You're right, he could be anywhere. We'll get wind in due course, and we'll monitor and wait. We don't want to frighten him off and start another chase. Is that clear?"

"Perfectly, ma'am."

"When we have a job that fits his skills, we'll then reel him in again; same as before."

Mr Jones relaxed.

She finished with, "your immediate task is to help fill the gap in the De Silva operation. We don't want ATS involved in any way."

THE END

ABOUT THE AUTHOR

I'm the third son of a Scottish father's and an Austrian mother's post-war romance. My early years were as a military brat in Malaysia. Apparently, I had a wonderful time there, but I don't remember a damned thing about all that fun. In the 60s, our family returned to cold and windy Scotland.

After graduating in engineering, I started my working life fixing computer systems. My brothers and I were always repairing 'stuff', so that career direction sorta made sense.

In the late 1980s, I was sucked into management, which pulled us down to England. After my bleating about our department's marketing, my boss found the perfect solution to shut me up. "OK, you do it then!" So, I did. That kicked off my marketing career and where I found my love of writing. It also enabled me to live and work in the Middle East and Asia.

My experience with tech, travels, and people have helped in my writing.

For many years, thriller and murder novels have bubbled around my head, desperate to pop out. In 2021, I officially retired, leaving the shackles of corporate writing. At last, I write my stories my way.

Logan's Rules is my first foray into writing novels. SPECTRUM is my second, and due out November'22. My third, a crime mystery set in Sri Lanka, is due out February'23. Our friend, Harry Logan, is back, fighting the bad guys in my fourth book, due June'23. More are on the way…

I hope you enjoy reading my books as much as I enjoyed their writing.

I'm married to a wonderful, long-suffering wife and have two children.

You can visit me on Facebook: Max.Holden.Author.

Printed in Great Britain
by Amazon